PERFECT RIVALRY

Acclaim for Radclyffe's Fiction

"Medical drama, gossipy lesbian romance, and angsty backstory all get equal time in [*Unrivaled*,] Radclyffe's fifth PMC Hospital Romance…[F]ans of small community dynamics and workplace romance without ethical complications will find this hits the spot."—*Publishers Weekly*

"*Dangerous Waters* is a bumpy ride through a devastating time with powerful events and resolute characters. Radclyffe gives us the strong, dedicated women we love to read in a story that keeps us turning pages until the end."—*Lambda Literary Review*

"Radclyffe's *Dangerous Waters* has the feel of a tense television drama, as the narrative interchanges between hurricane trackers and first responders. Sawyer and Dara butt heads in the beginning as each moves for some level of control during the storm's approach, and the interference of a lovely television reporter adds an engaging love triangle threat to the sexual tension brewing between them."—*RT Book Reviews*

"*Love After Hours*, the fourth in Radclyffe's Rivers Community series, evokes the sense of a continuing drama as Gina and Carrie's slow-burning romance intertwines with details of other Rivers residents. They become part of a greater picture where friends and family support each other in personal and recreational endeavors. Vivid settings and characters draw in the reader…"
—*RT Book Reviews*

Secret Hearts "delivers exactly what it says on the tin: poignant story, sweet romance, great characters, chemistry and hot sex scenes. Radclyffe knows how to pen a good lesbian romance."
—*LezReviewBooks Blog*

Wild Shores "will hook you early. Radclyffe weaves a chance encounter into all-out steamy romance. These strong, dynamic women have great conversations, and fantastic chemistry."
—*The Romantic Reader Blog*

In **2016 RWA/OCC Book Buyers Best award winner for suspense and mystery with romantic elements** *Price of Honor* "Radclyffe is master of the action-thriller series...The old familiar characters are there, but enough new blood is introduced to give it a fresh feel and open new avenues for intrigue."—*Curve Magazine*

In *Prescription for Love* "Radclyffe populates her small town with colorful characters, among the most memorable being Flann's little sister, Margie, and Abby's 15-year-old trans son, Blake...This romantic drama has plenty of heart and soul." —*Publishers Weekly*

2013 RWA/New England Bean Pot award winner for contemporary romance *Crossroads* "will draw the reader in and make her heart ache, willing the two main characters to find love and a life together. It's a story that lingers long after coming to 'the end.'"—*Lambda Literary*

In **2012 RWA/FTHRW Lories and RWA HODRW Aspen Gold award winner** *Firestorm* "Radclyffe brings another hot lesbian romance for her readers."—*The Lesbrary*

Foreword Review Book of the Year finalist and IPPY silver medalist *Trauma Alert* "is hard to put down and it will sizzle in the reader's hands. The characters are hot, the sex scenes explicit and explosive, and the book is moved along by an interesting plot with well drawn secondary characters. The real star of this show is the attraction between the two characters, both of whom resist and then fall head over heels."—*Lambda Literary Reviews*

Lambda Literary Award Finalist *Best Lesbian Romance 2010* features "stories [that] are diverse in tone, style, and subject, making for more variety than in many, similar anthologies... well written, each containing a satisfying, surprising twist. Best Lesbian Romance series editor Radclyffe has assembled a respectable crop of 17 authors for this year's offering."—*Curve Magazine*

2010 Prism award winner and ForeWord Review Book of the Year Award finalist *Secrets in the Stone* is "so powerfully [written] that the worlds of these three women shimmer between reality and dreams…A strong, must read novel that will linger in the minds of readers long after the last page is turned."—*Just About Write*

In **Benjamin Franklin Award finalist** *Desire by Starlight* "Radclyffe writes romance with such heart and her down-to-earth characters not only come to life but leap off the page until you feel like you know them. What Jenna and Gard feel for each other is not only a spark but an inferno and, as a reader, you will be washed away in this tumultuous romance until you can do nothing but succumb to it."—*Queer Magazine Online*

Lambda Literary Award winner *Distant Shores, Silent Thunder* "weaves an intricate tapestry about passion and commitment between lovers. The story explores the fragile nature of trust and the sanctuary provided by loving relationships." —*Sapphic Reader*

Lambda Literary Award winner *Stolen Moments* "is a collection of steamy stories about women who just couldn't wait. It's sex when desire overrides reason, and it's incredibly hot!" —*On Our Backs*

Lambda Literary Award Finalist *Justice Served* delivers a "crisply written, fast-paced story with twists and turns and keeps us guessing until the final explosive ending."—*Independent Gay Writer*

Lambda Literary Award finalist *Turn Back Time* "is filled with wonderful love scenes, which are both tender and hot." —*MegaScene*

Applause for L.L. Raand's Midnight Hunters Series

The Midnight Hunt
RWA 2012 VCRW Laurel Wreath winner *Blood Hunt*
Night Hunt
The Lone Hunt

"Raand has built a complex world inhabited by werewolves, vampires, and other paranormal beings...Raand has given her readers a complex plot filled with wonderful characters as well as insight into the hierarchy of Sylvan's pack and vampire clans. There are many plot twists and turns, as well as erotic sex scenes in this riveting novel that keep the pages flying until its satisfying conclusion."—*Just About Write*

"Once again, I am amazed at the storytelling ability of L.L. Raand aka Radclyffe. In *Blood Hunt*, she mixes high levels of sheer eroticism that will leave you squirming in your seat with an impeccable multi-character storyline all streaming together to form one great read."—*Queer Magazine Online*

"Are you sick of the same old hetero vampire/werewolf story plastered in every bookstore and at every movie theater? Well, I've got the cure to your werewolf fever. *The Midnight Hunt* is first in, what I hope is, a long-running series of fantasy erotica for L.L. Raand (aka Radclyffe)."—*Queer Magazine Online*

By Radclyffe

The Provincetown Tales

Safe Harbor

Beyond the Breakwater

Distant Shores, Silent Thunder

Storms of Change

Winds of Fortune

Returning Tides

Sheltering Dunes

Treacherous Seas

PMC Hospitals Romances

Passion's Bright Fury (prequel)

Fated Love

Night Call

Crossroads

Passionate Rivals

Unrivaled

Perfect Rivalry

Rivers Community Romances

Against Doctor's Orders

Prescription for Love

Love on Call

Love After Hours

Love to the Rescue

Love on the Night Shift

Pathway to Love

Honor Series

Above All, Honor

Honor Bound

Love & Honor

Honor Guards

Honor Reclaimed

Honor Under Siege

Word of Honor

Oath of Honor
(First Responders)

Code of Honor

Price of Honor

Cost of Honor

Justice Series

A Matter of Trust (prequel)

Shield of Justice

In Pursuit of Justice

Justice in the Shadows

Justice Served

Justice for All

First Responders Novels

Trauma Alert

Firestorm

Taking Fire

Wild Shores

Heart Stop

Dangerous Waters

Romances

Innocent Hearts

Promising Hearts

Love's Melody Lost

Love's Tender Warriors

Tomorrow's Promise

Love's Masquerade

shadowland

Turn Back Time

When Dreams Tremble

The Lonely Hearts Club

Secrets in the Stone

Desire by Starlight

Homestead

The Color of Love

Secret Hearts

Short Fiction

Collected Stories by Radclyffe

Erotic Interludes: *Change Of Pace*

Radical Encounters

Stacia Seaman and Radclyffe, eds.:

Erotic Interludes Vol. 2–5

Romantic Interludes Vol. 1–2

Breathless: *Tales of Celebration*

Women of the Dark Streets

Amor and More: Love Everafter

Myth & Magic: Queer Fairy Tales

Writing As L.L. Raand

Midnight Hunters

The Midnight Hunt

Blood Hunt

Night Hunt

The Lone Hunt

The Magic Hunt

Shadow Hunt

Visit us at www.boldstrokesbooks.com

PERFECT RIVALRY

by

RADCLY*f*FE

2022

PERFECT RIVALRY

© 2022 By RADCLYFFE. ALL RIGHTS RESERVED.

ISBN 13: 978-1-63679-216-3

THIS TRADE PAPERBACK ORIGINAL IS PUBLISHED BY
BOLD STROKES BOOKS, INC.
P.O. BOX 249
VALLEY FALLS, NY 12185

FIRST EDITION: MAY 2022

CREDITS
EDITORS: RUTH STERNGLANTZ AND STACIA SEAMAN
PRODUCTION DESIGN: STACIA SEAMAN
COVER DESIGN BY TAMMY SEIDICK

Acknowledgments

The first book in this series was written early in 2004, the year I founded Bold Strokes Books. The setting was a few blocks away from where I lived at the time—a "city" neighborhood whose spirit of community I hoped to capture. That book, *Fated Love*, was also one of the first medical romances I crafted, and at the time, I had no idea how my interest in writing medical communities and geographic ones would gradually blend to culminate in the Rivers community romance series. Writing the sixth book in this extended PMC series has allowed me to keep the stories current in time and spirit, and given me the pleasure of revisiting one of my favorite universes. As in the Rivers series, the hospital is modeled after a real one—one founded in 1850 as the Female Medical College of Pennsylvania. This was the first medical school in the world to admit and award women the MD degree and remained solely a women's medical school until late in the twentieth century when it became co-ed and eventually merged with several other medical schools in Philadelphia.

Thanks to the many people who helped me revisit this world—Ruth Sternglantz and Stacia Seaman for editorial expertise; Paula Tighe for enthusiastic beta-reading and style advice; Sandy Lowe, for invaluable personal and business support. And to my wife Lee, for always seeing the positive. Amo te.

To Lee, and the continuing adventure

CHAPTER ONE

Pennsylvania Medical Center (PMC) hospital, a Saturday night

Ren Dunbar adjusted the camera on the microscope to zoom in on the superoxygenated red blood cells in her most recent tissue sample, carefully advanced the O2 microprobe, and turned to her laptop sitting open on the lab bench beside her. Scanning the readouts scrolling across the screen, she gave a mental fist-pump. *Yes.*

These cells showed a definite improvement in oxygen carrying capacity, exactly what was needed for injured cardiac muscle cells. Busy importing the video of the procedure into her data feed, she absently registered the sound of a door opening and closing somewhere at the far end of the lab and ignored it. Usually at two in the morning, she was completely alone, but sometimes maintenance personnel working the night shift would come in to replace equipment or perform routine cleaning duties. Midnight to six a.m. were her most productive hours, and even when she was on call, she preferred spending the time she wasn't seeing consults working in the lab rather than wasting time in the OR lounge or on-call room. Quiet and solitude constituted her comfort zone. She flinched at the sound of her name.

"Ren," Quinn Maguire repeated, stopping beside her.

"Oh, sorry. Didn't hear you come in," Ren said, trying to hide her annoyance at the interruption.

The surgery chief and program director gave her a quizzical smile. "I had a feeling I'd find you here. Your beeper not working?"

Ren frowned. "Um, I'm not on call, Dr. Maguire. But if you need me for something…"

"No, but I've been having a hard time tracking you down. That wouldn't be because you don't want to be found, would it?" Quinn leaned her hip against the lab bench and folded her arms, looking relaxed but still very much in charge, which was pretty much how she always looked. Like Ren, she wore forest-green scrubs, the uniform for most surgeons while on duty in the hospital, especially in the middle of the night. At first glance, Quinn always reminded Ren a little bit of her older sister. Both of them were dark-haired, intense, and she guessed the word would be *handsome*, as attractive or pretty just didn't quite describe the strength in their faces or the absolute confidence behind their smiles. But Sax was leaner than Quinn and radiated an electric kind of energy twenty-four hours a day. Quinn projected a calm, controlled power that never wavered no matter how urgent the circumstances.

Ren schooled her expression to one of neutrality. She wasn't *hiding* in the lab—preferring solitude was different than avoiding company, after all. Not that she thought anyone would actually understand that—no one ever seemed to, although Quinn Maguire was very perceptive. A handy trait for someone in charge of training forty surgical residents, all of whom worked very hard at never revealing any kind of uncertainty or weakness. Or, in Ren's case, atypical behavior. Fortunately, she'd learned a long, long time ago how to prevent any of her emotions from showing on her face. She was pretty sure she'd successfully abolished even a blush after years of rigorous biofeedback practice. "I'm always very careful to keep my beeper charged and with me at all times when I'm on call."

"I know that," Quinn said. "You've always answered your pages promptly whenever there's been a consult or a case that we needed you for. But whenever you don't absolutely have to be available, I never see you around."

"My lab projects keep me very busy."

"No doubt," Quinn said with a nod. "You might want to join some of the resident functions happening in and out of the hospital for a break now and then, though."

Ren smiled. She hadn't really expected anyone to notice her absence, even though she intentionally avoided socializing with fellow trainees. That hadn't always been true, until she'd learned that just because she wanted to connect with others, the feeling wasn't necessarily reciprocal. She got along fine with the OR staff and even other residents when it was necessary, but when work didn't require it, she had no points of intersection, really. Nothing in common with any of the students, and later residents, on her career path.

"I'm very sorry if you've been trying to reach me," she said again.

"You don't have your voice mail turned on, on your phone."

Ren shrugged. "I have a new phone, and since I never had any messages on the previous one, I didn't see the point in setting it up."

"You might want to," Quinn said casually. "Congratulations on getting that paper accepted in *Circulation*, by the way. That's a real coup."

Warmth rose through Ren's chest, and she felt the flush in her cheeks. She couldn't avoid the response to some pleasures, and professional success was at the top of her list. "Thanks. Rinaldo deserves a lot of credit. If he hadn't been in charge of growing the tissue samples, we wouldn't have such great early results."

"He does, and his name is on the paper right after yours, where it should be."

Ren almost grinned but smothered it. A twinge of anxiety penetrated the brief glow of pleasure. Quinn Maguire would not have sought her out in the middle of the night just to congratulate her on the culmination of three years of laboratory research. She couldn't think of anything she'd done or failed to do that could have been a problem. She'd scrubbed on a trauma case a few nights before, but the last time she'd checked the patient, he was doing fine. No one could've complained about her. No one really noticed her.

"Do you need me to scrub on a case?" Ren asked.

"No. Mike Wu is taking a leave of absence for the rest of the year," Quinn said quietly. "He needs to be at home. His mother is very ill."

"Oh," Ren said quickly, "I'm so sorry to hear that."

She didn't know Mike well, but she'd worked with him a few times when her night call obligations had intersected with his coverage of the ER or general surgery. They'd done a few cases together, and he'd been friendly in a distant kind of way, as if he wasn't exactly sure what her role was, given that she wasn't part of the normal clinical rotation. Three years in the lab had put her out of step with all the residents who'd started in her year, but being out of step with everyone was the norm for her.

Quinn sighed and said, "You've done excellent work on this project—Larry Weatherby is very impressed. I'm sure he'd be happy to recommend you for a faculty position so the two of you could continue to collaborate."

"That's good to know," Ren said quietly, the quick surge of excitement giving way to caution. Her circumstances had always made what should have been straightforward much more complicated. If Quinn noticed her reservations, she didn't show it.

"I'm sure you'll have a few more papers once you get all your data analyzed," Quinn said, "but it's time for you to finish up your clinical requirements. I need you to take Mike's place for the rest of the year. You've got enough time accumulated in cases from your night call coverage to be able to meet the chief's year requirement with the rest of the fifth years."

Ren froze. Full-time clinical rotations now? She'd known she would have to do this in order to finish her residency requirements, but she hadn't prepared mentally for what it would take to all of a sudden switch from the secluded, protected world of the lab to the much more intimate, and much more ruthless, world of surgical residency.

"When?" she said briskly, reminding herself this was no different than anything else she'd ever had to do. She couldn't let Quinn see her uncertainty, and she couldn't be thrown by it either. She'd been uncertain of what she would face more than once before now. She remembered how to steel herself for the unknown, and how to protect herself.

"You'll start Monday morning on A service. For now I've moved Dani Chan over to fill in for Mike. You should talk to her tomorrow to get up to speed on the patients and go over the OR schedule for the week."

"Right, of course. Thank you."

"If this is still what you want," Quinn said gently.

"I'm sorry?" Ren said, lifting her chin. Quinn's gaze was deep and penetrating, making her feel as if Quinn could see beyond her carefully cultivated shields. Maybe she could—Sax could, and the two of them were so alike. That's why she'd chosen to train here, after all. That little bit of familiarity helped center her when there was nothing—no one—else. She didn't blink.

"You made a lot of decisions when you were a lot younger," Quinn said. "We don't always know what we want then."

Ren laughed. She couldn't help it. At Quinn's bemused expression, she said, "Dr. Maguire, I've been making decisions when I was a lot younger than everyone else my whole life. My age doesn't have anything to do with my capabilities or my decision-making process."

"I know you have," Quinn said, "and Sax is a great role model, but no matter anyone's chronological age, sometimes we make decisions before we've actually experienced the reality."

"I understand why you might think that," Ren said as politely as she could, "but I didn't actually know Sax until I was eleven. I knew *of* her, but I only met her when I told my father I wanted to go to medical school. He thought that Sax could talk me out of it."

Quinn laughed. "I can see that didn't work."

Ren smiled. "Well, he didn't really know either one of us. He didn't raise Sax, and he didn't understand me. I was in my first year of high school then, but he couldn't see me as anything but a child." She shrugged again. Past history. Only one of the many factors that taught her to depend on herself and her own judgment. "Sax was pretty neutral. She talked to me a lot about what the training would be like and how she felt about what she did. And she was… encouraging."

"It sounds like you're still sure," Quinn said.

"I am," Ren said. "I love the lab, but I don't want a full-time research career. I just didn't expect the timing." She smiled wryly.

"But timing has always been one of those things that's never been routine for me."

"The timing is right this time," Quinn said. "If you're going to apply for a cardiac fellowship, you need to do that now."

"I hadn't thought I'd be finishing so soon," Ren said, quickly calculating how competitive she would be at this point for the fellowship she wanted. On paper her clinical experience would look thin. "My case log won't be as robust as other residents' in my year right now."

"You'll catch up soon enough," Quinn said, "and you have your research credentials, don't forget."

"Of course." True, her research might help, but surgical fellowships were clinical positions, and that's where she needed to stand out. She needed not just cases, but a clinical accomplishment—like the Franklin Surgical Award, granted yearly to the outstanding chief surgical resident—to balance her years in the lab. That's what she'd need to focus on, in addition to bolstering her case load, for the next year. Now that she had a goal, she started to plan. "I'll text Dr. Chan right away to make arrangements to review the service."

"Good. I'll tell her you'll catch up with her."

"Right. Thank you."

"And Ren," Quinn said as she turned for the door, "you'll do fine."

Ren turned back to the computer and stared at the program, calculating how much she needed to get done before morning. She'd have to do fine. She didn't have any choice. She tried to recall what she knew about Dani Chan, other than she was one of the transfer residents from a medical center that had lost federal funding and closed their training program. She'd never done a case with Dani, but they'd crossed paths in the ER and trauma admitting a few times. Dani was one of those high-energy, gregarious, personable residents that everyone liked. They would definitely have nothing in common, but that wouldn't matter. They wouldn't have to work together.

❖

West Mt. Airy, 3:10 a.m.

Quinn pulled into the narrow drive between their Victorian and the one next to it. On the opposite side, Phyllis's half of their twin was dark. Her mother-in-law was due back from her latest cruise with friends in a day or two. She closed the Bronco's door quietly, in hopes of not rousing the neighbor's ever-vigilant watch-poodle, and walked around to the back porch. A faint light emanated from the kitchen, and she let herself in. The light under the microwave shone dimly onto the stove and left most of the kitchen in shadows, but she could see well enough to make out her daughter and her daughter's friend Janie at the kitchen table. She glanced at the time on the microwave. Yep. Three fifteen a.m. Way late for Arly to be coming in. Honor would have called her if Arly hadn't been home by the agreed-upon time, which at a few days shy of fourteen was ten p.m., and judging from their oversized T-shirts and from what she could see beneath the table—shorts and bare feet—they hadn't just come home. The half-eaten chocolate cake in the center of the table and the crumb-covered napkins in front of them attested to a middle-of-the-night snack.

"Hi," Quinn said, closing the door gently behind her.

Arly glanced at Janie, and then they both smiled brightly.

"Hi, Quinn," Arly said.

"Hi, Quinn!" Janie echoed.

Interesting. They didn't exactly look guilty, but they emanated that too-casual attitude that often meant they were sharing a secret. Of course, that could mean anything from an escapade that didn't bear repeating to parents to an interrupted discussion of something else—like sex—judged not fit for her ears. Quinn was working hard at giving Arly space to disclose what she wanted to share in her own time. She'd just never realized how hard it would be to let go, even a little, of her need to keep her safe. Honor was much better at it, although she knew it was just as hard for her. She pointed to the cake.

"Can anybody have some of that?"

"Yeah, but you better leave some for Mom," Arly said.

"Smart plan." Quinn pulled out a chair, carved off a slice of the cake, and plopped it onto a napkin. As she did, Arly cut several more slices for herself and Janie. The cake was indeed delicious. "So, what have you two been up to?"

Arly glanced at Janie.

"Not much," they both said simultaneously. Even in the dim light, Janie's blush was obvious.

Quinn paused. Okay. That had seemed like a neutral question. Apparently not. But since neither of them appeared injured or impaired in any way, whatever they didn't want to discuss likely wasn't dangerous.

"Right. Okay then." Quinn brushed off her hands and gathered up her napkin. "I'll see you in the morning. You two might want to get some sleep. Jack's going to be up in a few hours, and he'll head for your room first."

"Yeah, right, we're going," Arly said.

Quinn took a shower in the upstairs hall bathroom to avoid waking Honor and crept quietly through the darkened bedroom to her side of the bed.

"Baby?" Honor said from the stillness.

Quinn lifted the sheets and slid in beside her. Honor automatically turned into her body, wrapped an arm around her middle, and threw a leg over hers.

"Mm, hi," Honor murmured and kissed her throat.

Quinn circled her shoulders and stroked her hair, letting out a long sigh. "Hi. You smell good."

"Shampoo," Honor murmured.

Quinn chuckled. Honor was the sexiest, most beautiful woman she'd ever known, and she didn't need to try. Of course her shampoo was more alluring than any perfume she'd ever scented. She kissed her temple. "How was your day?"

"Blessedly boring," Honor said. "How did the aneurysm resection go?"

"Long, but I think she's gonna do fine."

"Good. Everything else quiet?"

Quinn stretched her aching back muscles—too many hours bent over the OR table—and Honor cuddled closer. The tension drained away as the pleasure, and peace, of being with Honor flooded in. "I decided to pull Ren Dunbar out of the lab to take Mike Wu's place in the fifth year rotations."

"Ren's very bright," Honor said softly, her breath a warm caress against Quinn's shoulder. "Do you think she's clinically mature enough?"

"She's got the cases accumulated, but you're right—she'd been in the lab longer than usual. She might need a while to get her feet under her. But I think it's time to see if she can."

"Mm. Well, you're a good judge of when they're ready."

"I'll keep an eye on her for a while." Quinn only wished raising a teenager was as easy. "So, Arly's downstairs in the kitchen eating chocolate cake."

"Is there going to be any left?"

"We saved you some," Quinn said.

Honor sighed. "Wise of you all."

"True." Quinn rested her chin against the top of Honor's head. "Janie is with her."

"Oh. I thought I heard voices when Arly came in. I was almost asleep, but she was home on time."

"They're acting funny."

"Funny? Like, how funny?"

"That super-casual nothing-going-on-here tone, and the little looks that they don't think anyone else will notice. Funny like that."

"Oh," Honor said in a knowing tone.

"*Oh* what?"

Honor snuggled closer and kissed the corner of her mouth. "I'm assuming if you thought they were in some kind of trouble you'd mention it, so I'm drawn to another conclusion."

"Care to share?"

"What kind of secret would you have had when you were their age if your parents walked in on you and a friend in the middle of the night?"

Quinn frowned. The only thing she *really* wouldn't have wanted them to walk in on— She peered at Honor, who had a little smile on her face. "What, Janie? Arly and Janie?"

"It's a possibility."

"But I thought Arly was interested in Eduardo."

"She told us she was bi."

"Oh," Quinn said. Arly *had* told them she and her friends were discussing sex. Maybe she'd been preparing them for what came next. And maybe *she* hadn't thought of it sooner because then she'd have to think about Arly being ready for sex. "Ah, okay. Do we have to have some kind of rule or something?"

"What else is there? We've already had the safe sex talk," Honor said. "And Arly promised she'd talk to us about anything that bothered her."

"Yeah, but what about the sex at home thing. Isn't there some universal rule that you can't have sex in your mother's house?"

Honor laughed. "I have no idea. Terry and I didn't have much of a chance to find out, since Phyllis caught us practically the first time we'd ever had sex, and that was on the back porch in a hammock. Phyllis just told us in the future to pick a safer—and more private— place. To us that spelled Terry's bedroom, and Phyllis, bless her, always pretended not to notice."

"Yeah, but Phyllis was ahead of her time."

"Well, we should be *with* the times, don't you think? And where would a safer place for them be than here? It's not like we want her having sex in the back seats of cars or who knows where."

Quinn digested that for a moment. "What if it's Eduardo?"

"I don't see that it's any different." Honor propped herself up on an elbow, enough moonlight coming through the unshaded window to illuminate her face. She studied Quinn. "Do you?"

"Knee-jerk, yes. But then when I think about it, no. We never told Arly she couldn't have sex. We've got reasonable safe sex rules in place, and she's the best kid I've ever known. So we'll just pretend we don't know about it?"

"We expect her to pretend she doesn't know we're having sex," Honor pointed out and slid on top of Quinn. "Besides, would you want your parents giving you little knowing looks if you'd just had sex?"

"God, no. Please don't even go there." Quinn groaned. "And if you want sex anytime soon, please stop talking about my parents."

"How about we stop talking altogether," Honor murmured, kissing Quinn in that way she did when she was making it clear exactly what she wanted.

Lost in the heat of Honor's body and the familiar excitement of her kisses, Quinn forgot about teenagers, house rules, and long-ago mishaps. This, right here, was her world, and all that mattered. She framed Honor's face, kissed her back, and gently tilted her hips to roll them over. Holding herself up with her arms on either side of Honor's shoulders, she kissed Honor's throat. "I'm in a mood to take my time."

Honor shuddered and wrapped her arms around Quinn's shoulders. "Let's see how long you last."

CHAPTER TWO

West Mt. Airy, 8:00 a.m.

"Where do you want this one?" Zoey said, hefting a cardboard box, the flaps open and an assortment of electronic gear sticking out the top.

"Um," Dani said, pointing vaguely toward a plywood-and-sawhorse worktable pushed under the window in her new bedroom. "Over there, I guess."

"You know," Zoey said, pushing a loose strand of blond hair behind an ear, "this is a really big place, and you can have more than one room, especially since Hank has now officially moved out."

"Yeah," Dani said, ignoring the ringing of her phone in the pocket of her cutoff sweats. She'd been spending most of her time hanging in this half of the twin Victorians with Zoey ever since Syd and Emmett got together, so moving in full-time just made sense. But now Zoey was hooked-up too, and she really didn't want to be the extra person yet again. "But you might want to get another roommate. You know, maybe Declan?"

Zoey laughed. Like Dani, she was wearing as little as possible on the already sultry August morning—a white Lycra tank and tight pale blue yoga shorts that looked a lot more fashionable than Dani's usual boxers and faded T. "Dec has her own place, and she's not really roommate material."

"If you move out of this place," Dani said, "I'm going to have to look for a roommate. A three-story Victorian is way too big."

"Not to worry. She's only a few minutes away," Zoey said, "and we're good with things the way we are." She smirked. "When we get together, it's always date night."

"Yeah, okay," Dani said, "you can stop showing off."

"Just saying…" Zoey protested.

Grinning, Dani dropped her duffel bag by the closet. "Maybe when I start sorting through all my stuff, I'll move some of it into another of the bedrooms up here."

"You should—there's not really enough space for that big-ass monitor and supersized gaming chair in your bedroom." Zoey shook her head. "That chair belongs in a *Star Wars* museum."

"Hey! You gotta be comfortable while you're conquering the world."

Zoey snorted. "I get that playing online games is a great distraction, the whole flow thing, right? But since you're up half the night doing it, maybe it's not exactly the most restful hobby."

"Not the point," Dani said, thumbing off her phone again when it rang. "It's not about rest. It's about"—she hunched a shoulder—"accomplishing something in the short term. Making a plan and seeing if it will work." She laughed. "And destroying the enemy forces."

"I totally get the immediate gratification thing, as opposed to being a resident where the goal line is so far in the future as to be invisible sometimes." Zoey looked pointedly at Dani's sweatpants. "Are you going to answer that phone?"

"Nope," Dani said. "It's my mother calling to tell me of yet another exceptional job opportunity that I can't possibly pass up at some pharmaceutical company or research center or, God forbid, think tank, probably on the other side of the country."

Zoey rested her hip against the footboard of the big old-fashioned four-poster bed. She couldn't recall exactly where that had come from—maybe Hank had found it on one of his antiquing expeditions. He liked old stuff like that. "Your parents still haven't quite figured out that you really don't want to be a research scientist, have they."

Dani tugged at her lower lip and tried to search for the

nonchalance that was her second skin. "No. They're convinced I'm genetically predetermined to win the Nobel Prize, like the rest of my family. And that sooner or later—and the later it gets, the harder they push—I'll find my way back to the true path."

"Well, your mom…"

"I know, she's amazing and I couldn't be prouder of her, but I'm not her. Or my younger sister or my younger brother or, for that matter, my father. He's no slouch and probably in the running for the Nobel in physics sometime in the next decade. Hopefully before that happens, I'll be done with a vascular fellowship, and they'll have given up on me changing my mind."

"I don't think I would've liked to have grown up with all that expectation on my head," Zoey said softly.

Dani blew out a breath. "I've got nothing to complain about. I've got a great family. My parents just don't…get me." Her phone rang again, and she shoved her hand in her pocket and yanked it out. Damn it. Whatever it was, her mother was not going to quit. She hit the accept button and said in a rushed tone, "Mom, sorry, I'm in the middle of an emergency here. I'll have to call you back."

Quinn Maguire said, "Something going on somewhere I don't know about?"

Dani looked at Zoey and mouthed, *Shit!*

Straightening to attention even though Quinn couldn't see her, she said, "Oh, sorry, Chief. I thought you were my mother."

"That's a terrifying thought. I take it you're not actually in the hospital, and whatever the emergency is, it doesn't have anything to do with surgery?"

"No, something totally, completely *not* surgical. Sorry." Dani winced. "Um, do you need me?"

"Just wanted to let you know Ren Dunbar will be taking over Mike's service tomorrow. Can you get together with her sometime today, do a walk around, make sure she's up to speed on all the patients?"

"Absolutely, I can do that," Dani said. "I'll page her right now."

"Excellent. Sorry to drag you away from whatever you're doing."

"Not a problem, Chief," she said briskly and slid the phone back into her pocket. Glancing at Zoey, she raised a brow. "That's weird."

She thought Dunbar was a lab rat. One of those MD PhD people that never actually wanted to be doctors, just wanted the MD part to go along with the PhD part, which never really made a lot of sense to her. She'd only seen her a few times and never worked with her.

"What's weird?" Zoey said, setting down another carton she'd retrieved while Dani was talking. "Where do you want this one? I think this is the last of your clothes. Unless you've hidden something away somewhere that isn't scrubs or sweatpants, I mean."

"I'll have you know I have civilian clothes. Somewhere." Dani peered at the few cartons of clothes and wondered if she actually had anything that had survived the last few moves that would be considered going-out-in-public clothes as opposed to going-to-the-hospital clothes or hanging-around-in-the-house clothes. It's not like she needed them for anything. Dating really wasn't her thing. In fact, she pretty much sucked at it.

"So what's up?" Zoey asked.

"That was Quinn." Dani relayed the conversation. "What do you think? Seems kinda strange to put someone on a service who no one knows."

"Oh, I know Ren. She's actually been in the program a few years longer than I have."

"Really?" Dani frowned, doing the math in her head. Theirs was a five-year program—six, sometimes, with a lab year—and if Ren started before Zoey, something didn't compute. "Like, what, she's part of the world's longest residency program or something? What's the deal?"

"She came in from one of those programs that combines MDs and PhDs with a research specialty. So she's been in the lab quite a while. I don't really know much about her."

"Well, if she's taking Mike's place, she's going to be finishing up with my year."

"That'll be interesting. I guess it really doesn't make much difference."

"Yeah, I guess not," Dani muttered.

"What?"

"Nothing."

"Calling BS here," Zoey said. "Best friends and all that. Something's up, and you're supposed to tell me your secrets. I told you about Dec."

"You never told me about any sex."

Zoey smiled, that smile she got when she was thinking about Dec, soft and satisfied. Dani tried to imagine what, or *who*, would make her feel that way, because she was pretty sure she never had, not about anyone. She wasn't celibate or anything, but she mostly got together with women she connected with online or maybe at the game center. Not all that often—who had time to play anything, especially this last year when she had a whole service to look after. But when she'd tried the girlfriend thing, she just didn't seem to connect. Maybe she just didn't get feelings. Her family were all eggheads, and emotions weren't a thing. If one of her sibs had a problem or a decision to make, it got talked out between them and the parents until a rational solution was reached. Feelings didn't enter into it.

Except hers. She'd been stubborn about wanting surgery for as long as she could remember. Her parents were aghast, and her siblings were just…confused. Despite all the rational reasons why she was better suited—genetically, constitutionally, and every other way—for the same careers they all intended to follow or had already established, she'd been adamant about a clinical career. So here she was, still wondering about the lives other people had, and still thinking she was running out of time to show her parents that the decision she made was not only a good one, but one they could be proud of. Maybe even proud of her. She'd had a plan, but this Ren Dunbar was a wild card she hadn't counted on.

She let out a breath. "So, you know, the Franklin surgery prize?"

Zoey's expression became serious, and she plopped down on the bed to face Dani. "Sure."

"I, um…am kind of hoping I'll be in the running for that. It looks good when you apply for fellowships, you know?"

"You *have* had a lot of big cases," Zoey said, watching her carefully. "You've been thinking about it for a while, haven't you?"

Dani shrugged. She'd be competing with some of her friends, and talking about it was weird. "I didn't get the sense anybody else was really going after it."

"What does this have to do with Ren Dunbar?"

"Seems like she's some kind of star. All that time in the lab and the double degrees and all." She knew a lot about that—her parents and sibs all had an alphabet's worth of letters after their names.

"I don't know if that will help," Zoey said. "The Franklin is clinically based for the most part. You know, the attending surgical staff have to vote on what kind of surgeon you are, not what kind of research you've done."

"Yeah, but you know how much emphasis there is in medical centers like this one on research. Making you better rounded. And I don't have any research experience." Dani tried not to sound angry about it. Her choice, after all. "You have a year in the lab, don't you?"

"I have lab time, most of us do here in this program, but I don't think you need to worry about Ren. You have her beat in every other way. She probably hasn't done more than fifty cases in the last three years."

"Yeah," Dani said lightly. "Crazy idea anyways. I'm not exactly competitive for it. I'm a transfer, after all."

"That's bullshit, you know," Zoey said. "You probably have more cases than any of us, and you're always lurking around the ER and the trauma unit looking for more."

"I don't lurk," she said defensively.

"You lurk."

Dani grinned. "You noticed."

Zoey hopped up, gave her a hug, and said, "Best friends, remember?"

"Yeah, I know." She loved Zoey, and there was a time, before Zoey met Dec, when she'd thought maybe…but things were better this way. And Zoey was right. Worrying about Ren Dunbar wasn't going to change a thing.

❖

PMC, later that morning

"Excuse me." Ren motioned to a young guy wearing earbuds, pushing a large canvas bin of folded linens toward the OR entrance. He pulled out one bud and smiled. "Where can I find small scrubs? The rack in the OR lounge doesn't have any."

"Oh, sure. Come on, I'll show you where there's usually some left."

"Thanks." Ordinarily if she got a page the night she was on call, she just threw her lab coat on over whatever she'd worn to the lab. She always stayed in-house on her call nights—and whenever she had something running in the lab. Which meant often, and bicycling to the hospital in the middle of the night wasn't practical or safe. If she needed to scrub on a case, she'd grab whatever she could find, but if she was going to be spending all day, every day in scrubs, which was de rigueur for surgery residents on clinical rotation, she wanted something that fit and didn't make her look younger than she already appeared. Thankfully, the discrepancy in her age from that of the other residents wasn't quite as obvious as it used to be, but she didn't want to be taken for a medical student.

The tech pushed open an unmarked door down the hall from the main OR lounge and pointed to the stainless-steel racks along one wall. Scrub shirts, pants, and green cover gowns lay in loose piles on the shelves.

"If you hunt around in there, you'll find some smalls."

"Perfect," she said as he closed the door behind her. She searched the stacks and took three sets of dark green shirts and pants and carried them back to the locker room. As she set her phone down on the bench in front of her locker, an IM popped up for Raven from Axe. She smiled, grabbed the phone, and read the message.

Have time for a duel?

She texted back: *Sorry, have to pass. Maybe later?*

NP. Hope you're doing something fun—or about to win one. Catch you later
For sure.

Later. Maybe. She hoped so. Her orderly life was about to go totally off-track. She wasn't sure when she'd have free time again, at least not that she could predict. One of the big differences about being in the lab as opposed to clinical rotation was despite how many hours she spent there, she was often waiting—waiting for a test to complete, waiting for a tissue sample to thaw, waiting for the spectrometer to spit out the information she needed. And while she waited, she gamed—some of the time, at least. She supposed she'd be waiting a lot now too, for a case to start, for lab results to come in, for a critical CT scan to be finished. Unlike in the lab, though, she probably wouldn't be alone, and she probably wouldn't be able to fill those wasted moments catching an online game.

She'd miss losing herself for a few moments in the challenge of a friendly but completely serious rivalry. She'd miss the connection with people who welcomed her—or Raven, at least—however distant the connection was. She'd miss Axe, even though they'd never met. Axe was one of her favorite competitors. Smart and clever and, fortunately, someone who enjoyed the same kinds of online gaming she did. They'd been playing together, one on one, for the last few months. She'd probably lose that connection now. One she'd gotten used to. One she liked. She sighed. A lot of things were going to change.

Her phone signaled another message. She didn't know the number.

Dani Chan here. Let me know when it's a good time today to do a walk around.

And so it began.

Ren replied, *I'm in the OR lounge. I can meet you anytime.*

30 min in the caf work for you?

Yes.

She messaged Axe.

Got some time—you still free?

Sorry. Something came up. Text you tonight
Sure

With a sigh, Ren slipped her phone into her back pocket and pulled on her white lab coat. Then, thinking better of it, she stuffed the white coat into her locker, grabbed a stethoscope from the top shelf, slung it around her neck, and pulled on a green cover gown. There. Now her uniform was appropriate for her new role. She'd gotten good at adopting uniforms—not just clothes but expressions, language, even attitudes. Nothing masked the fact that she was younger, always younger, always the one who didn't fit, but eventually not standing out allowed her to disappear.

She wasn't thirteen anymore, or even nineteen and just starting her residency, and she didn't plan on disappearing any longer. She wanted to look the part because she'd earned it—because she *did* belong. Hopefully soon she wouldn't have to keep proving it.

Twenty-five minutes later she waited outside the cafeteria. Being early was the first step in getting ahead, just like in gaming. Never come in second. She could hear her father's voice repeating that endlessly, but on that, at least, they had always agreed. She wanted to be the best at what she did.

Gaming had been a natural fit, and she'd picked Raven as a handle when she was ten. She admired the bird's size and stature, bigger than so many birds, and its often-underappreciated talents. Considered scavengers, they were actually skilled hunters—often hunting solo—and among the most intelligent predators. She liked that about them too.

She was about to text Axe to try to find a time to get together when Dani Chan came around the corner, dressed in scrubs like her, scuffed navy-blue clogs on her feet, and a cover gown flapping behind her. A bit of a bright yellow and black tattoo peeked out along her collarbone and the left side of her neck. A tiger, Ren surmised. Dani was about her height, dark-haired like her, but hazel instead of the almost black of Ren's. Like the Raven's.

Ren shoved her phone back into her pocket.

"Ren?" Dani said, holding out her hand. "Hi. I'm Dani."

Ren shook her hand. "Hi. Yes."

"I thought we could get a cup of coffee and do dry rounds first. You can make your list, and then we'll walk around."

"Fine."

"Do you want lunch or anything while we talk?"

"No."

Dani hesitated a second, and Ren wondered if there was something else she should have said. Or asked. She didn't think so. Then Dani pushed through the cafeteria doors, and Ren followed. She never took advantage of the free mid-night meals when she was on call, but she guessed that was about to change too. While Dani got her coffee, Ren got water for tea.

They sat at a round table on the far side of the cafeteria. Midmorning on a Sunday, the place was pretty deserted.

"Don't drink coffee?" Dani asked, adding a sugar packet to hers. It already looked like she had a quarter of a cup of cream in it.

"I do sometimes," Ren said. "But usually just first thing in the morning. Then I switch to tea."

"Hmm. I never get any kick out of it."

"You might with good tea," Ren said quietly.

"Coffee's more of a sure bet."

"Not a gambler?" Ren asked before she thought better of it. That was probably a weird thing to say.

Dani gave her a look, then smiled. "Just the opposite, but..." She shrugged. "Not with my coffee."

Ren had reached that point that she often did when she met new people. She wasn't any good at small talk and didn't know where to go next. She was surprised she'd been able to say anything at all. Maybe she just expected not to be able to talk to people, a self-fulfilling prophecy. Also far too late to worry about it. "The list?"

"Oh, right." Dani set her phone on the table and tapped it a few times.

Ren did the same and opened the notes function. She'd have to transfer all of this to her mini-tablet. She should have thought of that. She frowned. Already not on top of things.

"Problem?" Dani asked.

Ren was careful not to blush when she looked up. Dani's eyes were curious, but warm. Friendly. "No. Nothing."

"Okay, let's start with the ICU," Dani said, a sudden seriousness replacing the playful note her voice had held earlier.

Ren bent her head over her phone. For some reason, knowing Dani might still be watching her disturbed her focus.

For fifteen minutes, Dani recited names, room numbers, diagnoses, OR dates, pending labs, recent vital signs, and outstanding tests.

Not looking up, Ren asked a few questions and took notes. By the time Dani was finished, Ren had forty-five names in front of her. She sat back, looked at Dani. "Big service."

"The A service covers a lot of attendings, including the big three."

Ren raised a brow. "Maguire, Naji, and Chung?"

"Yep," Dani said, "along with three or four others who only have a few admissions a week, if that."

"What about ER consults?" Ren asked.

"The attendings rotate, which means you'll get called when they're up. You'll need to check the ER board to find out who you'll be covering. Same for trauma call." Dani slid a beeper with a red band around the middle across the table. "And today's your lucky day."

"Okay." Ren clicked the trauma beeper to her waistband, collected her empty tea container, and stood up. "You ready then?"

Dani sipped the last of her coffee and grinned. "Always."

Ren wondered if she should know what that smile meant. She didn't, but she liked it all the same.

CHAPTER THREE

PMC, later in the day

Dani spent several hours with Ren making rounds, seeing each patient on A service, making chart notes, reviewing labs, and generally assuring that everything was buttoned up for the rest of the weekend. And to be sure that Ren had a good handle on what would need to be done come Monday morning. Dani didn't envy her at all. It was tough running a service for the first time for anyone, and Ren had been in the lab for years. She didn't have any experience running a team and probably wouldn't even know the other residents on the service. Talk about a hard entry. If she was Quinn—ha—she'd pull the best fourth year they had and put her with Ren, someone who wouldn't undermine her authority, but who would have her back if—make that when—things went FUBAR. Because they always did. Enoch Sloan, the fourth year on A service now, was an okay resident, but they already had a slot in an ophtho fellowship lined up and were pretty much just putting in time. But…she wasn't Quinn and not her call.

She still couldn't help thinking it was kinda crazy to stick surgical residents in the lab for even a year, let alone three years. Sure, there were things to be learned—she wasn't an idiot. Her parents and siblings were scientists. She valued what they did, even if it wasn't for her. But still, surgeons needed to be in the OR.

"You good?" she asked Ren when they left the ICU after seeing the last patient.

Ren looked surprised for a second as if that was a weird question, and then that smooth, totally chill expression came over her face. Dani'd noticed that despite everything that had been dumped on her *and* a service full of new—and pretty sick—patients, Ren never seemed to get ruffled or worried by anything. Pretty impressive. Yeah, she was some kind of star, all right. Lab rat or not, she had to be in the running for the Franklin. Dani mentally squared her shoulders. Not like she was afraid of a good fight or anything. Even though she infinitely preferred her battles to be virtual. She'd just have to find a way.

"Quite fine." Ren colored a little—a first—and added hastily, "I mean, I'm great. Thanks for meeting me. I'm sure it disrupted your day."

Dani smiled. "Nah. I was just moving boxes around."

"Sorry?" Ren frowned as if she was trying to decode another language.

"Literally, I mean. I live—lived—with Syd Stevens, but I just moved over to the other half with Zoey Cohen this morning."

"Oh," Ren said, and a smile slipped through. A nice smile. Soft and a tiny bit playful. "I see. You live on one of those blocks with the Victorian twins by the park."

"Yep."

"That's a very nice neighborhood." Ren paused. "Very convenient. I mean, to the hospital and everything."

That faint blush appeared for a heartbeat or two and then faded. Ren was damn cute when she did that. Dani did another mental double take, this one totally not about surgery or prizes or who could outshine who. Ren was seriously hot.

How had she not seen that instantly? *Aaand* now she was probably staring. She cleared her throat. "So, uh, I'll see you around then, I guess."

"Yes. I expect so," Ren said quietly. Her eyes—dark gray with fine flecks of darker black now that Dani looked closely—searched Dani's.

Looking for what? Dani swallowed, and heat flooded her

midsection. Wow. Okay. This was new. "So…call me. I mean if you have questions! Or anything…"

Slick. Very slick.

"Thank you."

"Since I'm here, I'm going to check on my intern. Make sure she's on top of things." Dani backed toward the stairwell. Ren was still watching her. "See you around."

An hour turned into two as she helped the intern start a central line in an ICU patient and checked on the next day's pre-ops to be sure all the labs and X-rays were done. Finally finished, she hurried down the stairs and burst out onto the main floor, nearly colliding with Emmett McCabe. "Whoa, sorry!"

"What's up?" Emmett asked. "Is there a code?"

"No—I, uh, nothing. Just finishing rounds."

Emmett, taller than her with dark hair and deep blue eyes, gave her a quizzical stare. "I thought you made rounds this morning?"

"It's complicated," Dani said, falling into step with Emmett.

Emmett laughed. "All right. Did you get moved okay?"

"Yeah. Zoey did all the heavy lifting."

"I bet." Emmett paused. "You know, you don't have to move out. Syd and I like having you—"

"It's all good," Dani said hastily. She didn't want to embarrass Emmett or herself by explaining that their intense couple-ness, if that was even a word, made her…want something. Something she'd rather not have to think about. "This works out for Zoey too."

"That's good then," Emmett said and thankfully let it drop.

"Something going on?" Dani said as she realized they were heading for the ER.

"Consult," Emmett said. "I just finished in the OR with McCleary doing an ischemic bowel resection on one of the ICU patients. The ER called me earlier about a consult but said it could wait."

Dani frowned. The ER liked to move patients through as quickly as they could, especially on nights and weekends, and would often keep calling around until they found someone free. "I didn't get a call, and I've been here since morning."

"I think it's a direct admission sent in from an attending covered by B service. Didn't sound urgent."

"Oh," Dani said. They were already there, so she might as well tag along and see what else was happening in the ER. There was nothing worse than leaving the hospital in the middle of the afternoon and just getting home to find out a consult had been sitting there for an hour that no one had called in. Then she'd have to turn around and head back. She followed Emmett over to the central station where ER residents, nurses, techs, and PAs filtered through, checking labs, completing patient charts, and triaging patients who needed to be seen or admitted.

"Hey, Philippe," Emmett called as she walked up and leaned on the waist-high counter that ran around the open square of the station, "you got a consult somewhere down here for me?"

The ER nurse slashed a signature across the bottom of a digital form and looked up. "Oh, we did, but it's taken care of."

"Sorry?" Emmett frowned. "Did one of my residents get down here then?"

"Hold on." Philippe grabbed the ringing phone. "ER, Rodriguez." He nodded, pulled another tablet toward him, and swiped it open. "Yes, the report just came in. I'll see she gets it. Thanks."

He hung up the phone, texted something on his phone, and glanced back at Emmett as if surprised she was still there. "I wasn't paying too much attention to who came down. But I'm pretty sure the patient's slated to be admitted already."

"Great," Emmett said slowly. "What room is the patient in?"

Philippe swiveled to look at the digital intake board on the wall opposite the station. "That would be Andrew Gilmore, in seven."

"Thanks." Emmett headed down the hall, one of three that emanated from the station like spokes on a wheel.

"I'll wait and walk home with you," Dani said. Maybe Emmett would have some thoughts on the best way to get noticed by the staff voting on the Franklin. Or, hell, maybe she expected to get it herself.

Emmett was slated for a trauma fellowship, and that was Quinn's thing. Might as well know now. Not that she planned on quitting just because she had a little—okay, a lot of—competition. They'd almost reached cubicle seven when the curtain slid back and Ren Dunbar stepped out, tablet under her arm.

"Hey." Emmett skidded to a halt. "Dunbar."

Ren smiled at Dani, a smile that disappeared as she nodded to Emmett. "That's me. Ren. I just talked to your junior resident—Wesley Curtis?"

She pulled the curtain closed behind her and stepped a few feet down the hall. Emmett and Dani followed.

"What's the story?" Emmett asked.

"This is Dr. Akeema's patient—Andrew Gilmore, forty-seven—sent in for an evaluation of abdominal pain."

"Did Akeema actually see the guy?" Emmett asked mildly, a hint of scorn in her voice. Quite a few of the non-hospital-based surgeons used the ER as their own private acute care center and expected the residents to take care of the patients they told to go there to be seen.

"A video consult," Ren said neutrally. "His symptoms—acute onset of severe pain and fever—warranted a workup. He's got an elevated white count and some tenderness in the left lower quadrant. The CT just shows a little edema consistent with diverticulitis. I think that's likely. Anyway, Akeema wanted him admitted. It's all set now."

"Uh, thanks," Emmett said with a questioning tone in her voice. "Are you covering the ER or something?"

"No," Ren said, "I just happened to be down here, and one of the ER docs said they were waiting on a surgery consult. I figured I might as well take care of it while the rest of your team was busy." She tilted her head and frowned at Emmett. "Problem?"

"No, as long as everything is covered, and our guys know what's going on."

"Oh, I explained to the patient, and also to Dr. Akeema when I called him, that I was admitting him to your service. As I mentioned, your resident was busy in the ICU, and I filled him in too."

"Well, I guess thanks then for taking care of it." Emmett shot Dani a look.

Ren smiled. "You're welcome." She edged around Dani and made her way back toward the central station.

Dani turned and watched her go, then muttered, "I think that might be a first."

Like, super unusual for a busy surgical resident to be concerned about patients who were the responsibility of another surgical service. But on the other hand, they were all there for the same reason, to take care of patients. Hard to complain about someone doing all the right things, even if it was a little odd. Maybe Ren just wanted to get back into the swing of things quickly. Couldn't blame her. And come to think of it, Dani'd been in the ER plenty of times when someone had grabbed her and asked her to see a consult even though she wasn't technically responsible for seeing anyone. She'd done it because it needed doing and, ultimately, because it was her job. That was probably all there was to it.

"Well," Emmett said, "at least she wasn't trying to steal the case."

"No," Dani said thoughtfully, "I don't think that's her style."

"You know her?"

"Not really. We just met. She's taking A service."

"As service chief?"

"Yeah."

"Huh." Emmett shook her head. "Hell of a crazy year we've got."

Dani shrugged. She was part of the reason it was crazy. She and Ren had that in common. They both were outsiders, in a way. And Emmett was the chief surgical resident responsible for all of them. "You need me to do anything?"

"Nah—go home. I'm just gonna introduce myself to this guy and check the ICU. I'll be a while."

"Okay. I'm outta here then."

As she gathered her gear and headed home for the second time that day, Dani thought about Ren Dunbar. If she hadn't known better, she would've thought at first sight that Ren was a first year at best. Most fifth year surgery residents, like Dani, were around thirty, but Ren didn't look much older than early twenties. She had to be at least a little older than that, though, even if she *had* been part of some accelerated program. Her build probably added to the impression she was younger too. Like Dani, she wasn't much above average height, but thinner—not fragile or weak-looking, but the lean suppleness of the dancer as opposed to the more muscular build Dani had acquired thanks to years of martial arts training. They weren't similar in any other ways, though. At least none that showed. Ren was very focused, very intense, and as far as Dani could tell, without much sense of humor. All business. Nothing wrong with that either. She'd probably be pretty reserved and intense herself if she'd gotten tossed from the lab into the middle of a busy service overnight. Not that she'd let a case of nerves show. She smiled to herself—Syd called her a swashbuckler. She'd always secretly liked that.

Ren was way more quiet than Dani but, no question, also supersmart. She warmed up almost instantly whenever she talked to a patient—almost a different person. Softness came into her voice, and even her expression changed. Dani could tell when someone cared as much about the people as the science. Ren did. Her kind of doctor.

Too bad they'd be on different services the rest of the year. She kind of liked her. Ren was different, like her, and well, there was the fact she was hot. Dani grinned as she turned the corner toward home. There was that.

Humming to herself, Dani bounded up the steps on the wrong side of the porch. She'd moved that morning, remember! Now she lived on the other side. She vaulted over the railing that divided the mirror-image front porches, dug out her keys, and unlocked the front door.

"It's me," she called.

The house was silent. Zoey was either asleep, in which case nothing short of an earthquake would wake her, at the hospital, or with Declan. Because what else was there for a resident besides sleep, work, or—with luck—sex. Which for some reason made her think of Ren, and thinking about hot girls she didn't actually have a shot at left her restless. Better to think about a slow afternoon, a cold beer, and a good game.

That picture was almost perfect. Almost. In the back of her mind, she couldn't quite shake the sense of time running out. When this year was over, she'd be one step closer to her career goal, and one year further away from the chance that her parents would ever understand what she was doing. That she would ever be part of their lives, or them part of hers. She probably should be used to it by now—the odd silences on the end of the phone when she tried to tell them about her newest rotation or a case she'd scrubbed on. Those things didn't matter to them. For her parents, for her whole family, awards and recognition were symbols of true success. She hadn't had anything to show them yet. She had a year to change that.

But she didn't have to think about the Franklin award for the rest of the day. She scanned the inside of the fridge until she found the last two cans of beer. She pulled one out and tucked the box of Cap'n Crunch under her arm on her way out of the kitchen. Right now, she could spend a few hours with a friend in a friendly competition. Smiling with a buzz of anticipation she didn't get anywhere else these days, she pulled out her phone and texted Raven.

I got the afternoon free. You?

Raven answered almost instantly. *Looking for revenge?*

Dani laughed. *Hey, you're only three games ahead of me. Close enough to go either way*

close only counts in horseshoes

What? Dani laughed and then put in *???*

horseshoes it's a game

I know what horseshoes is

Well then you understand the saying

Dani sat on the top porch step and leaned back, phone in hand, and drank some beer as the unsettled sensation faded away. Sunlight slashed across her thighs, and the sounds of neighborhood kids calling to one another shaped a kind of relaxing background melody. Yeah, this was good. She typed, *I guess I do, except I've never heard anyone under 75 use it.*

Her phone stayed blank. No return message. Uh-oh. Sometimes what she thought was funny, other people…not so much. She really liked Raven. Raven was the best gamer she'd ever faced, subtle and swift and smart. Playing with Raven upped her game a lot, and she routinely beat almost all of her other opponents. Raven, though… she had the really bad feeling that sometimes when she did win, Raven was probably doing three other things at the same time. Because when she could feel the focus burning through her phone or emanating from the monitor, Raven annihilated her.

She didn't know the ordinary things about Raven that she'd know about someone else she counted as a friend. Where they lived, what they liked to eat, hell, what they looked like. But still, Raven was as real to her as Zoey.

She didn't want to lose Raven. The thought made her a little queasy.

Rave?

The IM popped right away, and Dani let out a breath.

I guess you're probably right. All my mentors were older. Blame it on my childhood.

Dani laughed again. *Safe bet for us all*

A smiling emoji came back. *Isn't it?*

So you ready? Dani typed.

For sure, Raven replied in her signature response.

Dani opened the app and saw the invitation from Raven waiting for her. Happy, excited, she clicked *Join*.

CHAPTER FOUR

Ren moved her token, claimed the last victory point, and smiled as the scores tallied up. A moment later the message from Axe appeared.

That's only one point. Close only counts in horseshoes.

Ren laughed out loud, the sound strange in the otherwise silent on-call room. She curled up on the bottom bunk with her back against the wall and her legs drawn up, her computer balanced on her knees. She'd hoped all evening that no one else would come in to share the space, and she'd been lucky. She was alone, as she'd hoped. The hours had passed so easily, as their victories bounced back and forth, first Axe winning, then her. She liked to win, but she liked to play even more, especially with an opponent like Axe who was never predictable and always forced her to vary her strategy. Axe wasn't just smart—she was perceptive. If Ren hadn't learned long ago how to avoid making the obvious draw or building on a predictable series of moves, she'd almost think she was telegraphing her play. But she wasn't—any more than she telegraphed her plans, or feelings, in person. Axe just sensed what she was thinking…somehow.

She texted back: *It counts when you're the one closest to the pole*

It's stake…and you say that now. Not what I heard earlier :-)

If it wasn't close, what fun would it be?

Not as much fun as this.

A warm feeling spread through Ren's chest. Axe enjoyed playing with her, maybe as much as she did. Silly, that she cared about what someone she'd never met thought about her. But it was such a change, to have a friendship with someone, after finding over and over again she was bad at it. Maybe if they actually played in person...No. She already knew how that would turn out. She wouldn't know the right things to say, or not say, and she wouldn't be what she was expected to be. Just not right, somehow. She understood she was the odd one, the one who didn't fit. But here, she could be herself, and all that mattered was what she said and how she played. Here Axe liked her.

Another game? Ren asked.

Bummer. Can't, Axe texted. *Work in the morning.*

Work. Not school. Not class. So at least Axe wasn't a teenager, most likely. Not that it really mattered. They were just gaming friends. Ren sighed. She didn't sleep much. She was like Sax that way, never seeming to need much sleep and always being just a little bit wired. She knew sleep was important, though, for her and everyone else. *NP. Will catch you again soon for sure. later*

later, Ren texted with just a bit of sadness. Missing someone whose face she'd never seen, whose voice she'd never heard. Maybe that made her kind of pitiful. But there it was.

She thought about trying to sleep, but she wasn't the least bit tired. If she got two or three hours, she'd be fine. She set her computer on the narrow desk tucked against the wall at the foot of the bunk beds, left her backpack in the middle of the bed to claim her spot, and walked down the hall to the ER.

The charge nurse, Linda O'Malley, watched her coming, and when she stopped to look at the intake board, said, "Surgery?"

Ren nodded.

"I was just about to call a consult. Who are you covering?"

Ren perked up. "I'm covering A service, but I'm not busy right now."

Linda glanced at the on-call board. "This is just a routine unreferred patient who needs to be cleared for discharge. Perkins is the attending on call—he wants the patient seen by a resident before we send him home." She lifted a shoulder. "Kim Rae is covering consults, but she's down in radiology getting an a-gram on a cold foot."

"No problem. I can take it."

"Great. He's in four."

Ren turned to pick up the tablet from the rack of patients to be seen, then reminded herself that she ought to be working on her communication skills. The first step was to ask something about the other person. Studies had shown it didn't even have to be a personal question—any question usually enhanced the positive response to the interaction. She wished she'd known that when she was twelve. Of course, she hadn't really tested the theory herself. She cleared her throat. "How is your new baby?"

Linda smiled, her eyes shining. "Feisty and doing great."

"You just came back, didn't you?"

"Yes, after almost four mostly glorious weeks off. I miss her, but it feels good to be back."

"Well," Ren said, anxious to get to the consult, "it's good to see you."

"Thanks. It's Ren, isn't it?"

Ren paused, surprised. "Yes. Ren."

"Let me know if you need anything."

"I will."

Maybe the studies were right. Linda's warm smile followed Ren down the hallway toward room four. Most of her ER calls had been at night, and she'd found the quiet to be a silent comfort. Curtains were drawn, lights were dimmed, and voices were lowered. She caught muted bits of conversation and an occasional moan or sigh, but nighttime in the hospital always felt like some slip of time, tucked in between the chaos and bright lights of waking hours. She paused outside the closed curtain of cubicle four to scan the chart. A forty-three-year-old man complaining of headache after being hit in the head by a wild pitch during a summer league baseball game.

The kind of blunt injury to produce a hematoma or fracture. The ER resident had noted soft tissue swelling in his left temple region, but nothing else on exam. A notation said he'd had a CT scan a half hour before. The reading had been normal other than some suggestion of mild contusion. Not surprising after taking a blow to the head.

Expecting this to be a brief check and discharge, she slid the curtains back and stepped inside. A man looking his stated age lay on the stretcher, eyes closed, a faint pallor to his face. An IV line ran from a bag of saline hanging on a pole beside the bed to a catheter taped to his right wrist.

"Mr. Mancuso? I'm Dr. Dunbar," she said as she walked over to the counter adjacent to the stretcher, set down her tablet, and leaned over the sink to wash her hands. "How's your headache doing?"

"Worst headache ever," he said slowly, with just a hint of a slur to his words.

Ren narrowed her eyes and turned to look at him more closely. The right lower corner of his mouth sagged. Subtle, but it was there. She looked around for a flashlight and found one in the cabinet above the counter. She needed to start carrying one. Leaning over the rail by his side, she said, "I'm just going to check your pupils. Can you open your eyes?"

He did, slowly, and she shone the light in first his left then his right. Anxiety fluttered through her stomach, and every muscle tensed. "Are you having any blurred vision?"

"No," he said. "Don't...know. Maybe."

Definitely slurred speech now. Ren put the flashlight aside and grasped both his hands, one in each of hers. "Squeeze my hands. Hard as you can—I'll tell you when to stop. Don't worry."

He did, except his right hand barely closed around her fingers. Now the tightness in her belly spread to her chest, and she had one paralyzing moment of terror. Then, as if a prism had slipped in front of her gaze, the world grew sharp and bright.

"I'm going to raise the back of your stretcher a little bit more." She found the controls and put him upright, hoping to relieve some of the pressure in his head. She turned the IV down as low as it would go. "I will be right back."

She dropped the tablet on the counter, slipped out of the curtain, and raced down the hall. Linda heard her coming and stood up. "What?"

"He's got an intracranial bleed. He's about to herniate. We need neurosurgery, right away."

"Are you sure? The CAT scan—"

"I don't care what the CAT scan shows. He's got right-sided symptoms, and his left pupil's blown. Get somebody. In the meantime…" She mentally flipped through the emergency protocol for intracranial bleed. The page came into view, the words scrolling through her memory. She reeled off the meds and dosages.

"Got it." Linda didn't hesitate, already on the phone while flagging down a PA who'd heard their conversation and stopped with a questioning look. "Kareem, you're with Dr. Dunbar. Get the meds she needs started in four, stat."

Ren jogged back down with the PA while a nurse wheeled the med cart to the opening of the cubicle and began to prepare the drips and drugs she'd ordered to help control his intracranial pressure until neurosurgery could get there and do a definitive procedure.

"What's happening?" the patient muttered. "Fuck, my head hurts."

Spasms started in his right hand, traveled up his arm, and suddenly his entire body began to shake.

"He's seizing," Ren said in a voice that came out steady and calm. Another page from the emergency protocol manual flickered into view, and she barked out instructions. "Call the code. Let's get him intubated." Within seconds, the room filled with even more people—starting IVs, drawing bloods, pulling out the intubation equipment. She paid little attention to who was around her, too busy watching the monitors, assuring the right meds were being given, adjusting dosages until the seizures stopped and he appeared stable. She spun around to look for Linda and came face-to-face with Honor Blake. "Is neurosurgery here?"

"On their way. Nice job, Dr. Dunbar."

Honor didn't seem at all surprised or taken aback by her perfunctory tone. Honor *was* the ER chief after all, and Ren was… Well, Ren was just a resident. She frowned. "I might've been a little bit slow in making the diagnosis. I read the results of the CAT scan first, and it threw me off. They read it as normal."

Honor nodded. "That happens. Especially when the bleed is small and there's some swelling around the site. That's what you would expect with a blow to the head and a mild contusion. We'll probably find out this is an epidural bleed. They expand quickly, and the symptoms accelerate fast."

A big man appeared behind Honor. Ren recognized him. Kos Hassan, the neurosurgeon. At his side, Sydney Stevens, the senior neuro resident.

"I heard he seized," Kos said. "Let's get this guy upstairs." He regarded Ren for a second. "Who are you again?"

Ren tensed. "Ren Dunbar. Senior surgery resident."

"Huh. Okay, then. You want to scrub with us?"

"I do." She glanced at Syd, who in this instance was her senior. "If there's room?"

"Sure," Syd said. "I'll get the consents from his family, if you help get him upstairs."

"Of course."

Syd gave her a long look, then smiled. "Thanks."

Ren relaxed, pleased. She'd done her job, of course, and that was what mattered. But she liked Syd's smile too. Maybe she'd be able to do this after all.

❖

Dani slept in a tank top and boxers on top of the sheet with the windows wide open. She still woke up sweaty and restless a little before the sun came up. Maybe part of the hot and unsettled feeling was due to her crazy-ass dreams. Something to do with a cliff and a woman with wings—but definitely not the fairy princess kind of woman—one who led her on a chase through foggy forests that turned into deserted city streets, and then the woman—fairy... whatever the hell she was supposed to be—dragged her into the mist and kissed her. A freaking hot kiss and then...she flew away. Looking like some dark bird against the moonlit sky. Totally *WTF?* and typically frustrating.

How come every time she was in the middle of a sexy dream,

something would happen to interrupt, and her subconscious would go veering off in some other direction before the finale. She sighed. Probably a metaphor for her life that she hadn't yet deciphered.

She sat up and ran her hands through her hair. The damp strands just touched her shoulders. An inch longer than she usually wore it. She needed to find time to get it cut. She needed to find time to get to the dojo. She needed to find time to get a life, but that wasn't gonna happen this year. Not during the busiest, most important year of her residency. Not now especially, when she had the crazy-ass idea to try for the Franklin. She probably should give that up. She would, maybe, if she wasn't always hearing her mother's urgings to reconsider and her father's subtle frustration. If she didn't think, *hope*, achieving something they could understand and appreciate would somehow change things. Somehow make her not the disappointment. The one no one could understand.

And she was going to have to do something to figure out exactly what she needed to do to win the stupid thing. Every time she got to this point, she wanted to think about anything but, and she instantly thought of Raven. A game and some easy chat with Raven, that's what she needed. She grabbed her phone and winced. They'd just said good night a few hours earlier. Raven was almost always around, no matter the hour, but Dani still didn't want to chance waking her up. And she knew Raven was a she—not because of anything Raven had said, just…because of a feeling. Yeah, right. Like she was so good at those—still, she trusted this one. And she was going to let Raven sleep.

She left her phone on the bedside table, shed her clothes, and padded down the hall to the bathroom. She'd been under the shower three minutes and was just contemplating doing something about the lingering arousal left over from the unrequited lust of her dreamscape when the bathroom door banged open and Zoey exclaimed, "You are *not* gonna believe this."

"Naked in here," Dani shouted. "Taking a shower."

"What, you think I don't know that," Zoey said. "What do you think I'm doing in here?"

"Interrupting me?"

"You're taking a shower, what's to interrupt?"

Dani rolled her eyes. Like she was going to say something to that. *Not.*

"Go away, and I'll be out in ten minutes," she said instead.

"Who needs ten minutes in the shower," Zoey said. "Nothing takes ten minutes. Besides, I want to talk to you."

Annoyance killed the last of her flagging arousal, and Dani surrendered. "All right, what do you want, then?"

Before Zoey could answer, Syd Stevens said, "What are you guys both doing in the bathroom?"

"What, is there some kind of party I don't know about," Dani yelled. "I'm taking a shower. Zoey is bothering me. Why are you here?"

"Because I've been up all night, I needed coffee, and there's cinnamon rolls downstairs."

Dani hurriedly rinsed the rest of the soap from her hair and turned off the water. "Get out, both of you. I'll be downstairs in two minutes."

She opened the door of the shower a few inches. "Wait—hand me a towel."

Zoey handed her a towel. "Hurry up."

Grumbling, Dani wrapped a towel around herself and hustled back to her bedroom. She pulled on jeans, T-shirt, and beat-up loafers and finger-combed her hair. By the time she got to the kitchen, Zoey had poured three mugs of coffee, and Syd was sliding cinnamon rolls into the toaster oven.

"I don't need mine toasted," Dani said. "Thanks for the coffee."

"Wait five minutes, Dr. Impatience," Syd said. "The payoff'll be worth it."

"Nothing's worth waiting five minutes for, when you really want something," Dani said.

Zoey rolled her eyes. "You'll change your mind someday."

"And you complain I'm always thinking about sex," Dani said, grinning.

"Never mind the cinnamon rolls," Zoey said, holding up her phone and waving it in the air in Dani and Syd's direction as if they could actually read the blue bubbles on the text screen. "I'm trying to tell you something important."

"What?" Dani asked.

"I got a text from the chief a few minutes ago. I'm getting pulled from transplant to general surgery."

"Um, so," Syd said, sounding only slightly mystified. "What's the crisis?"

Dani felt a chill. A real chill. "Let me guess. You're going to A service."

Zoey narrowed her eyes at her. "What did you do?"

"*Me*," Dani said. "Nothing. Why does it always have to be me?"

Syd grinned, and Zoey pointed at her. "Because it usually is."

"Got a point," Syd said, setting the rolls on the table.

"Hey!" Dani shot Syd a wounded look. "You're supposed to have sympathy for me. Fellow transfer and all that."

Zoey snorted. "As if anybody cares about that anymore."

Dani grimaced. "I bet they do. Maybe not the residents, but... never mind. Is it A service?"

"Yes."

"Well, that makes sense then," Dani said. "Mike's leaving, and the new chief doesn't have a lot of clinical experience. You do."

"I don't want to spend the next four months babysitting," Zoey said.

Syd snorted. Dani rolled her eyes. "You're saying Quinn Maguire asked you to babysit a fifth year resident?"

"Well, no, but..."

"You're not gonna have to babysit Ren," Dani said, feeling unexpectedly protective. "I made rounds with her yesterday. She's smart. You'll—"

"Supersmart," Syd put in. "She just scrubbed on a case with me and Kos. Very brainy. Pretty good hands too, for somebody who's been in the lab all that time. I think she said she was dissecting beef hearts under the microscope or something."

Dani swiveled in her chair to stare at her. "Wait a minute. Ren just did a case with you? Last night."

Syd nodded. "Yeah. Well, this morning really. She saw a patient in the ER with a developing epidural hematoma. Really fast pickup too. If she hadn't seen him and made the diagnosis right away, the guy could've died."

Syd had left general surgery to go into neuro and launched into a lot more detail than Dani really wanted to hear just then. Not that it wasn't an interesting case, but what interested her a lot more was figuring out what the hell Ren was doing in the emergency room in the middle of the night when she wasn't even on call.

"I don't get it," Zoey said. "If she's so good, why pull me then?"

"It makes sense," Dani said. "I was just thinking earlier today, if I was Quinn, that's what I would do."

Zoey sighed. "So she *does* need a babysitter."

"No," Dani said. "That's not what I meant. It's just that when you have a new chief who doesn't know the residents, it helps to have a senior who supports them and can ride herd on the juniors. The other residents all know you. And, well, you're the best resident in your year."

Syd said, "Aww. That's really sweet."

"Shut up," Zoey said, a blush coloring her cheeks.

Dani ignored the teasing. "And you're not going to have any reason to steal cases from her, since you want transplant. Like I said, perfect choice."

While Syd and Zoey went back to discussing the neuro case, Dani kept turning over and over in her mind the question of what Ren was doing in the ER in the middle of the night. The only answer she could come up with was that Ren was making an all-out push to show she was clinically up to speed. To make an impression. As if the lab experience wasn't enough. Of course, Dani could think of a lot of reasons Ren might want to do that, but the biggest one was she wanted to be competitive for the Franklin. Dani'd figured the other residents in her year all had a good shot at it—probably better than she did, but Ren suddenly joining the field changed things. She never liked starting a game against players she didn't know. Maybe she needed to change that.

CHAPTER FIVE

Ren finished scrubbing on the neurosurgery case around four thirty. No point in trying to sleep then, and she was too wound up physically and too excited mentally to even consider it. Besides, in a little over an hour she'd be meeting with her new service, and she had plenty to do before then to get ready. First impressions mattered, especially for her. She knew what people thought when they first saw her. Beyond the obvious—too young, too inexperienced—their next thoughts often carried a hint of subtle suspicion—who was she, where had she come from, what special privileges had she been granted. She kept her private life private, which wasn't hard since she never developed close relationships anyhow, but she was doubly glad now that no one knew Quinn Maguire was a family friend. She'd known Quinn since she was fifteen, and that *was* partly the reason she was here. But she'd had other offers from other training programs. None of that mattered now. What mattered was that she belonged here, even if no one but her knew it. That was up to her to change.

She planned to make rounds even before the other residents did, so she'd know the patients as well as, or better than, they did when they first sat down to discuss them at morning rounds. If she wanted to be in charge, she'd have to banish their doubts as to her abilities before they had time to form doubts. So no time to get home and even think about a change of clothes, not that she needed anything other than clean scrubs. She had all of her necessary items in her backpack. After a quick shower in the locker room, she dried her hair with a towel and a quick minute or two with a blow-dryer. She never worried much about styling it. It was thick enough and had just enough wave not to need anything special. She'd never really gotten the hang of makeup, as if she'd had time or reason to learn, or even *wanted* any when wearing a surgical mask all day long. And she'd never really had to worry about any other occasions, like having a date or anything. That had never been on her mind. When she was the age other people began doing it, she'd been in college and a full five years younger than everyone else. No, dating had not been on her horizon then, and by the time she might have been able to breach the distance between herself and her colleagues, other things seemed more important. Or at least more comfortable.

As she got dressed for the day, she kept thinking about the surgery of the night before. She'd scrubbed on only a couple of neuro cases a long time before, and they hadn't been anything other than routine. This had been an emergency. A life-or-death situation, and she'd felt it, every second of the immediacy, the intensity, the controlled speed and pressure of getting him upstairs, getting him anesthetized, getting the access through the bone into the intracranial space, finding the large hematoma pressing on his brain, clearing it away, relieving the pressure, watching his vital signs stabilize. All within what felt like seconds, but had really been minutes. Twenty minutes that had spelled the difference between a future for him and a tragedy. She'd been part of that.

At one point Kos—Dr. Hassan—had told her that if she hadn't moved as quickly as she had, hadn't done the right initial emergency treatment, they might never have gotten him upstairs in time. She had saved a life. The very thing that had made her decide to go into medicine in the first place, to use the skills that she was good at—her brain, her focus, her eidetic memory—not just to impress teachers and mentors, but to make a real-life difference. She'd felt it even when she was so young no one else had taken her seriously. She'd believed it all the years she had to face the challenges alone, but she'd never before truly experienced it. Those few hours with

Kos and Syd Stevens had shown her that everything she'd thought she'd wanted was true. She'd had success in the lab, she'd impressed people—not that that was new or even had much meaning to her—and she'd published papers, significant scientific findings that would make a difference, in theory and, hopefully, in practice at some point. But those successes would never come directly from her hands. Her research mattered. She was proud of her work, and she would finish her work, but this, this was like nothing she'd ever felt before. *This* sense of accomplishment, of fierce victory, was what she wanted. And she wanted more of it.

Still heady with the feeling of success, of triumph, she got coffee, toast, and eggs and splurged with a helping of the hash the cafeteria was famous for. Her usual breakfast was a protein bar while sitting at her computer in the lab. But last night warranted a celebration. She carried her tray to a small table on the far side of the cafeteria where she could look out the window and watch the sunrise. The view was one of her favorites, across the green lawns that sloped down to the fringe of trees that separated the grounds of the medical school and hospital complex from the neighborhood that surrounded it.

She'd just started on her toast when Dani Chan came in with Zoey Cohen, both of them in green scrubs like her and almost every other person in the cafeteria. Ren watched them for a few seconds and then averted her gaze back to the window. She didn't want Dani to think she was staring at her, which she was, but just seeing Dani—someone she knew, even just a little—made her feel as if she was a part of things somehow. Even though she wasn't really. She didn't really know Dani, and Dani had probably forgotten all about her.

Dani said, "Hi, Ren, mind if we join you?"

Ren looked up, hiding her surprise, pleased that she hadn't jumped at the unexpected sound of Dani's voice. "Of course. I mean, of course I don't. Mind. Please, sit down."

Dani pulled out a chair, and Zoey sat beside her, facing Ren. After a second, Zoey extended her hand.

"Hi, I'm Zoey Cohen. I don't think we've ever actually met, but you know, we've passed each other here and there."

"Of course." Ren extended her hand and, as they shook, added, "You're a fourth year, right?"

"That's right," Zoey said. "And as of right now, I'm *your* fourth year."

Ren frowned. "I'm sorry?"

"I'm on A service—fourth year."

"Not according to the list I received from Dr. Maguire."

"Well, apparently there's been a switch," Zoey said lightly. "I got a text this morning from Dr. Maguire that I was being transferred over to your service."

"Oh," Ren said, mentally calculating what that might mean while surreptitiously checking her phone for a missed text. She knew there wasn't one—she'd been checking for a message from Axe for the last hour. She couldn't come up with a reason for replacing her fourth year resident except that Dr. Maguire either wanted her to have a more experienced senior resident to watch her and report on her, or help her out. She could either be paranoid about that, which wouldn't change whatever the truth was, or she could simply start out believing that Zoey was there to do what every other fourth year resident did—make sure the chief was well-informed at all times, never surprised by anything, and always had all the answers that an attending might want, and to see that the junior residents faithfully carried out the chief resident's instructions. In other words, Zoey was there to be her right hand.

"Well then," Ren said, stretching her hand across the table. "Welcome, and thank you. I'm glad to be working with you."

Zoey took her hand, squeezed it firmly for a few seconds, and nodded. "Same here."

Ren glanced at Dani, who'd been watching them intently, probably judging how the two of them were going to get on. Dani, it seemed, was an observer. Ren understood that. What it was to watch the interactions of others, to draw conclusions about them from what she saw. There was safety in observation, but there was very often also truth.

❖

Dani leaned back in her chair while Zoey and Ren discussed the day's OR schedule. They'd forgotten all about her as they settled into the familiar routine. She took in the little details, their body language and tone of voice, trying to get a fix on how they'd get on. And, she discovered, Ren *did* drink coffee in the morning—strong too, from the looks of it.

"I'm going to take Omati's aortic aneurysm resection with one of the juniors. I was thinking Shelby. What do you think?" Ren said, glancing at Zoey before making a note on a handwritten list she'd laid on the table by her coffee cup.

"Shelby's had a rotation on vascular already. Omati almost never lets the juniors do anything, so the case would be wasted on Patten…so yeah. Shelby."

"Good," Ren muttered. "Do you want the colon or the liver resection?"

"Liver," Zoey said instantly. "You can put Patten and the first year on the colon. Daniels ought to be done with the floor work by the time that case starts."

Dani sipped her coffee, light and sweet the way coffee should be, while she watched them work. All that was missing was the Cap'n. Ren was going to do fine. Her aura of quiet self-containment might look like shyness to some people, but Ren wasn't shy. She was deliberate, and there was a world of difference. She was careful in what she said, but always definite. When she'd spent a little time with Ren that first day, Dani'd perceived a slight flicker in her gaze that most people probably wouldn't notice. That fleeting sign told her Ren was a little surprised by something. And then just as quickly, the unwavering intention in her gaze returned. That's when Dani knew she had sorted through the probabilities and come to a decision. She'd seen Ren do that on rounds when she'd been presented with patients in serious condition, who needed decisions about what to do next. She'd been silent, inwardly appraising, and then she stated her plan. With finality. Dani knew then she would do well as a chief with that approach. One of the first things she'd learned was that indecision was worse than no decision, even a wrong one. Indecision meant delays, halfway treatment, or even worse, no treatment at all. In an emergency, in a life-or-death situation, indecision was literally deadly. Ren was not indecisive. She made her moves with assurance. She'd make a good gamer.

Idly, Dani wondered if she played.

"I think you're set," Zoey said, just a hint of surprise in her voice. Ren didn't seem to notice but smiled at Dani.

"Dani was a big help," Ren said, dragging Dani back from her reverie.

"You didn't need it," Dani said, "but happy to serve."

Ren laughed.

Dani rose. "I've gotta make rounds myself. Good luck, you guys."

"Thanks," Zoey said.

"Thank you," Ren said, still smiling at her.

That little bit of formality. That was Ren too. Another of those little things she'd noticed, that she liked. Dani grinned, unaccountably lighthearted, and walked through the cafeteria toward the administrative wing. She'd decided to do this on a whim, somewhere between her truncated shower and the ten-minute walk with Zoey to the hospital. She'd been thinking about her family and questioning if anything, including a nationally recognized honor, would change their image of her, and how much any of that mattered. Thinking about the Franklin brought her face-to-face with the almost-certain reality that Ren was probably the stronger candidate. And Ren wasn't the only competition—just the one who'd appeared out of nowhere and who occupied her mind more than anyone else she knew, other than her best friends. And Raven. Dani laughed to herself. If the best friend category was based on the strength and importance of a connection, then Raven qualified there too.

And since she was losing sleep over the whole Franklin thing, it mattered enough, it seemed, to propel her toward Quinn Maguire's office. Really, she had nothing to lose. The question was, did she even have a chance.

The administrative wing was quiet at a little before six in the morning. The regular staff wouldn't arrive until seven thirty or eight, and the surgeons all headed straight for the OR first thing in the morning. Except she'd often seen Quinn heading this way well before the first OR cases of the day were ready to start. She took a chance, which was, after all, kind of how she lived her life.

Sure enough, light shone in Quinn's office. Dani walked past the empty reception desk and tapped on the inner office door. Quinn sat at her desk with files in front of her. When Dani knocked, Quinn looked up, saw her, and gave her a quizzical smile.

"Come on in," Quinn said.

"Sorry to bother you, Chief, if you've got five minutes."

"Have a seat," Quinn said, obviously picking up on the fact that Dani wasn't there because of some surgical emergency.

Dani sat and, before she could think about it, did what she always did. Plunged ahead without any plan besides her gut feelings. Overthinking never really helped her when she'd made a decision. "I wanted to talk to you about the Franklin award."

Quinn nodded but said nothing.

"I, um, I know I'm a transfer, so I don't have much of a track record, but I'm hoping to change that. So I might be considered."

"You know I can't talk about anything other than the general basis for the award, right?" Quinn said.

"Oh yeah, it's not about that. Well, maybe it is. I guess I have a question. No, two questions."

"Okay, go ahead. I'll answer what I can."

"I'm wondering how important research experience is, and if it matters, how I can get some."

Quinn smiled. "That's a request I don't get very often."

Dani laughed. "Yeah, I bet."

Quinn blew out a breath. "You know the Franklin is voted on, and the votes are counted—no discussion. The parameters under consideration are pretty broadly drawn—the surgical resident who demonstrates the outstanding principles and ideals of the surgical profession. The senior staff can interpret that any way they like."

"Department heads all vote," Dani said.

"That's right."

"Okay, well, I've rotated on almost all the services but not everyone's. Does that disqualify me?"

"No. Surgical residents get exposure to all the staff when they see ER and trauma patients. Not everyone rotates on every service, depending on what direction they're planning to go in after they finish general surgery," Quinn pointed out. "So you've still got plenty of opportunity to interact with all the staff."

"Well, no place I'd rather be than the ER or the trauma unit."

Quinn laughed again before saying, "As far as research is concerned, it varies as to how much emphasis each voter places upon it. But, in all honesty, it doesn't hurt."

"Yeah, that's what I thought. It doesn't seem reasonable that there's anything I can do in the lab at this point," Dani said almost to herself.

"That's true," Quinn said. "You don't have time, realistically, to spend in a research lab with the number of cases you need for your chief's year."

Dani nodded. She'd known, but she'd just needed to hear it.

"But," Quinn said, and Dani alerted, "surgery is a clinical specialty. *Medicine* is clinical. Of course, great advances are made in patient care as a result of bench research. Those are long-term goals. But what we have," Quinn said, sitting forward, her voice intensifying, "is an amazing wealth of clinical material—hundreds, thousands, of clinical cases. Records of patients who presented with all manner of diseases, who've been treated in different ways, with different outcomes. Clinical studies, even retrospective studies, can be elucidating. Can give us springboards for treatment and further research."

"Clinical studies. You mean, patient studies."

"I mean outcome studies. Looking at the data from focused groups of patients who presented with similar conditions, but whose treatments may have varied, or whose treatment was similar, but the outcomes were different. Analyzing that data can give us valuable information about a disease and its treatment."

"What would I have to do?" Dani said.

"Talk to Allison Carducci. I know she's interested in looking at the impact of various nutritional regimens on kids with cardiac atresia. She's got enough data there you could get a paper out this year, and it would mean something."

"I'll do it." Dani didn't even need to think it over. She didn't have any idea exactly *how* she would go about doing it, because she'd never given it any thought, but she'd figure that out.

"Good," Quinn said. "I'll give her a call and let her know you'll be coming by to talk to her."

"I'll do it today," Dani said, rising.

"You know, Dani," Quinn said quietly, "no matter who wins the Franklin, what matters is the kind of surgeon you'll be this time next year and five years from now."

"I understand," Dani said, and she did. But this mattered too—more, she realized, every day.

CHAPTER SIX

PMC Hospital, early evening one week later

Ren got a soda from the machine in the OR lounge, flopped down into the corner of one of the well-worn leather sofas, and propped her feet on the coffee table. She took a long swallow of the wonderfully cold liquid, leaned her head back, and let out a long sigh. Her entire body ached, in a good way. She'd been standing for the last six hours, doing a complicated bowel resection and reconstruction. Buzby, the attending surgeon, had nodded absently when she'd walked into the OR, and when she'd stepped up to the table opposite him had asked, "What year are you again?"

"Fifth." She'd met him the day before when she and Zoey had rounded with him, and they'd been introduced. He'd directed most of his questions to Zoey.

"You're one of the Franklin transfers, right?"

"No," Ren said, taking the sterile sheet the scrub tech handed her to drape out the surgical area. Her first year resident crowded as close to her side as he could. She hip-checked him before he could cramp her arm movement. "PMC regular."

"Huh." He glanced over the drape at the head of the table. "Can we start?"

"He's good," the anesthetist said.

"Fifth year?" Buzby repeated, his eyes above his mask drifting over hers. Relaxed. Appraising.

She looked back steadily. Answer what she was asked—make no excuses where none were needed. "Yes."

"Well then, go ahead."

Ren hesitated a millisecond—not long enough for him to notice, just long enough to register the meaning. She held out her right hand. "Scalpel."

Buzby made the procedure easy—easier, Ren knew, than it would have been if she'd been doing it alone. He had a way of directing the dissection without actually saying anything, just moving tissues and lifting organs into the field for Ren to expose, cut, suture, and repair. When they finished, she had learned something and taken note of what else she needed to know for next time. And she'd had a very good time.

"Thank you," she said.

"Nice job," he said. "I have a splenectomy day after tomorrow. You should scrub."

"I'll try," she said, pleased that he wanted her to scrub with him but wary of committing to a case that ought to go to Zoey or a third year. Attendings always wanted the most senior residents to scrub with them. And as much as she needed as many cases as she could get, she wasn't going to take them away from the junior residents.

Happily, she'd done more surgery in the last week than in the last six months. The elective service schedule was full, and summer in the city kept the ER busy with recreational and home improvement injuries as well as routine surgical illnesses. Trauma alerts sounded steadily with vehicular and violent injuries, and since she hadn't left the hospital for more than a few hours, catching as many cases as she could, the days and nights had been a blur. She'd slept in between cases, grabbed food in the cafeteria, showered in the OR locker room, and pretty much had the most exciting week of her life. What she hadn't done was spend any time in the lab. She should've missed it, but she didn't, not really. She did miss the quiet and the solitude. But the trade-off was worth it. The residents on her service had been strangers a few days ago, but she was coming to think of them certainly not as friends, but as people whose names she knew and who knew hers. People whose priorities she understood. They knew almost nothing about her past and didn't have the time or energy to care. What they cared about was how she ran the service—whether or not she allotted the work fairly, gave them a chance to do the cases they needed or wanted to do, and got them out of the hospital at a reasonable hour whenever she could.

She hadn't appreciated right away how important it was for most of the residents to be able to get away from the hospital for a few hours when they weren't on call. She'd never cared very much about being anywhere else. Everything that interested her had been here. That was still true but, she'd quickly realized when Zoey subtly suggested they start sign-out rounds every night around six, not for everyone. Oh, they were all hard-working, competitive, and would've stayed if it meant they would've missed out on something. But most of them also wanted, needed, something else in their life.

She set her soda on the coffee table and rolled the tension out of her shoulders. She'd never had a particularly balanced life, but she did have one thing that took her away from the pressure of constantly needing to succeed, that gave her a space to unwind and replenish her mind and spirit, if not necessarily her body. She checked her phone for the first time since early that afternoon and saw the text from Axe.

You around?

The time stamp said the message was three hours old. That often happened. She would text Axe or find a text waiting for her, and sometimes they would be able to connect, and other times it would be another day. She hoped she'd get lucky this time.

Ren answered, *Just got free. What are you doing?*

Dying of boredom.

Really? Why?

Long story. Paperwork, sort of.

Ren couldn't remember Axe ever complaining about anything before. *Work?*

Sort of. Special project, Axe came back.

Bad time?

No. Was hoping you'd save me.

Ren laughed. She'd never heard her voice, but she felt the smile in her words.

Time to play then

For sure. Always

Ren smiled. She knew that wasn't true, but she'd come to count on the comeback. Like a secret code. *Perfect. I'll see you.*

Ren opened the app to the game site, logged in, and sent the invite. She watched the screen, waiting with anticipation. Twenty seconds later, Axe's icon popped up. A stylized warrior, gender indeterminate, with a shield and sword. Hers, of course, was a raven perched on a branch, waiting, watching for prey. They started a new game, and she quickly moved into the alternate reality, her senses alert and her adrenaline flowing. She loved to flex her mind, meeting the new challenges Axe always came up with, reveling in the competition. They didn't chat while they played, but she sensed Axe with every probing move, every rapid block and parry.

When the game ended, this one going to Axe, she typed, *Nice one. I didn't expect that countermove*

Wouldn't want you to get too confident.

Oh, of course not

:-)

Ren laughed again.

"Hey." Zoey plopped down beside her. "You busy?"

Ren flipped her phone over and pressed it against her thigh, shifting to face Zoey. "No, is there a problem?"

"Nope. All the rooms are done. I was just getting ready to check the post-ops, and a couple of us were going out for pizza. You want to come?"

Ren stared. "I'm sorry? What?"

Zoey half smiled and shook her head. "Dinner, Ren. You know, food. You want to come out for pizza?"

"Oh." She was just finding her way on the new service, establishing herself. Starting to fit in. Things had gone easier than she'd expected, but that had been about work. She understood her role there even if she needed the practice. Socializing wasn't a necessary skill. Going out with the residents crossed boundaries, moved her into a zone where she might lose all the progress she'd gained. For something she didn't need. "I have some reading I need to do later, but thank you."

"Okay then." Zoey stood and stretched. "I'll see you in the morning."

"If you're making post-op rounds," Ren said, "I'll come with you."

"Great. We'll get done twice as fast."

Ren clicked on her phone as she followed Zoey through the locker room to the hall and texted quickly, *Sorry, have to go.*

Me too—thanks for the company

Ren hesitated. *Always*

Flushing a little, wondering if that had been the right thing to say—even though it had felt quite right to her—she slipped her phone into her back pocket. Part of her wished she'd said yes to Zoey—perhaps she would be a more effective resident if she attempted to integrate more. But her success had always been rooted in what she did best, using her drive and determination to excel. She could hardly take credit for her brain, after all. Those things had gotten her this far, and she only had this year to prove herself. Pizza, and everything else, could wait.

❖

"If you change your mind," Zoey said as she and Ren left the intensive care unit, their last stop on evening rounds, "we'll be at Big Dom's for a few hours."

"Thank you," Ren said.

Zoey waved and disappeared down the stairwell. Ren walked to the opposite end of the hallway and went down one flight to the bridge that connected the clinical floors to the newer section of the hospital that housed the research offices, animal facilities, and labs. She crossed the bridge that spanned the staff parking lot and glanced down at the steady stream of vehicles, mostly residents and medical staff, leaving for the night. Some were undoubtedly going home, but many, like Zoey and the other residents, were going to take advantage of the few free hours they had to socialize. Ren'd made the walk hundreds of times, had looked at the same scene just as many, but tonight for some reason imagining everyone setting off to enjoy the other parts of their lives, parts she didn't have, touched off a pang of melancholy.

She'd barely ever thought about what she might be missing. She was lucky. She'd discovered early what she wanted and had been happy in the pursuit of those goals. She still was. But every day she spent in her new role outside the lab, some small experience, like Zoey's invitation or a passing remark from one of the residents about a party or barbecue, reminded her of what she hadn't done. She wasn't given to introspection, and now was definitely not the time to worry about that, or even think about it. Not when she had challenges on every front.

She pushed through the fire doors at the far end of the walkway, leaving her ruminations and regrets behind. As was the norm, the research building was quiet at midevening. The administrative staff and many of the researchers kept normal business hours, though PhD students were often coming and going, setting up experiments, checking data, or working late to finish a paper. As she walked toward the lab, light would occasionally splinter into her path from beneath a closed door or illuminate a section of the hallway through an open one, but for the most part, her footsteps echoed through the deserted building. Larry Weatherby's lab—what she thought of as *her* lab—was at the far end of the right wing of the T-shaped building. As she passed the open door of the library that sat at the junction of the three corridors, she heard a familiar voice say quite clearly, "I'll be a hundred before I get through all of this."

Ren stopped abruptly in the doorway and stared into the long narrow room. Two large windows filled the center of the wall opposite the door. Several oak tables, each with six navy-blue chairs around them, occupied the middle of the room. Floor-to-ceiling dark walnut bookshelves lined all the available wall space.

Dani sat at one end of the closest table with several stacks of charts in front of her. A wire cart stood next to her chair, laden with more.

"Dani?" Ren couldn't have been more surprised if she'd looked through the door and seen a snowman.

"Hey, Ren," Dani said with just a hint of dejection in her voice.

"Um..." Ren raised an eyebrow and looked pointedly at the charts.

"Yeah, I know." Dani surveyed the stacks. "I don't know what I'm doing here either."

"Oh," Ren said quickly, "I didn't mean to imply that you shouldn't be here. I'm just used to seeing people from the lab in here. It's perfectly fine for anyone in the complex to come in here."

"Well, it's a first for me." Dani pushed back in her chair, looking at the charts as if they were radioactive. She wore a scrub shirt and jeans with running shoes. Her hair was mussed but somehow still looked attractive, with a few strands hanging over her forehead and others drifting over her neck to the collar. The short-sleeved scrub shirt left her arms bare, and well-defined muscles rippled beneath her tanned skin.

Ren had only vaguely thought of Dani as slender, but she wasn't at all. She was quite toned and...well-built. Ren imagined if she touched her, she would find her solid and strong.

"Something wrong?" Dani asked quietly.

When Ren pulled her gaze upward to meet Dani's eyes, Dani gave her a lazy smile. Ren jumped, her heart suddenly pounding. How very odd. She swallowed, her throat unusually dry.

"You looked...bothered?" Dani added when Ren didn't answer.

"No, I...no. You look awfully busy," Ren said, embarrassed to have been staring. "I didn't mean to interrupt you."

"Oh, please, do. I could use a reason to escape."

Dani sounded so frustrated and forlorn, Ren couldn't help but laugh. Dani grinned, and the moment of worry that Ren might have given the wrong impression disappeared. She took a step closer, indicating the charts with one hand. "What are you doing?"

"Now, that's a very good question," Dani said. "I'm supposed to be making sense out of these cases." She waved at the pile. There must've been a hundred folders.

"You're doing some kind of study, I take it. I can't think of anything else to be doing with all those charts."

"Well, in theory, yes, I'm doing some kind of study. That's about where I am right at this point. Theory." Dani stood and stretched. Her jeans, faded blue denim with a ragged quarter-sized hole in the center of her left thigh that did not appear to be a fashion element but a real sign of wear, outlined sculpted thighs and calves.

Ren marveled at how different Dani's body was from hers, even though they were roughly the same size. She never thought about her body, which she supposed she'd have to describe as soft and slightly curvy, so why in the world was she so fascinated by Dani's?

Nonplussed, Ren tentatively backed up. "I am interrupting, then. I'm sorry. I'll go."

"No, don't." Dani sprawled in the chair again, her legs stretched out before her, and motioned to the chair beside her. "Stay, unless you have to be somewhere. You're the best distraction I can imagine."

"Well, I…I have some things in the lab, but they're not urgent." Feeling the flush start again, Ren shut it down with a firm mental hand and sat down next to Dani. Research papers were her comfort zone, even if talking to women she hardly knew wasn't. "You must be going back a ways—pre-digital conversion?"

"Yep," Dani said.

"It looks like you're just getting started."

"I wish that was the case. I mean, yes, I'm trying to get started, but basically you can think of me as someone who is learning how to swim by being tossed off an ocean liner into the middle of the Atlantic. Without a life preserver."

"I remember the feeling," Ren said.

"You do?"

Ren nodded. "When I was working on my master's, the first time I showed up in the lab, my advisor informed me that he was leaving for a meeting and would be gone for two weeks. He handed me the research proposal and said I could get started while he was gone." She shook her head. "I didn't really have a clue."

"That's it? No instructions or anything?"

"Oh no—we were expected to be able to design our own experiments to address the research question."

"Wait...you have a master's degree too?"

Ren sighed, knowing what would come next. The surprise, the faint suspicion, the inevitable distance. "No, I actually have a PhD. The master's was just the midpoint."

"Oh—you're one of the MD PhD people."

"Yes."

"Well," Dani said, "that sounds worse than what I'm doing."

Ren stared for a beat and then laughed. No one had ever simply brushed that aside without even a question—or a comment. Relieved, intrigued, she said, "What's your study about?"

"I'm looking at the impact of nutritional regimens on outcome in surgical treatment of cardiac atresia in preemies."

"Oh," Ren said, trying not to sound as surprised or disconcerted as she felt. "With Dr. Carducci?"

"Yes."

"I didn't realize that you were in her lab." Ren would've preferred to be in Allison Carducci's lab for her surgical research, but when she'd arrived at PMC, Allison hadn't yet been on staff. Larry Weatherby was an excellent surgical researcher, and she'd done interesting work in his lab, but that wasn't where she wanted her career to focus. She wanted to focus on pediatric cardiothoracic surgery. Allison Carducci's specialty. "I didn't realize you were interested in cardiac surgery."

"I'm not." Dani shrugged. "Well, I don't know, I suppose, technically, I am now. But not really. I'm doing a project with her, looking at patient outcomes. Dr. Carducci was looking for someone to do this project, and I could use the research experience."

"I see," Ren said, and she thought she did. There weren't a whole lot of reasons that Dani might want to get a publication at this point in her residency. In fact, the only one she could think of was to enhance her chances at winning the Franklin. And Dr. Carducci would almost certainly lobby in support of her when the voting occurred. And unlike Ren, Dani would be well-known to most of the clinical staff too. A clear advantage.

"Anyhow," Dani went on, oblivious to Ren's consternation, "that's the project. Honestly, I've read everything about the clinical end of things, and I pretty much know what I'm supposed to be looking for, but then"—she indicated the piles of charts—"how do I know what's important and what isn't?"

"You'll figure it out after you get familiar with the cases," Ren said noncommittally. She could have said more, could have offered to help her set up the study parameters and data tables, but she wasn't responsible for helping Dani. But Dani wasn't likely to ask Dr. Carducci for help. Ren wouldn't either. That wasn't the way to impress staff about anything, and the first thing every resident learned. Ask your fellow residents for help—not staff. But Dani's research project was not her problem.

Dani grimaced. "Never mind. I'm just complaining. It took me three hours to pull all these charts, and I missed dinner."

"I know, that happens to me a lot when I'm busy with a project. The forgetting to eat."

"So, what are you doing here tonight?" Dani asked. "Isn't it way after lab hours? This place is deserted."

"Oh. I've got some samples I need to run in the lab. I've been so busy with the surgical service, I've been putting it off."

"Yeah, it's hard to juggle, isn't it."

"Well, it's a lot more fun to be in the OR," Ren said.

"Tell me about it." Dani leaned forward, pushing the charts aside with her elbow. "You want to grab something to eat? I don't know about your samples, but these charts aren't going anywhere."

"I really should get those samples running..." Ren hadn't wanted to join a group of people when Zoey'd invited her out just a short while before, but now she considered it. Why did this seem different? And harder to say no to. "I don't have a lot of time."

"There's a tapas place two blocks away, San Pedro's—you know it?" Dani said.

"No, I don't eat out much."

"Service is fast, and the food is great. You'll be back here in an hour."

Dani watched her, a glint in her eyes, as if she was trying to persuade Ren to say yes by sheer willpower. And it was working.

Ren surrendered to the urge to step outside her routine. The lab *would* still be there in an hour, and Dani was surprisingly easy to talk to. "Okay. Yes."

"Great!" Dani jumped up and strode over to the door. When Ren joined her, Dani's hand lightly grazed Ren's elbow as she reached past her to switch off the light, leaving the library and the piles of charts in the dark. She said softly, "Ready?"

Ren caught the gleam in Dani's eyes even in the semidark. "Yes."

CHAPTER SEVEN

Dani squelched the urge to grab Ren's hand and tug her along down the hall. She wasn't in the habit of getting physical with women she hardly knew who hadn't invited her attentions, but she had the feeling that Ren would disappear any second—bolt down the nearest stairwell and disappear into the night. She glanced at Ren, but her expression, like usual, was composed and nearly unreadable, as smooth as the still waters of a mountain lake just after dawn. Without a ripple, without a hint of current, with no suggestion of what might be teeming just below the surface. Not shallow, anything but. Endless depths.

"Something wrong?" Ren asked.

Dani jumped. "No. No. Not at all. I was just thinking…" They'd reached the elevator, and she pushed the down button.

"We could take the stairs," Ren said.

"Great idea," Dani blurted, spinning around and hurrying to the stairwell. She pushed the fire door open and held it for Ren. What was the matter with her? She was acting like she was thirteen and on her first date. Which she was so not—and this was so not a date.

"Thinking what?" Ren said as they started down the concrete stairs, their footsteps echoing in the stairwell, keeping time, it felt, with the beat of Dani's heart.

What had she been thinking? Dani struggled for a response. She wasn't about to say she'd been half mesmerized by looking at Ren, by trying to figure her out. When they pushed through at the bottom, they were on the far side of the hospital, separated from the street by a wide grassy expanse bisected by a brick walkway. The summer heat and the smell of fresh-mown grass and the distant smoke of barbecue hit Dani all at once. She almost stumbled as she stopped and said the first thing that came to her. "God. *Life*. It feels so damn good to be out here."

Ren stared at her, and then her calm expression turned bright and warm, her face suffused with pleasure. She laughed, an airy, musical sound that accompanied the thunder of Dani's heart like a teasing refrain.

"What?" Dani said, slightly louder than she meant.

"Nothing," Ren said, but she was still smiling. "I just like your…exuberance."

Dani frowned. "Why does that make me sound like a puppy?"

The corner of Ren's mouth twitched, as if she was trying not to laugh again. "Don't you like puppies?"

They'd reached the street now and made their way through the neighborhood of mostly single-family homes. One of the things Dani really loved about being at PMC was the sense of the community all around it. She'd wanted a big-city hospital program, but she hadn't wanted to live in the heart of the city. Luck wasn't something she was used to, and certainly nothing she ever counted on, but the closure of her first surgery program had turned out to be just that. She'd ended up at exactly the kind of place she wanted to be. And she'd met Zoey, an amazing new friend. And Ren—someone she hadn't expected. Someone who…fascinated her.

Dani caught her mind wandering again and said quickly, "Everyone likes puppies, until they're not puppies anymore. The affection is an illusion." She frowned. "Or maybe the puppies are."

"I had a puppy, and I loved her just as much when she grew up," Ren said softly, her expression distant.

"That's good to know," Dani said. Maybe puppies weren't as disappointing when they grew up as children often were.

"But," Ren said, recovering her light tone, "I was just thinking about how joyful they always seem to be, and now that I think of it, that's how I first thought of you."

"No one has ever suggested that about me." Dani pointed to the left. "It's this way."

"Why is that, do you think?" Ren asked.

Dani narrowed her eyes and shot her a look. What the hell kind of conversation was this? Not the kind she was used to when she was just trying to get to know a woman. Of course, come to think of it, she didn't usually need a whole lot of time for anything more than the usual: name, age, relationship status, and were they ready to leave yet? She definitely needed to rearrange her expectations. Ren was nothing like those women, and she should've known that. Every encounter she'd had with Ren so far had made that clear. Ren was waiting for an answer, strolling along as if she hadn't been poking at places Dani preferred to keep safely buried. She could just not answer, signal she wanted to keep things superficial, easy. That's how she always managed it when relationships got too heavy. The rest of her life was plenty heavy. But then, nothing about Ren signaled superficial or easy, and she found she didn't want Ren to be disappointed. She took a breath. "Not being joyous, you mean? There's a lightness to it, isn't there. Optimism. And I don't think I have a lot of either."

"It's kind of hard to hold on to anything like that, sometimes, with what we see, don't you think?"

"Maybe that's it." And Ren was right, dealing with life and death and what often seemed unfair made a person wary, but there were so many other reasons not to expect a perfect ending. And that was *way* beyond what she wanted to talk about.

When Ren remained silent, Dani wondered if they'd strayed too far from what was comfortable already. For her it was a pretty narrow path, maybe for Ren too.

"You don't really know someone just from brushing up against them, not literally necessarily, but even when you work beside them," Ren said contemplatively. "I would've said you were not exactly happy-go-lucky, but not bothered by much of anything. Carefree, maybe."

"But you changed your mind?" Dani said. An unexpected wave

of disappointment passed through her, as if she'd failed Ren somehow.

"No, *you* changed it." Ren smiled. "You just showed me my assumption wasn't true."

"And that's all it takes?"

"You told me something about you, and who would know better?"

"Well. Okay. I never figured it to be that easy."

"What?" Ren asked.

"Being actually seen by someone."

"Oh, I understand now." Ren's brows drew together, leaving a tiny crease between them. In that instant, she went from really attractive to really sexy.

And Dani really wanted to brush her thumb over that little crease. Actually, she wanted to kiss her. Whoa. Not her usual modus operandi. Ren had somehow turned everything upside down. She all of a sudden wanted to kiss her because Ren said she understood her. A little? That was just…not her.

"I don't think it's easy—letting someone see you," Ren said, "at all. If you hadn't told me something about yourself, I never would've known. I would've just kept on thinking that my very distant and probably superficial and obviously incorrect impressions had been true."

"Okay, then you have to tell me something about yourself."

"I might need to think about it." Her tone suggested she thought Dani might argue or push her to say something she might not be ready to reveal.

"Fair enough." Dani slipped her hand under Ren's elbow. "The restaurant's just over there." A few seconds later she realized what she'd done, but Ren hadn't pulled away, and she didn't want to move her hand. So she didn't. Being that close to her felt nice. "Is it okay with you if we eat at the outside tables? I know it's a little hot, but—"

"No, that would be great," Ren said. "I love that it doesn't get dark until almost nine during the summer. We even get to leave the hospital sometimes when it's still daylight."

"I know." Dani laughed, and the lightness she'd felt when Ren had agreed to come out with her returned. Ren had a way of chasing away the shadows.

The hostess showed them to a two-top against the short wrought-iron fence that separated the seating area in front of the cantina from the sidewalk.

"Can I get you two something to drink?" she asked as she handed them the menus.

Dani glanced at Ren. "I'm not on call. You?"

Ren shook her head.

"I'll have whatever's on tap. Ren?"

"I'll have the same."

"You girls got ID?" the hostess asked.

Ren retrieved the thin ID case she carried in her shirt pocket and extracted her license as Dani took out her wallet.

The hostess glanced at them, took a second look at Ren, and handed them back. "Okay, thanks."

"At least they've stopped asking me if my ID's fake," Ren muttered.

"Did you get that a lot?"

"Yes," Ren sighed.

"That's annoying."

Ren gave her a grateful look. "It *is*."

"So, have you decided what you wanted to tell me? That I should know?"

"I'll add persistent to my impressions of you," Ren said.

"I kinda like that one," Dani admitted.

Ren laughed, making Dani want to tease her some more.

"Misdirection won't work," Dani said. "I won't forget."

"No," Ren said quietly, her expression so intense Dani held her breath. That kind of intense scrutiny was rare—and unexpectedly exciting.

A server dropped off two sweating glasses of beer, and Dani muttered an absent thanks, waiting. Watching Ren.

"I…" Ren leaned her chin on her palm, the corner of her mouth dipping down as she seemed to be studying Dani, or simply lost in thought. "People think I'm shy, but I'm not. I'm just not very good at casual conversation."

She said it all in a rush as if she was afraid if she didn't get it all out quickly, she wouldn't say it at all.

"Oh hell, you're not shy," Dani said with a smirk. "Anybody who's been around you more than a few minutes would know that."

Ren straightened. "Is that what you think?"

"Sure. It's obvious. You're not having any trouble talking to me."

Ren caught her breath. "Oh. Well. You're different."

Dani felt the blush. Oh, so uncool. She coughed and sipped the beer, trying to find her game face again. After a few seconds, she realized that was long gone. Ren was totally derailing her. "I am, am I?"

Ren smiled. "Well, you're really easy to talk to and you're very interesting and…" Her voice trailed off, and she caught her bottom lip between her teeth. As if wishing she could take the words back.

Dani so did not want her to do that. She couldn't help the surge of satisfaction. She'd seen Ren looking at her. Looking at her, the way a woman who might be interested would. She liked that. She leaned forward a little and lowered her voice. "And?"

"And I don't know anything about, you know, anything."

"That's a lot of something. Could you be more specific?" Dani stayed leaning forward on her elbows, watching Ren's eyes. They were really beautiful. Dark, almost black, with little slivers of gold sliding through them. Ren was very easy to look at. And right now, she couldn't think of anything else she'd rather do.

"And you don't make me nervous," Ren said quickly.

Dani felt her eyebrows rise. "Well, I'm glad to hear that. Do most people?"

"As a matter of fact, yes."

"You're not that way with patients."

"Well, that's different. I know what I'm doing there. I know what they need, and I know that I can give it."

"And you're saying in other circumstances you don't feel that way."

"I've never quite figured out—you know, how to be sociable."

"I'm not sure there are any rules," Dani said. "But now you've told me something, and I see you better."

Ren's eyes widened and her lips parted just a little, and damn if Dani didn't want to kiss her again. This was crazy. Crazy in a way she'd never experienced, and that she liked a lot.

"Can I ask you a personal question?" Dani said.

"I think we've been pretty personal already," Ren said just a little hesitantly.

"It's one of those common social questions."

"Oh, you mean the ones I don't usually ask?" Ren said.

"Maybe."

"Okay."

"Are you seeing anyone, you know girlfriend, boyfriend, fiancé?"

"No," Ren said and laughed. "What a crazy idea."

"Why is that crazy?"

"Because I'm not interested in those kinds of things, and even if I was, I don't have time."

"You're not interested," Dani said slowly. "Like tonight, or this week, or…ever?"

"Well, I don't know," Ren said. "I've honestly never had time to think about it."

"How old are you?" Dani asked.

"Why does that matter?" Ren straightened.

A faint bit of heat colored her cheeks, and Dani could almost see the bristles erupting. "I'm just wondering how long you haven't had time to think about it."

"I'm twenty-five."

Dani did some quick mental math. Four years of college, four of med school, four or more for a surgical residency. Even with a few years shaved off in a combo program, the math was off. "Twenty-five. How is it possible that you're a fifth year now—*and* after three in the lab?"

"How do you know how long I've been in the lab?"

Dani flushed. "Zoey is my housemate. She mentioned it."

"Oh." Ren sighed. "This is why I'm not sociable. I always end up explaining, and then…"

"Then what?"

Ren shrugged. "And then people usually disappear."

"First, unsociable and not socializing are two different things," Dani said. "You are sociable, you're just not into socializing."

"I'm not so sure about the distinction," Ren muttered. "What's second? You said first."

"Second, I'm not disappearing."

"Oh." As if not sure what to say, Ren sipped the beer and made a little bit of a face. "Is this a good beer?"

"Yeah, maybe not the best, but a good one."

"I don't think I like beer."

"Is this your first beer?"

"Yes."

Dani tried and failed to hide her surprise.

"I've had wine," Ren said defensively.

"I don't think you want that here. Hold on for a second." Dani signaled the hostess, who threaded her way between the tables.

"Can I get you something?"

"Strawberry margarita, on the rocks with…salt."

"Sure thing. I'll pass the word."

"Thanks." Dani tilted her chin at Ren. "So, now you're going to tell me about how you got to where you are now."

"I am?"

"Uh-huh. It's one of those things you do when you're getting to know someone." Dani rested her elbow on the table and her chin in her hand. "I've got all night."

"No you don't," Ren exclaimed, but the tension left her shoulders. "I started high school early, that's all, and…well, then I started college early too. And then I was in the accelerated medical school program, and after that, you know, it was accelerated."

"Yeah, I got that, a lot of acceleration. How old were you when you started high school?"

Ren looked away. Dani reached across the table, lightly slid two fingers around Ren's wrist, and gave her a little shake. "You don't have to answer. It's okay. It's just interesting. Fascinating, really. It must've been exciting and hard at the same time."

"It *was* exciting," Ren said quietly. "And I guess, yes, it was hard too."

"Well, I think it's pretty amazing."

"I was eleven," Ren said quickly, "when I started high school, I mean. I finished in three years, and then everything just went faster after that."

"Well. Okay. You were a superstar."

"I'm not sure what defines that, but I'm pretty sure it isn't me," Ren said. "I just have a quick brain."

Dani laughed. "That goes without saying. Oh, here comes your margarita. Let me know if you like it better than the beer."

Ren took the glass and sipped. She caught her breath and looked at Dani. "That's really good."

"Yes," Dani said, grinning. "Success."

After they ordered, Ren said, "So, it's your turn."

"For what?"

"To do the social thing. When did you know you wanted to be a doctor?"

"I was seven."

Ren didn't act as if that was at all unusual.

"Okay. When did you know you wanted to be a surgeon?"

"First year medical school. You?"

"I was twelve."

"Of course you were."

"No, you see, I'd just read a biography of Dr. DeBakey and the first heart transplants, and it was so incredible, so fascinating, that I knew right then that I wanted to be a cardiothoracic surgeon."

"You were twelve."

"Well, yes."

Dani grinned. "Are your parents doctors?"

"No, my father's on Wall Street and my mother wasn't around—divorced. My older sister is, though. She's a trauma surgeon in New York City."

"No kidding. Cool."

"Are your family doctors?"

Dani winced before she could stop herself. "No. They're all scientists at Cal Tech."

"Really. All of them?"

"Mother, father, sister, brother."

Ren studied Dani for a second. "Veronica Chan?"

Dani blew out a breath and nodded. "My mother."

"Wow. That's...your mother is a Nobel laureate. That must be...What *is* it like?"

"Complicated."

Ren must've heard something in her voice, because she didn't ask anything else. Dani steered the conversation away from the personal. She'd already told Ren more about herself in an hour than she told Syd the whole first year they'd roomed together. She still hadn't let Zoey know some of the things that she struggled with. If this was a date, and she wasn't sure that it was, she absolutely never revealed these things on a first date. Or second. Or on the rare occasions there was a third, even then. She didn't even know how this had happened.

"I should get back," Ren said when they'd finished eating. "I really do have some work I need to get done in the lab."

"I don't think I can face those charts tonight," Dani said, "but I'll walk back with you."

"You don't have to," Ren said.

"I want to. Besides, it's on my way."

"Okay. If you're sure."

"Never surer."

At the hospital, Ren said, "Thanks for taking me there. I've never been, and it was really good." She hesitated. "And I had a really good time."

"Me too." Dani turned and walked backward a little bit as Ren stopped on the brick walkway to the lab. "We should do it again sometime."

"Oh," Ren said, as if surprised by the idea. "Okay. Yes. We could do that."

"Good. Friday?"

"What about Friday?" Ren called.

"Friday, again."

"Oh," Ren said, sounding even more surprised. Dani kept walking backward, watching Ren. Her heart pounded in a weirdly exciting way.

"All right. Yes. Friday."

"I'll find you." Satisfied, and something more she couldn't quite define, Dani turned for home.

Chapter Eight

Dani had been walking to and from the hospital whenever she had time—meaning she hadn't been called in stat or it wasn't raining buckets. Heading home when it was still light out, when she so rarely got the chance to do that for at least half the year, lifted her spirits the way few things could any longer. She was jazzed after her dinner with Ren, but she didn't hurry. Instead, she took her time and replayed the evening. When she'd asked Ren to dinner, she hadn't been thinking of anything more than getting something to eat. Only after she'd offered the invite did it hit her how much she'd been enjoying the easy conversation they'd fallen into in the library. Not that the topic was one she really wanted to dwell on. The research project was going to be more of a hassle than she'd anticipated. No, scratch that. It was going to be every bit as much of a hassle as she'd worried it might be. Not that the research question wasn't interesting, because it was, and Quinn was right, the information was probably going to be helpful, something other surgeons could use, and that at least made it feel worth it. But it was time-consuming, not her natural comfort zone, and she couldn't let up on getting the practical kind of clinical experience she needed. So she'd just have to fit in more hours of work and spend a lot fewer doing anything else.

Venting to Ren had just...happened, and when Ren hadn't brushed off her worries, or offered useless advice, but had simply *understood*, the problems didn't seem so insurmountable.

Dani almost laughed out loud. Nothing had changed—not the whole Franklin quest, the time suck of the study, or most of all her parents' dim view of her life—but for a few hours, the weight of it all had lessened. She'd shared a little of her anxiety and shared a really interesting hour with an intriguing woman, while the pile of charts she had to go through, the pressure of being on a deadline when her career hung in the balance, and the ever-present, bone-deep wish that she could make her parents happier, despite resenting them at the same time, had faded.

She had Ren to thank for that. And try as she might, she couldn't find the will to worry about any of it now either. All she wanted to think about was Ren Dunbar. Whom she'd apparently asked out on a date. An actual bona fide date. As in setting up a time and place to meet—not a casual *oh by the way, a bunch of us are going out* kind of thing. Although they hadn't really discussed what they would do beyond getting together after work for dinner, it was still an advance plan, for just the two of them. And not something she'd done with anyone else since she'd been at PMC. Thinking back, even before that. Oh sure, she went out with Syd and Jerry and other friends when she'd been at Franklin, but always in a group or well after hours when the only reason anyone was out was to hook up. Not something she did very often, and totally given up when she'd moved across town to PMC. Being faced with finding a place in the new surgery system and shouldering a lot more clinical responsibility really quickly had pushed the idea of expending energy on hunting for sex totally out of her mind. And now, when she had so much more of everything—clinical responsibility and this research project—demanding her time, she'd found something far more interesting than a late-night score. Ren.

She'd never met anyone like her. She'd been surrounded by high achievers her entire life, but none with the combination of incredible drive and surprising humility that Ren seemed to have in equal measure. Her accomplishments were extraordinary, and yet far from seeming to realize it, she was, instead, beguilingly unaware of her own specialness. That's probably what Dani found most appealing about her. Ren not only didn't realize how amazing she was, she presented a compelling—hell, fascinating—combination of quiet sensuality and innocence.

She'd talked to Ren for an hour, and she would have been happy if that had been ten. Thinking about her was almost as pleasurable, a habit she could get used to. That was new. And nice. Very nice.

She didn't expect Zoey to be home yet, but a light was on in the kitchen when she walked into the house. She dumped her gear bag at the bottom of the stairs and went on back. Zoey sat at the table with a cup of tea and an open pizza box, looking oddly forlorn.

"Hey," Zoey said. "Brought home leftovers."

"Big Dom's?" Dani pulled a beer from the refrigerator. She sat down opposite Zoey, checked the pizza, and took a small slice of the leftover Greek.

"Yeah, short night, though. Everybody was kind of tired."

"You okay?" Dani asked.

Zoey looked surprised. "Yeah. Oh…" She laughed and shook her head. "The ER is backed up and Dec is second call."

"Aw, no sex for you tonight." Dani flipped the pizza box closed. "You can have it for breakfast."

"Go ahead, have the rest," Zoey said.

"Nah, I'm good. Actually, I just ate a little while ago. I'm just stockpiling in case I get called in."

"Sorry," Zoey said. "I should've texted you that we were all going out. I thought you said you were going to be busy."

"No problem. I was. Sort of. Mostly I was staring at a pile of charts. Ren came by, and we ended up grabbing something to eat."

"Really? You and Ren? Where'd you go?"

"San Pedro's."

"Really?" Zoey said, her voice rising a little bit higher. "That's interesting. I asked her if she wanted to go out for pizza with us, and she didn't want to."

"I guess she just got hungry," Dani said, shrugging.

Zoey leaned her chin on her hand and studied Dani through narrowed eyes. "Who asked who to go out to eat?"

"What?"

"Come on. How did this come about?"

Dani knew that look. Zoey was about to start digging for intel. Weirdly, she didn't want to talk about Ren. Not that there was anything to hide—just, the whole unanticipated evening with Ren shone in her memory still. She didn't want to dim the images. "Well, I suggested we grab something to eat."

"Okay. So how was it?"

"It was fine, Zoey. It was dinner." Dani stood. "I think I might grab a shower."

Zoey hooked a finger in the pocket of her jeans and yanked, pulling her back down again. "You asked Ren Dunbar out on a date?"

"It wasn't a date," Dani said defensively. "It was…spur of the moment. Just dinner."

"Uh-huh. And Ren went."

"I told you, it was just dinner."

"I didn't think she'd be your type," Zoey said casually.

Dani stiffened. "What do you mean by that?"

"Dani," Zoey said with exaggerated patience. "Ren is just… she's all about the work. You can tell that's all she ever thinks about. She's not, I don't know, experienced."

Dani snorted. "Oh, come on. What is *that* supposed to mean?"

"You know what I mean. She's younger to begin with, and I don't know, she feels sometimes like she's my younger sister."

"She can't help how old she is, but she's not that young." Dani frowned. "And besides, she's the same year as me in training—she didn't get there without making it through a lot of hard crap."

"I wasn't talking about that kind of experience."

Dani flushed. Ren had given her the impression that she wasn't super experienced with women, but so what? They were just having dinner. "Why does it bother you?"

Zoey tilted her head. "It doesn't. Not really. I guess I'm just surprised."

"Well, if you're worried about Ren, you don't have to be. There's nothing serious going on. Dinner now and then is just that."

"Wait." Zoey pointed a finger. "You have plans for another date?"

"Not a date, just dinner."

"You asked her to have dinner," Zoey said.

"Well, yes."

"That's a date."

Dani blew out a breath. "Okay. A date. A simple, uncomplicated one."

"Why?"

"What do you mean, why?" Exasperated, Dani tilted back in her chair and stared at the ceiling. If she'd wanted to dissect her feelings about Ren, she would have done it herself already. All she wanted to do was hold on to the curl of excitement in her middle that kindled when she thought of her, without asking why. But Zoey was Zoey—a dog with a bone. "Why does anybody ask someone out? Because she's interesting, and easy to talk to, and I like her."

"You like her," Zoey said slowly. "Wow."

"Wow?" Now she sounded defensive. She *was* defensive. Why shouldn't she like Ren? Ren was amazing and interesting and hot. "What's this all about, Zoey?"

"It's just...I don't think you've actually had a date since I've known you."

"Of course I have. You think I'm a monk?"

"I know you're not a monk," Zoey said. "I wasn't talking about you getting laid. I was talking about a date that didn't start and end in bed."

"Well, okay. So?"

"I think it's cute, and I'm sorry that I said Ren wasn't your type. I don't even know what your type is."

Dani relaxed. This was Zoey. Her best friend who was needling her the way best friends did. And she knew why. "I don't know what my type is either," she said slowly. "But it's not about that, Zoey."

"Oh, really? So you're not attracted to her."

"Am I still breathing?"

Zoey grinned. "That's better."

"But I'm not asking her out to dinner so I can get her into bed. I just...I like being around her. She makes me feel, I don't know, like I'm okay just the way I am."

"That's because you are," Zoey said softly.

"Tell that to my parents," Dani muttered.

"I would if I got the chance." Zoey's phone rang and she grabbed it. "Hey." Her whole face transformed. "Really? Now?…Sure. I'll be there in fifteen minutes." She pocketed her phone. "They cleared up the backlog in the ER, and Dec is getting out earlier than she thought."

"So go," Dani said. "See you tomorrow."

Zoey ruffled Dani's hair on the way past. "I'm glad about Ren."

Dani sighed, dumped her empty can in the recycling, and went upstairs to shower. Her phone signaled a text as she climbed the stairs. How come whenever her friends got hooked up, they thought everyone else should too?

She showered, pulled on clean boxers and a tank, and stretched out on the bed to check her phone.

Raven.

How's the boring work going?

Dani smiled. *I blew it off for dinner with a friend.*

! Me too :-)

Raven wasn't usually into chatting. She was always about the gaming. Dani was good with that, but tonight even Raven seemed more relaxed. *Do you feel guilty?*

Not a bit. Just…surprised.

Why?

Not what I expected.

Dani propped a pillow behind her head. She knew what Raven was saying. *Good unexpected or bad unexpected?*

Good, I think. No, definitely good.

Dani thought back over her evening. Yep—definitely good. More than that. *Sounds special.*

Raven was silent a few moments. Dani wondered if she'd crossed some line, let her own emotions get in the way.

Yes. That's a good word for it, Raven finally said. *Want to finish the game?*

For sure, Dani typed.

Meet you...
Dani switched into the app and the invitation was waiting. She thought about Ren. And clicked join. Her night had been special too.

❖

I'm done, Ren typed. *You're killing me tonight*
You're distracted
Ren smiled. She was never distracted. Tonight was a first. She hadn't been able to get out of her head and into the game, and when she didn't bring her A game, she didn't have a chance against Axe. Her concentration kept wavering, and she'd start remembering snippets of conversation she had with Dani at dinner. Had she said the right thing? Had she said something foolish? Was there something she should've said or done? Or not?

She often had those misgivings when she met new people, especially in situations where she didn't have professional ground rules to guide her. If there were rules for socializing, especially with people—girls...*women*—who she liked, she didn't know them. She hadn't had girlfriends in high school to learn from. She really wanted to have gotten it right this time. Dani was so much fun. And so matter-of-fact about who she was, and who Ren was. She'd never felt awkward, at least not after the first few minutes, about her age or her experience or her lack of it. She hadn't needed whatever the rules were she didn't know.

And she'd made discoveries, wonderful ones. A woman's voice could change so quickly in a matter of seconds, going from light and teasing to low and husky in a way that heated her all the way through. Dani's voice did that. So did her eyes, when they flickered and turned darker.

She could reveal bits of her past without becoming an oddity, or worse, just plain odd. She could forget herself listening to someone else's story.

And she hated beer. Who knew she would love strawberry margaritas? They were perfect, and Dani had known.

Raven?

Ren jumped. *Oh hey. Sorry. I guess I am distracted. Sorry.*

LOL. I hope whatever's on your mind is something good.

It is. Thanks.

I'm sure you'll get me back next time, Axe messaged.

For sure. Ren hesitated. *Thanks for listening*

:-) Anytime. night Raven

Ren smiled. Something else she'd learned. Sharing something special was a little bit like reliving it. *Night Axe*

❖

"How are you doing in here?" Honor asked, stepping inside the curtain. She smiled at the seven-year-old on the stretcher, Leo Marcoux, a pale, wide-eyed, dark-eyed boy clutching his father's hand. Martin Marcoux, his father, an older version of the boy with a bit of scruff, a tangle of dark brown hair where he'd run his hand through it, and worry in his eyes, forced a smile.

"We've got a bit of a fever, but we're doing okay."

"And a stomachache too, I understand, right, Leo?" Honor said.

"A little," he said softly.

"Can you show me where?"

Leo rubbed a hand over his lower abdomen. "Down here."

"Okay. Thank you." Honor glanced at Ren and raised an eyebrow. She'd been waiting for a surgical consult to evaluate the young boy, a renal transplant patient, who presented with a low-grade fever and complaints of abdominal pain. The transplant team was in the OR, and the general surgery resident covering the ER had been pulled for a second trauma alert. Ren had shown up in his place.

"I've Dopplered Leo's kidney," she said, smiling at the boy. "We can hear the blood flow, can't we?"

Leo nodded vigorously. "Ren said that means that my kidney is working."

Ren nodded. "It means that the *blood flow* to your kidney

is working. We still have to wait for the results of the urine test, remember?"

The boy grimaced. "I know. But my pee looked good, right?"

"So far, but we need to look at it under the microscope too."

"Right," Leo muttered.

Ren switched her gaze to Honor. "CAT scan was backed up, but they're ready for him now."

Honor stepped to the bedside and said, "Can I listen to your abdomen too?"

"Yes, if you want to," Leo said.

"I would." Smiling, she settled her stethoscope in her ears and listened to the very quiet abdomen. Not much in the way of bowel sounds. "Let's listen with the Doppler again—that's the little probe."

Leo nodded. "Okay."

Honor rolled the gel over the lower part of his abdomen where the graft would be situated and touched the probe to his skin. A strong arterial pulse echoed from the machine. While she couldn't be sure of what the venous outflow was like from the kidney, had it been obstructed, the arterial pulse would've eventually stopped. The CAT scan would give them a good view of the transplant, and with contrast, they should see more of the blood supply as well. She nodded and looked up at the boy's father. "The CAT scan will tell us a lot more."

He cleared his throat. "I can go with him, right?"

"Of course."

"My husband should be here soon," Martin said. "He had a seven o'clock counseling session, and I didn't want to interrupt him until we knew something. Father Domingo Lopez."

"Of course. Dr. Dunbar or I will speak to you both when he arrives," Honor said.

"Thank you."

"Ren, can I go over a few things with you while we get Leo ready to go to CT," Honor said and stepped outside the curtain. Ren followed her down the hall a few feet.

"What are your thoughts?" Honor asked.

"Everything suggests that the transplant is all right. His CBC shows a shift in his white count, but normal for an infectious process. Not a lot of lymphocytes or anything suggesting rejection." She was quiet for a second, her expression contemplative. "I think there's a good chance he has appendicitis."

"It would fit for the age and the history," Honor said. "And if he does?"

"There's going to be a problem if the graft is in the way. And there's likely to be adhesions, so technically challenging."

"Have you looked at his OR records from the transplant procedure?"

Ren took a slow breath. "I haven't, and you're right. I should have already," she added quickly with a bit of a wince, "because they may have taken his appendix when they put in the graft. If that's the case, it's something else."

"Check it. They may have left it. It would depend on where they put the graft and how pressed for time they might've been during that procedure. And you're right, the CAT scan will likely give us a definitive diagnosis."

Ren shook her head. "Still, I should've thought of it."

"Well, next time you will," Honor said. "And thanks for picking up the consult." She paused. "You've been doing that a lot lately."

"I was in the lab, and I'm often around," Ren said with a deprecating shrug. "And that's what I'm here for, right?"

"As long as you're not overextending. A service is busy."

"It is, and I won't."

"All right then, thanks."

"I'll go down with Leo to CT," Ren said.

"Good. Call me with the reading."

Ren went off to organize transport, and Honor scanned the board, which finally looked like it was under control.

A welcome voice said from just over her shoulder, "How's it looking?"

The timbre of Quinn's voice and the faint warmth of her breath against the side of her neck sent a shiver down Honor's spine. She leaned back slightly until her shoulder touched Quinn's. "We're winning."

Quinn grinned. "Aren't you always?"

"Eventually."

"Did Arly call you?" Quinn asked.

"No," Honor said, turning quickly. "Is she all right?"

"Yeah, sorry. I didn't mean to scare you. It's one of those situations where she wants permission to do something, and she's checking with the parent she thinks is going to say yes first."

"Family conference time then. I've got about five minutes." Honor linked her arm through Quinn's. "Come back to my office."

Once there, she shut the door partway and gave Quinn a quick kiss. "So, what did she want to do?"

"Are you ready for this? Apparently the Billie Eilish US tour has added the Wells Fargo Center to their schedule over Labor Day. Arly wants to go."

"Really?" Honor said. "Billie Eilish? We should all go."

"I don't think that's what she had in mind." Quinn laughed. "She wants to go with Janie, Eduardo, and four or five other kids. Parents were not on her list."

Honor sighed. "She's never gone to anything like that alone. What do you think?"

"Janie's older brother's Raymond is going, sort of a de facto chaperone. He's driving them all, so they'll have an adult with them. I sort of hedged…No, I definitely hedged and said I needed to talk to you."

"Oh, so if *we* say no, it'll be my fault. Smart move, Maguire."

Quinn grinned. "I'm learning."

Honor sighed. "I suppose she can go as long as there's a responsible adult. I know Janie's brother Raymond. If he's willing to drive them and keep an eye on them, I don't think we have a good reason to say no."

"I pretty much agree, and there hasn't been much in the last year or so for them to do. It's tough to say no."

"All right then. We're united."

"Aren't we pretty much always?" Quinn took her hand and kissed her knuckles, something she'd always done and that Honor still loved.

"While I've got you, there's something else I wanted to mention," Honor said.

"Problem with one of my residents, or one of my staff?"

"What makes you say that?"

"Because it usually is."

"A resident this time," Honor said.

Quinn frowned. "What's going on?"

"Actually it's the opposite of a problem. Ren Dunbar. She's been seeing consults on a regular basis. Not stealing cases, but whenever we've been waiting on the consult and there's been some delay, she's been picking it up. She's very bright."

"Well yeah, we know that. So what's the problem?"

"I just thought you should know, because considering the hours she's keeping, I think she's living at the hospital."

Quinn blew out a breath. "Yeah, she practically does. Always has. Sax never seemed to sleep much either. But that's who she is, Honor. She puts every bit of her energy into whatever goal she's trying to accomplish. She wouldn't be here if that wasn't true."

"I understand that's normal for her," Honor said, "but it's early in the year, and if she keeps up this pace, she might burn out."

"I'm glad you told me." Quinn rubbed her forehead. "I may have created a couple of monsters lately."

"What do you mean?"

"Well, I pulled Ren out of the lab and put her into the fifth year slot because I needed a strong resident there. Plus, if she's ever going to move on clinically, she needs to get out of the lab. But of course she feels pressured to catch up to everyone."

"You couldn't help that," Honor said.

"I know. But then I pointed Dani Chan toward a research project because she expressed interest in being competitive for the Franklin. So now *she's* got a double load. If I'd known she was serious about competing for the award too, I could've gotten her started on something sooner."

"So you're worried that she's not going to be able to handle everything."

"Dani is an excellent resident. Not driven the way Ren is, but she hides her intensity. The two of them going head-to-head is going to present a quandary when we get around to voting."

"Do they know that?"

"I don't know. It's not usually an issue. Most of the residents are too busy keeping their heads above water and looking toward the finish line to actively go for it. Hell, usually whoever wins is totally surprised. This year it's looking different."

"Well, all you can do is keep an eye on them."

"Yeah," Quinn said, rubbing her forehead. "There's a lot of that going around these days."

Laughing, Honor looped her arms around Quinn's shoulders and pressed close. "I love you, you know."

Quinn closed her eyes and sighed. "And lucky for me."

CHAPTER NINE

Dani slouched in the corner of the lumpy, mustard-colored sofa pushed up against the wall in the OR lounge and propped her feet on the edge of the coffee table. She cradled the phone against her shoulder and dialed the dictation extension.

"This is Dr. Dani Chan, dictating an op note on Marsha D'Angelo, date of birth four, four, 1947, hospital number 100-3729. Attending surgeon, Ronald Chu MD, assistants, Dani Chan MD and Lawrence Chatell DO." She closed her eyes and continued dictating, working her way through the case from the time they brought the patient into the room, prepped and draped, made the incision, exposed the vital organs, isolated the blood supply, resected the tumor, and repaired the large bowel. She felt someone sit down beside her as she finished up.

"Once the anastomosis had been completed, the abdomen was irrigated with two liters of sterile saline, a suction drain was placed in the left lower quadrant, brought out to separate stab incision, and the abdomen was closed in layers using Monocryl on the peritoneum, two-oh running Prolene on the fascia, and a running subcuticular three-oh Prolene on the skin. The drain was secured in place with a figure of eight, two-oh Prolene and attached to suction. After the application of sterile dressings, the patient was extubated uneventfully and transported to the recovery room. Thank you very much, Dani Chan, MD dictating." She set the phone down and glanced to her neighbor. Zoey munched a Mr. Goodbar, her pea-green clogs on the floor beside her and her feet tucked beneath her.

"I didn't even know they made those anymore," Dani said.

"They're in the vending machine," Zoey said. "They must make them somewhere."

"They probably ran out of everything else and found those in the back of some warehouse. Give me a bite."

Zoey held out her hand with the half-unwrapped candy bar, and Dani leaned over and took a bite. It was good.

"Thanks," she said, after she swallowed.

"I thought you had plans tonight," Zoey said.

Dani grimaced. "Yeah, me too, but I haven't heard from Ren."

Her GI case had run pretty late, but she'd been hanging around killing time, and it was after six. She'd texted Ren but hadn't gotten an answer. She hadn't even been able to reach Raven to get a game going to occupy herself.

"She can't be in the OR," Dani said, "because I've looked and I didn't see any cases running."

"No, we finished all the cases about four—in fact I was just about to hunt her down myself so we can make sign-out rounds. I've got a date."

"What, you and Dec are still at the dating stage?" Dani snorted. "You're practically living together."

"So what, we can't have dates? That's part of the reason we don't live together. I told you, every night is date night with us."

"Please," Dani said, "spare me."

"Well, you did ask."

"I didn't ask—I made a comment. That's a statement not requiring a response."

"Well, if you mock me, then there will be a response." Zoey stretched out a leg and poked her with her toe. "You're just in a bad mood because you were counting on getting some tonight."

"I most certainly was not."

Zoey cocked her head. "You sound serious."

"I am serious. Dinner, I told you that."

"Well, that's the beginning of the evening," Zoey said as if Dani was a little bit slow. "But then there's after dinner, and after-after dinner."

Dani shook her head. "No, it's not like that."

"Yeah, that's what you told me. I'm wondering what it *is* like since you can't find her."

"Hey, be nice, I'm suffering." Her phone vibrated beside her, and she grabbed it.

So sorry. I got stuck in the ER. Clear now. Still need to do sign outs. So sorry!

Dani let out a breath. *No big deal. It's still early. Seven?*

Yes!

Zoey's phone beeped, and she looked at it.

"Well, Ren's appeared."

"She was in the ER," Dani said flatly.

"That's not surprising," Zoey said. "She literally lives there."

"I noticed. I'm kinda glad I didn't have to compete with her every single year of our residency," Dani muttered.

"You can say that again. Doesn't she ever get tired? Doesn't she ever sleep?"

"I don't know. I'm usually sleeping."

Zoey laughed. "Or staying up half the night playing *World of Warcraft.*"

"I'm not playing *Warcraft*," Dani said and grinned.

"Whatever."

"Besides, that's different. That's relaxation, not work." Dani frowned. "I haven't even been able do that all that much lately. Super busy."

"How's your project coming?"

"Slow." Dani grinned. "I'll get there, though."

"I know you will." Zoey stood and stretched. "I should go, so we can finish sign-outs, and Ren can put you out of your misery."

"I don't think that's exactly what I was hoping for."

Zoey laughed. "I hope you have fun."

"Yeah," Dani said, half to herself. "Me too."

She'd been looking forward to it all week. In between everything else she had to do on the floor and in the ER and working on her research project, she'd think about Ren and imagine spending more time with her. She hadn't been as anxious to do anything like that in longer than she could remember. The only thing that really gave her any kind of thrill was doing a challenging case in the OR and knowing it had gone well and that she'd done a good job. That never got old, but sometimes it felt like there ought to be more.

This week she had the feeling maybe there was.

She still had a good forty-five minutes to kill and texted Raven again, hoping to fill the time with something more than the impatient jangling of her entire nervous system.

Hey, you around for a quick game?

After a minute or two, she figured she wasn't going to get an answer. That happened. Online connections were hit or miss, and she wondered why she'd never made any move to find out more about Raven. Raven was a constant in her life, someone she communicated with almost as much as she did with Zoey, and yet other than her texts, she had no place to put her. No face, no image of her at work or play, no sense of who she was in the world. Except the last couple of times, when she sensed Raven's excitement. That something had changed for her. Raven'd even said as much when she'd mentioned meeting someone. That probably explained why she wasn't around as much. Dani laughed. What an idiot. *Of course* that's why Raven had disappeared. She was probably in the middle of some hot love affair.

The twinge of jealousy came out of nowhere, and she shook her head. Boy, was that dumb. She certainly had no hold on Raven, but she missed her. That was real. And they were friends, in the way that the internet allowed for friendship, and she would miss her if she lost her. But that's what happened. You connected and got really tight, you maybe shared some things, and then life went on, and the internet didn't create enough of a fabric to hold things together. You drifted apart, and the cycle started again. She'd had it happen a few times, but Raven had always seemed different. More real. And that's why she missed her.

Her phone vibrated. Raven replying.

Still at work, pretty busy. Can't now but later on tonight or tomorrow

Dani grinned. *Sounds good have fun tonight*

?
Hey, Friday night. Got plans?
:-) Maybe
I'll take that as yes
:-)
I mean it, Dani texted, and she did. *Have fun and I'll catch you soon*
for sure

Dani slid her phone in her pocket and went to change. Ren would be ready soon, and the surge of excitement, along with the nerves, came back.

"Okay," Ren said, "we're done. Laila, I'll meet you at six tomorrow for rounds?"

The intern nodded vehemently. No sign that she was upset that her chief wanted to make rounds an hour ahead of everyone else's.

"Great. I'll have my beeper if there's a problem. Call me before anyone else, okay?"

"Yes, I understand," Laila said, apparently trying not to sound like she'd heard it every night at sign-out rounds.

Ren caught the inflection in her voice and grinned. "Okay, I know, you've heard it before."

Laila colored. "I…um…"

Ren laughed. "It's fine."

Zoey slid her tablet into her backpack. "Well, I'm outta here. You walking out, Laila?"

"I have to check a couple of post-op X-rays," Laila said. "You go ahead."

"I'm done," Steve, one of the juniors, said. "You want a ride, Zoey?"

"Sure, thanks." She shot Ren a grin as she stood. "Have fun tonight."

Ren blushed. She didn't have time to stop it. She'd instantly thought of Dani, and the flood of anticipation that came over her every time she did caught her before she could tamp down her response. "Oh, right. Thanks."

Zoey quirked a brow, gave her a little wave, and left with Steve.

Ren checked the time. Almost seven. She gathered her tablet and her empty water bottle and hurried through the cafeteria, dropping the empty container in the recycling bin as she passed. She rushed through the halls, up the stairs, and into the OR locker room. Five minutes. She could do it in five minutes. She slammed open her locker, grabbed the bag with her change of clothes, and scurried into the shower room. Two minutes to shower, a minute to dry off, a quick zap of the dryer to her hair, thirty seconds for a splash of lip gloss, and another minute to jump into capris, sandals, and a short-sleeved linen shirt. She stuffed everything back into her bag and stopped abruptly. Where was she supposed to meet Dani? Wonderful. She could remember every single page of every one of her textbooks, but she couldn't figure out how to manage something as simple as a date.

Which of course was because it wasn't simple at all. Especially not when it was all about doing something she had no experience with. No textbook, no mentor, no besties to tell her the step-by-step procedure. Beyond wanting to look at least clean and in something other than scrubs, she wasn't sure what came next. But she was pretty sure finding out where Dani was waiting was probably a good idea.

Hi, where should I meet you?

Downstairs by the main entrance. Be there in a minute

me too

That crisis averted, she hurried downstairs, made her way through the lobby, and stopped when she didn't see Dani. Of course, she'd been looking for someone in scrubs, and Dani was in tight black jeans, lace-up black boots, and a charcoal T-shirt that should've looked super-casual but looked anything but, clinging to Dani's sharply defined shoulders and chest. Simple, and totally... wow.

Dani grinned. "Hey, Ren."

"Oh. Hey," Ren said, hurrying to join her. How long had she been standing there gawking? Even though Dani was way gawkable.

"You look nice," Dani said softly.

"You look…amazing?"

Dani's grin widened, and she laughed. "I think that was a question?"

"No, it absolutely wasn't. It was a statement. Most definitely a statement."

"Well then, thank you." Dani motioned toward the door, pushed it open, and held it as Ren walked through.

"Hungry?"

"Yes," Ren said, although what she was feeling was anything but. Her stomach was a mass of swirling sensations that she now understood to be butterflies. She'd never actually thought that statement could be true, but it clearly was. Dani even smelled good. Something citrusy and darkly fragrant, like oranges and oak, maybe. She'd had Scotch the one time in her life she'd tried going to a dorm party. She'd liked the smoky taste, but not much else about it. Dani had a hint of that smoky flavor about her.

"Whatever you're wearing, it smells great," Ren said.

Dani step hitched a beat, as if she was surprised. "Thanks. Again."

"Sorry," Ren said.

"For what?"

"I don't actually know how to do this."

"This?" Dani asked softly.

"Date?"

"There's not a rule book."

Ren was grateful that Dani wasn't laughing. "There isn't?"

"Nope." Dani reached down and took her hand. "For example, there's no rule that says you can't tell me that you like the way I look or the way I smell. Anytime. I like it."

"Well, you do and you do, and so do I."

"You know, it's weird," Dani murmured, linking her fingers with Ren's, "but I got all that."

Ren took a breath and tried to think past the amazing sensation of Dani's soft, warm hand entwined with hers. She'd touched hundreds of patients. She knew what skin felt like. But Dani's— Dani's skin tingled against hers. "I'm glad there's no rule that says we can't hold hands, either."

Dani glanced at her, and her eyes glimmered. "Definitely not that one."

"I bet there are some, though," Ren said thoughtfully. "And if there are, I don't know them."

"So how about we just make up our own," Dani said.

"That should make for interesting dinner conversation."

"Ren," Dani murmured, "every conversation with you is interesting."

Ren knew there must be an appropriate response to that, but between the heat rising in her throat and the swirl of butterfly wings in her middle, all she could do was whisper, "I'm glad."

CHAPTER TEN

Dani'd spent so much time thinking about seeing Ren alone, outside of work, she hadn't thought to ask Ren where she might want to go for dinner. She was pretty much a grab a pizza or cheesesteak kind of person, and that probably wasn't a great idea for a date. At least she'd dressed for a date, sorting through her closet, or rather the boxes in her closet that she hadn't actually unpacked, and finally deciding that if she wasn't going to wear scrubs, it was going to have to be jeans. She was happy with the choice now, especially having caught the look in Ren's eyes when Ren'd first spied her waiting in the lobby. She was pretty certain, at least she really *hoped* she was right, that Ren's slow scan of her body and the slight look of surprise meant appreciation. Hell, Ren got her pulse racing, and she at least wanted to return the favor.

Since they'd walked two blocks without any particular destination, she probably ought to get her head in the game.

"Is there something in particular you'd like for dinner?" Dani asked.

"Anything except Thai," Ren said. "That seems to be the go-to takeout in the lab, and I think I've probably had it for eighty percent of my meals for the last three years."

"Spend a lot of time there, do you?"

"Um. Guilty," Ren said. "But I'm not completely weird. I do have my own apartment."

"Roommates?"

"Oh no, just me."

Dani hoped that wasn't too obvious. Not that she was planning on them needing all-night privacy or anything. Just...considering contingencies. She'd never brought a woman home to the house when she'd lived with Syd and Jerry. Not subjecting her house-mates or the woman she'd slept with to a potentially embarrassing encounter just seemed the considerate thing to do. Zoey wouldn't mind someone staying over, but she'd be relentless about the details. Something else Dani'd prefer to avoid. And if she ever got that far with Ren... She dragged her wandering mind back from possibilities she'd sworn to Zoey she wasn't contemplating.

"Okay, no Thai," Dani said. "There's a family-owned place just around the corner. It's not very large, and it's not fancy, but the food is really good."

"Sure. Okay. Do they have margaritas?"

Dani laughed and stopped in the middle of the sidewalk, turning to grin at her. "I told you you'd like it."

"I did."

The serious expression on Ren's face was damn cute. The swelling of tenderness in Dani's chest was new. Nice. She had a lot of nice feelings around Ren. Some of them went beyond nice into breathless, aching territory. Those she was trying to tamp down. She was used to moving fast, but not this time. Not with Ren. "I'm not sure about the margaritas, but we can find something else that you'll like."

"Well, that probably won't be hard, because I'm really not much of a drinker. I definitely don't like beer. And I don't like the way Scotch tastes. But I like the way it smells on you."

"Come again?"

Ren blushed. "Okay, that's not exactly what I meant. I was thinking earlier—when I first saw you—that you smelled kind of the way Scotch tasted." She made a rueful face. "Boy, that sounds bad, doesn't it."

"Ren," Dani said, "you're pretty much killing me here."

Ren's eyes widened. "I am? I told you I was bad at it."

"No. That's not what I meant at all. What I meant was...oh, hell." Dani leaned closer and kissed her very lightly on the mouth.

"I meant you're so *not* bad that I'm having a hard time sticking to the rules."

"You mean there are some—because we said we'd make them up as needed."

"I needed a couple."

"Like what?"

"Like spending time getting to know you...for us to get to know each other...before, you know. Anything more serious."

"Such as...?"

Dani sighed. "Well, kissing was on the list."

"Oh. Does that count as a first kiss, then?"

"Let's just say it's a preview," Dani said. "Because I can do better."

"I don't think better is the point," Ren murmured. "But if there's a repertoire, I'm open to you demonstrating."

Dani groaned. "Are you sure you've never done this before?"

"You mean date?"

"I was thinking more along the lines of seduction."

Ren laughed, a genuine happy laugh that lightened Dani's heart. "Oh, absolutely not. I think I've had two almost-dates in my life, and they didn't last very long. So really, untried ground."

Dani tugged her hand and started walking again. "Well, I like covering new ground with you. I'm sorry if that kiss came out of nowhere. It's just that you make me want to kiss you sometimes."

"I think a kiss out in the open, in the middle of the sidewalk, that lasted about three seconds is pretty much okay, and if I hadn't wanted a repeat, I would've said so."

"You didn't say so," Dani said.

"No. I didn't."

Dani let out a long breath. "That's...good. Very good."

Ren laughed again. "Sometime we should talk about the other rules you thought you needed."

"I might have trouble remembering them if you keep distracting me," Dani muttered. Ren was driving her crazy. The way she looked, the way she laughed, the things she said. She believed every word Ren said about not having much practice dating, but Ren didn't need practice. She was a natural. She was open and easy and said what she meant. No games. They were barely touching, but just the brush of their hands left Dani wanting. Wanting more. Funny, though, she was enjoying the buildup. Sex for her was usually the case of an urge first, then finding a willing partner second, and taking care of business third. Then done. This was totally different. The person... Ren...was the beginning and the end of what turned her on. Being with Ren was what was making her hot.

"Waiting will work too, then," Ren said. "No point if we don't need them. I guess we'll find out."

"Dinner first. This is the place." Dani pointed to the pale blue Victorian with the wide front porch and ornate trim and hoped she could make it through a meal without some part of her imploding.

"Really?" Ren said. "This is a restaurant?"

"Oh," Dani said, "I should've mentioned it's on the first floor of a regular house, hardly altered at all to fit the restaurant. It's really kind of like having dinner at home—if you lived in a cool house like this."

"I love these Victorians," Ren said. "They're probably the same era as the brownstones in DC, but homier somehow. More approachable."

"I know what you mean. Things were a whole lot more modern where I grew up on the hillside outside LA. I like it here better too."

They crossed the porch and walked through the archway of the double doors into a small marble-tiled foyer. Beyond that, what had once been the central hall with sitting rooms off either side now held white-tablecloth covered tables filled with diners. Chandeliers with fluted shades provided mellow lighting and a warm welcoming atmosphere. A middle-aged woman with wavy dark hair streaked with silver in a plain white shirt and dark pants met them just inside the foyer.

"Hi, Dani. Dinner for two?"

"Rachel, hi—yes, thanks. Sorry I don't have reservations."

"That's okay. We're past the rush. I've got a nice table in the bay window at the back. Will that work?"

"That would be great, thanks. Oh"—she tugged Ren forward a little bit—"this is Ren Dunbar."

"Hi, Ren," Rachel said.

"Hi," Ren said, holding out her hand. "Pleased to meet you."

Smiling, Rachel shook her hand, turned to grab two menus hand-printed on parchment, and led them to a round table for two tucked into a shallow alcove in front of a set of bay windows overlooking a garden.

"This is great," Ren said as they settled at the table and a younger woman, probably in her early twenties, approached to fill the water glasses.

"Take your time with the menus," she said, "but the pasta dish tonight is great. Homemade rigatoni with a vodka cream sauce and a vegetable medley."

"Thanks, Vickie," Dani said.

Vickie looked from Dani to Ren, smiled, and disappeared.

"You come here a lot, I guess?" Ren asked.

"As often as I can," Dani said, "which with our schedule isn't often enough."

"Is it your go-to date place then?"

Dani laughed. "Uh, no, actually, it isn't. I like to come here by myself, or maybe with Zoey or Syd. It's just nice to relax, and it feels like I'm here with friends even if I'm alone."

"Should I not ask about other dates?" Ren asked.

"You can ask me about anything you want, Ren," Dani said gently. "But just to clear up a few things, I'm not dating anyone, and I haven't been in a serious relationship for ages, and if I *am* dating someone, I don't date anyone else at the same time."

"Oh," Ren said, sitting back and studying Dani contemplatively. "I think those are rules, aren't they? But not like universal rules. Just rules for us."

"Not really rules," Dani said. "More information about me. *You* might have different rules, and if you do, it's probably a good thing that I know them pretty soon."

"Oh. You mean monogamy and sex…things like that."

Dani tried not to sputter as she laughed. "Okay, yeah, that's getting to the chase. Good topics to discuss. Maybe we should start with how you like to handle dating before, you know, we get to the sex. Talking about sex, that is."

Jeez, could she be any more obvious? She really needed to stop letting her hormones dictate everything coming out of her mouth.

"Well, that's an easy one," Ren said offhandedly. "I'm dating you."

"That's easy?" Dani murmured. "Just me?"

"Shouldn't it be?"

"Yeah, maybe it should. It would be a first for me, though."

Ren smiled. "Good."

Dani paused as Vickie returned.

"Made a decision?" Vickie asked.

"I'll do the special," Dani said. "And I'll take a stout."

"So will I," Ren said, "except not the stout. I'll have…um… something new." She glanced at Dani. "Recommendations?"

"A White Russian," Dani said quickly.

"You know I have to ask," Vickie said.

They both got their IDs out, and after a quick look, Vickie went off to get their drinks.

"So, a White Russian," Ren said, then listed the ingredients. "I think I'll like that."

"Did you memorize a bartending manual?" Dani said, duly impressed.

"Oh, I scanned one while I was waiting for a case the other day. I didn't want to go through life ignorant of the possibilities."

"You scanned one." Dani leaned on a fist. "How about a Manhattan?"

Ren regarded her steadily for a minute, and then quietly reeled off the ingredients.

"You can do that with everything?" Dani asked.

"Yes," Ren said quietly.

"That's amazing. I sure wish I could do it," Dani said. "Is it annoying, to, you know, remember everything you read?"

"No one has ever asked me that before," Ren said. "No, it isn't. It's not like I'm constantly thinking about everything I've read. It's just that when a topic comes up that I've read about, just like you would remember having read about it, I do too. Except I remember *everything* that I read about it—verbatim."

"I can't see any downside."

"Other than the fact that people think you're strange or weird?"

Dani frowned. "Why would they? It's a great ability. Besides, it's just the way you're made."

"Differently."

"Ren, there's nothing wrong with being different. In fact, I think it's one of the things that makes you so interesting."

"You do." Ren regarded her solemnly, as if the idea was new to her.

Maybe it was. Dani frowned inwardly. How was it possible Ren didn't know how fascinatingly unique she was? How intriguing, how…amazing. Right at that moment she wished she could gather her close and whisper some of that to her. Instead, she held her gaze and said emphatically, "I do."

"You don't mind that I don't have a lot of practice at this."

Dani shook her head. "All I care about is that you're enjoying yourself. I hope as much as I am."

"Oh, I am."

"Good. Me too."

The drinks came, and Dani asked, "How's the little boy with the kidney transplant doing?"

"Oh, Leo, with appendicitis. He did great. He went home this morning."

"That was a nice case."

"I was glad I got to scrub on it. I haven't done a lot of endoscopic surgery. I'm going to have to make up for that this year." She shook her head. "Along with a lot of other things."

"I guess you got thrown into things out of the blue, huh," Dani said as she made room for Vickie to put their food down.

Ren sipped her drink. "Oh, I like this one. Definitely add it to my favorite drink list. There are now two."

"So noted."

"I was surprised to be moved out of the lab so suddenly, but"—Ren sighed—"I knew it was coming. My research project is nearly completed, and we've had a couple of papers published. It was time. I just thought that Quinn—Dr. Maguire—would give me a little more of a heads-up."

"You're catching up fast," Dani said.

"Maybe—but it's more than just the number of cases I can manage to do. I need to make connections and learn how to direct a team. Inside the OR and out. You're way ahead of me there."

Dani nodded. "You're obviously capable of doing anything you set out to do, so I wouldn't worry."

Ren tilted her head with a curious expression. "Based on what?"

"You mean my opinion?"

"Yes."

"Everything about you—you're supersmart, goes without saying, but being smart isn't enough to accomplish all the things you have even if you didn't have to deal with the challenges of being accelerated."

"I...well, thank you," Ren said quietly.

"You're welcome."

Ren smiled shyly. "So, how is your project coming along?"

"The case studies?" Dani shrugged. "I'm getting there."

"Are you enjoying it at all?"

"Sometimes, yeah, I can see the appeal. And I like thinking that maybe something I dig out is going to help someone treating some kid somewhere." Dani shook her head. "It's not exactly what my parents had in mind for me...Hell, I don't know, maybe it'll mean something to them."

"What do you mean?" Ren asked.

"Oh, family stuff." Dani considered changing the topic again. She didn't talk about private stuff with girls on dates. Except, Ren wasn't any girl. And this wasn't the usual encounter. And if she didn't tell her, how many other things would she never tell her. And then what would they end up with? "I told you my family are all research scientists, right?"

Ren nodded. "Possibly an understatement?"

"True. It's kind of the lifeblood of our family. Genetically predetermined. Somehow, I didn't get the genes."

"Oh, but you're a doctor, a surgeon, so you got some of the science genes."

"Yes, but not the intellectual ones, at least not from where my family sees it."

"Families," Ren muttered. "I'm sorry, that's hard. So they pressure you?"

Dani laughed. Telling Ren just that little bit of the story took a little of the bitterness away. "Yeah, you could say that. Oh, not so much when I was growing up, because they just expected that I would follow along like everyone else in the family. But when it became apparent that I was diverging, then the subtle and eventually not-so-subtle pressure started." She lifted her shoulder. "Now, my mother calls every few weeks with suggestions for research positions that I might consider."

"So," Ren said, sounding as if she'd been turning something over in her mind and reached a deduction, "the Franklin. That's why you're doing a research project in your last year."

"Yeah," Dani said.

"You've certainly got the clinical background, and that's a very strong position."

"Stronger than having published a few research articles in *Circulation* and *The Journal of Cardiology*?" Dani said quietly.

Ren put down her fork. "Should I ask how you know that?"

"Easy. Medline. I looked you up."

"Why?"

"Because you impressed me, and I wanted to know more about you."

"So you looked up the journal articles I've written? Dani, you're weird."

"Hey, I thought that was supposed to be my line."

Ren stared until they were both laughing.

"Maybe we should agree to table work for the rest of the night," Dani said, "and get back to the more important things."

"You mean like monogamy and sex?"

"Oh, so you haven't forgotten."

Ren tugged her lower lip between her teeth for an instant, the way she did when she was thinking seriously about something. The little tell made Dani's stomach clench. They really needed to finish eating soon.

"Yes, I've definitely been thinking about it," Ren said. "I think probably the sex should come first, and then the rest of the discussion."

Dani sucked in a breath. "Ren, you're *seriously* killing me here."

"I told you I didn't know the order of things."

"Oh no, you're doing just great."

"So we can start with sex?" Ren tilted her head. "The talking part, I guess?"

"We can start with any part you want." Dani held her breath. If she didn't at least get to kiss her again, she might not be able to make it home without incurring bodily damage.

"I don't know if I mentioned it, but I live in the neighborhood," Ren said. "About five minutes from here."

"Are you two interested in dessert?" Vickie asked brightly as she stopped by the table.

Dani asked, "Ren?"

She thought she might have sounded in pain.

"No, thank you," Ren said to Vickie. "Everything was wonderful."

"I'll bring your check," Vickie said.

"So, your place then," Dani said, still watching Ren.

"Yes." Ren pulled out a credit card and handed it to Dani. "For my half. And Dani?"

"Yes?"

"I do have one rule."

"Let's hear it," Dani said softly.

"You have to trust me to know what I want."

"From what I know about you," Dani said, "you always have."

Ren smiled. "Then you already know me better than almost anyone in my life."

"Good. Because that's what I want."

CHAPTER ELEVEN

"My place is on the far side of the park," Ren said. "I usually walk home past the duck pond. It's still light enough out if you want to go that way."

"Sure." Dani slowed a little. "One thing before we get there. No expectations. I just wanted to say that."

Ren glanced at Dani. "You mean *you* have no expectations. I might possibly have all kinds of expectations." She grinned. "No pressure, though."

Dani looked startled, then amused. Then something else passed over her face. Something that looked a lot like hunger. "Ren, I'm trying to think *slow*. But you don't make it easy."

Ren smiled inwardly. Dani had said she was good at seduction, but she was pretty sure Dani was teasing. She was very certain she didn't know the slightest thing about seduction. She didn't have any experience at all with what she thought they would be doing. If not tonight, soon, if they kept seeing each other. And she hoped they would. Reading people was another of her undeveloped skills, but Dani—unlike anyone else she'd ever met—was open and undisguised with her feelings.

Ren might be inexperienced, but she wasn't naive, and she recognized what she saw in Dani's eyes. And she knew what she felt in her body. Dani looked at her and thought about sex. And when she looked back, she felt it too, a reflection of that desire. A tingling deep inside that was at once warm and exciting. An ache that worried at her concentration and made her forget about all the things that always seemed so important. She hadn't thought about the lab or her career or what she needed to do to be competitive for the best fellowship in the country in hours. Those things were always on her mind. Those were her goals. Those were the things that defined her. She should be worried that she'd lost sight of those things. But at this moment?

Dani's kiss had consumed her awareness, an instant so light and fleeting that if she didn't still feel it in the featherlight vibration in her lips, she could almost believe she'd imagined it. But she hadn't. The heat left behind still haunted her.

Her breath, when she drew it, shuddered into her depths to some place just coming to life, opening with equal parts joy and ferocity. Oh, she had much more than expectations—she trembled with urges that defied anything so simple.

"I agree. We should abandon expectations. I think we'll do better," Ren said, "if we don't have any."

"I'm not sure if I should be disappointed or optimistic," Dani said.

Ren reached for Dani's hand as they turned into the park and traveled toward the duck pond down a gravel path between patches of oak and evergreens. Taking Dani's hand would have been unfathomable a week before. She had not known then how intriguing the sensation of another's touch—the subtle texture of skin, the strength of bone and flesh—could be when intimately pressed to hers. Dani's hand was a thing of wonder. How that hand would feel moving over her body in other ways, in other places, was still a mystery, but one she wanted—yearned—to discover. "I was thinking that without expectations, anything could happen. No automatic stops."

"That definitely leans in the optimistic direction."

Ren squeezed Dani's hand. "Maybe that's not the direction you were going, though."

"Remember I said I was working on the idea of *slow*? That's my head talking." She laughed a bit hoarsely. "I can't say the rest of me is totally on board with that concept. But pulling out the stops—metaphorically—could be risky. Some things take on a life of their own, and a pace of their own. I'm not saying I wouldn't stop the minute you said to. You don't have to worry about that. But if you don't, I might not."

"Let's agree that we'll both be responsible for what we do, and then you don't have to worry."

"I'm not worried," Dani said quickly.

"Aren't you? Because I get the sense you think you might need to protect me from something I don't understand. I like that you think about that and care about my feelings, but you're not responsible for my comfort or my safety." Ren shook Dani's hand playfully and brought it to her lips, kissing the knuckles where Dani's fingers curled over hers. Dani gasped, and an entirely foreign and sharply exciting thrill coursed through her. "I'm inexperienced, but I'm not uninformed. I haven't been living in a bubble my whole life. I know what sex is about. I even know what sex feels like, under some circumstances."

Dani closed her eyes and emitted a soft groan. "Okay. That's it. I'm dying now."

Ren laughed, the sound cut short when Dani released her hand and unexpectedly swung an arm around her shoulders, pulling her close. The move was so assured, and so possessive, and so completely natural for all its newness, all Ren could do was go with it. And enjoy it. Dani's body was warm and firm, and this close, she smelled even more wonderful than Ren remembered. She'd seen couples walk this way, of course, but never stopped to wonder why. What message they were sending through the simple act of walking that they couldn't communicate some other way. Now she knew. A visceral sensation of being claimed, even as she claimed. An awareness of belonging, of *fitting*, that was at once amazing and effortless. The fluttering in her midsection grew heavy, and a thousand butterflies settled down into the pit of her stomach, leaving an ache at once sweet and insistent.

"This feels nice."

"Yeah." Dani kissed her temple and breathed in softly. "You smell like...lilacs?"

Ren laughed softly. "Close enough."

"I never thought you were naive," Dani murmured as they began walking again.

"Good. I like how careful and caring you are. But I don't need to be taken care of."

"I get that."

Ren followed Dani's lead and tightened her arm around Dani's waist. She'd never been as close to another woman in her life. Every place they touched turned electric. "I love the way your body feels."

"Do you?" Dani asked, her voice low and husky.

"Yes." She let her hand slide down Dani's flank and over the curve of her hip until her fingertips rested on the crest of Dani's hipbone. "So strong and sleek."

"You realize when you touch me like that, it turns me on," Dani said.

"Does it." Ren repeated the motion. "Is the effect cumulative?"

Dani's laugh came fast and strong. "Oh, it is. How much farther is it to your house?"

"Just opposite the park. Three minutes."

"Then maybe you should just keep your hand still until we get there."

"You know if you tell me not to do something, it's just going to make me more curious. But all right. I'll wait."

They were alone on the short path out of the park, and Dani stopped abruptly, turned Ren toward her, and kissed her again. This kiss went on much longer than the brief one they'd shared on the way to the restaurant. Dani's arms were around her waist, holding her close to Dani's body. Dani's mouth sealed to hers, soft and firm and warm. The tip of Dani's tongue skirted across the surface of her lower lip, and the churning deep inside her grew heavier, lower, with a pounding ache that was both pleasure and urgency. Ren wrapped her arms around Dani's shoulders even more tightly against her, fitting her breasts to Dani's chest. The pressure against her nipples created a sweet aching she'd never imagined. She moaned very softly, and the sound astounded her.

Dani drew her mouth away and rested her forehead against Ren's. "You're so sexy. I could kiss you like that all night."

"I think if you did…" Ren struggled to catch her breath. "I think it might drive me crazy."

"You want to find out?" Dani asked.

Ren gripped Dani's shoulders and kissed her back. "Yes."

Ren stopped in front of a narrow, three-story, pale yellow Victorian single with green and red scrolls along the roof lines and eaves, that sat behind a wrought-iron fence and a small yard bisected by a flagstone walk. The first floor windows were nearly as tall as a person, and white lace curtains fluttered behind them.

"Nice place," Dani said, turning to look over her shoulder at the park and the faint glimmer as the setting sun turned the pond to gold. On any other night she might have suggested they sit for a few minutes on the wide stone steps and just breathe air that didn't carry the ever-present scent of tragedy while they watched the sun set. But not tonight. Not when she'd already accepted she had no way to rein in the need Ren had set off within her.

"I was lucky to get it," Ren said, pulling keys from her backpack. "A lot of the staff live here. Quinn and Honor are three doors down. Quinn let me know about the opening."

"You're friends with them, aren't you?" Dani asked as she followed Ren across the wide mahogany wood porch to the ornate filigreed doors.

"I know them, through my sister Sax. She and Quinn worked together in Manhattan. But I don't socialize with them, if that's what you mean. I don't really socialize, actually."

"Why not?"

Ren shrugged. "The usual reasons. No time. And then there's the other thing. The acceleration problem."

"I think I'm starting to get that," Dani said. "Your not being at the same place as everyone else a lot of the time."

"It was a bigger problem when I was younger."

Ren's flat tone suggested she didn't want to give the topic any more consideration, so Dani let it drop. But she wouldn't forget it.

Ren pushed the doors wide and held them open. Dani looked past her down the parquet floor to a staircase ascending to the next level and rooms opening off either side.

"This isn't an apartment."

"No, it's a house."

"The whole house. Wow."

"It seemed simpler," Ren said, dropping her backpack on a parson's bench that sat beneath a tall, ornately framed mirror.

"How do you mean?" Dani asked, placing her backpack next to Ren's.

"I'm not all that comfortable with roommates," Ren said. *Or them with me.* Dani didn't seem to find that odd, and Ren added quickly, "I bought some beer."

"I thought you didn't like it," Dani said.

"I don't. The store owner said it was similar to the one you ordered."

"Thank you. For thinking of that." Dani cupped Ren's nape and drew her gently closer so she could kiss her. They were alone in a gorgeous house, and Ren had thought to buy beer for her. Ren had been thinking about her visiting. Just the idea was enough to stoke the fire that had been simmering in her for what felt like days. When Ren threaded her arms around her shoulders, Dani sensed the remnants of her restraint pulling loose and falling free. She tugged Ren closer, edging her thigh between Ren's, and slid a hand down Ren's back to the hollow at the base of her spine. Ren made that little sound she'd heard once before, not quite a moan, but close enough to make Dani's head pound.

When she angled her head to deepen the kiss, Ren's tongue flicked out, a little hesitantly at first, then much more assuredly. Surprised and instantly aroused by Ren's advance, Dani opened for her. Ren must've taken that as a sign to keep going, and her kisses took on a more insistent edge.

On unfamiliar but tantalizing ground, Dani surrendered to Ren's explorations, her head swirling and her skin on fire. She closed her eyes, distantly aware she was swaying slightly, her limbs trembling with urgency.

After a few breathless moments, Ren leaned back and murmured, "Do you still want that beer?"

"Not just now." Dani gasped a little as she struggled to even her breath.

"Good." Ren took her hand and tugged gently. "Let's go upstairs."

Dani's instinct was to back off, to ask if Ren was sure, to give Ren time to reconsider. Why, though? Was she as guilty as all those other people in Ren's life who'd underestimated her or overlooked her? Ren had already told her, hadn't she?

You have to trust me to know what I want.

Dani nodded. She'd let Ren set the pace and determine exactly how far they journeyed tonight, even if keeping that vow was going to be near impossible. Every nerve and muscle in her body quivered, and the blood rushing between her thighs pounded with a wild demand that made her dizzy. Somehow, she was standing in front of an open doorway, through which she could make out a bed next to a wide tall window. The last rays of the sunlight cast a faint glow over everything.

"All right?" Ren asked.

"Perfect," Dani rasped.

Ren smiled, an eager, altogether unselfconsciously pleased look that shot straight to Dani's clit. Oh, she was in trouble.

Ren sat on the edge of the bed, and Dani followed, leaning back on one arm as she turned to Ren to kiss her again. Somewhere in the middle of the kiss they ended up lying half on the bed and half off, her arm around Ren's waist, Ren's hand on her chest. Kissing Ren was like time-traveling. She lost herself in the sensations, and when she became aware of her surroundings again, eons had passed. Ren kissed with her whole body, shifting and pressing against her, sweeping her tongue over her lips and teasing along the inner surface. Dani'd always liked kissing, but Ren turned it into an experience so sensuous, so all-over pleasurable, she almost forgot there could be more. Almost didn't care that there might be.

Until Ren tugged up her T-shirt and slid her hand across her stomach.

"Hell," Dani blurted.

"Okay?" Ren asked, her breath warm against Dani's throat where her lips brushed the lower edge of her jaw.

"Good. Really good. Don't stop."

Ren laughed softly and somehow knew to draw her fingernails lightly down the center of Dani's stomach until her thighs clenched and her hips lifted.

"Ren," Dani said. "Do you have any idea what you're doing to me?"

"Not entirely," Ren said, her teeth grazing the angle of Dani's jaw.

Dani quivered.

"But I definitely like it," Ren said, and the teasing note in her voice was nearly Dani's undoing. She slapped her hand over Ren's as Ren's fingertips edged beneath the waistband of her jeans.

"Wait."

Ren stilled. "No?"

"That would be the point of no return." Dani could think of only one way to apply the brakes, at least for a few minutes. She slid her hands to Ren's waist and twisted, stretching Ren onto her back and sliding on top of her. Her leg fit just as naturally between Ren's as every other thing they'd done, as if their bodies were built to meld. She braced herself on bent forearms on either side of Ren's shoulders and smiled down at her. "My turn."

Ren's eyes widened, and her mouth, her eminently, deliciously kissable mouth, parted slightly, as if surprised. Dani dove in for a kiss and, as she did, cupped Ren's breast through her shirt in the palm of her hand.

"Oh." Ren surged beneath her, back arching as if Dani had pressed her palm between her thighs. Her response was so electric Dani's clit swelled and pulsed.

"You like that," Dani said, her voice so husky she could hardly get the words out.

"Yes," Ren whispered.

Dani fumbled with the buttons on Ren's shirt until Ren pushed her hands away and unbuttoned the rest of them herself. Her bra was cut low, and Dani swept her hand inside, closing her thumb and fingers around Ren's nipple. She squeezed gently, and when Ren cried out, Dani's vision hazed. Blood pounded at the base of her belly.

"Can I—"

"Yes," Ren said. "Please."

Dani braced herself on one arm and quickly pushed aside Ren's shirt, slipping a hand behind her back to open her bra. When she managed to release the clasp, Ren shrugged out of one sleeve of her shirt and shoved her clothes aside. Dani didn't wait. Couldn't wait. She needed, craved, to feel the soft fullness in her mouth. Ren's hand came into her hair when she put her lips to Ren's breast. The grip was tight, assertive, and Dani let herself be led. She skimmed her mouth over Ren's nipple, heard a sharp cry, and took her in completely. Ren's hand twisted in her hair, and the tug of sensation was like a finger on her clit. Her hips surged, her thighs closed around Ren's leg, and a moan escaped. Urgently, Dani twisted away before the pressure, and the promise of release, took her too far too fast.

Ren made a protesting sound and gripped her hips, pulling her back.

"Baby," Dani muttered, her mouth against Ren's breast, "give me a break."

"Why?" Ren asked, hooking her leg around the back of Dani's calf.

"You make me so hot."

"I know. Me too." Ren tugged Dani's hair until she looked up. Ren's eyes were huge, her skin flushed. She was gorgeous.

"We're not stopping," Ren said. "There's no reason to."

"I don't think I can," Dani said.

"Take your clothes off," Ren said, her tone half plea, half demand.

Dani didn't ask if she was sure. She could see that she was. She could hear it in her voice. Ren wanted her as much as she wanted

Ren. She got to her knees and ripped off her shirt. Ren's hands were on her jeans, opening them, tugging at the zipper, and just watching her do it almost made her come.

"Easy," Dani gasped. "Take it easy. I'll lose it before you even get me naked."

Ren, her hands clenched on either side of Dani's open fly, grinned up at her. A grin so self-assured and triumphant, Dani's stomach tightened in that gotta-come-soon way that made her vision haze.

"I'd like that," Ren said.

Dani pushed Ren's hands away, laughing. "Would you."

"Oh yes."

"Man, you are dangerous." Dani shoved her pants down over her hips and twisted to get them off along with her sneakers. While she did, Ren shed the rest of her clothes. Turning back, naked, Dani paused to take her in. She was soft in all the places she should be, smooth and delicate in some, firm and strong in others. Her breasts were just full enough, falling gently toward her sides, the soft curves calling for her hands again. Ren watched her looking, her gaze skimming Dani's body, lingering where Dani's thighs straddled her hips. Dani sucked in a breath as Ren reached for her, stroked her fingertips along her flank, traced the curve of her hipbone, and brushed across the delta between her legs. Her thighs quivered, and she gritted her teeth.

"Don't touch me," Dani gasped. "I really will come all over you."

"I really want you to," Ren said, her fingertips oh so very close.

"Just let me have a few more minutes of you," Dani murmured and lowered herself carefully, slipping one thigh between Ren's, easing her sex against Ren's skin, feeling Ren hot and wet against her. Knowing that Ren could feel her the same.

"Oh," Ren said again, as if making a delicious discovery. She cupped Dani's ass in her hands and pulled Dani even tighter.

Dani's head whirled. She had seconds—just seconds—left.

"You're not gonna let up, are you?" Groaning, she kissed the angle of Ren's jaw.

"I just want to feel you everywhere. I love the way your body feels all over me."

"If you keep doing that with your leg between mine, I'm going to come," Dani whispered.

"I think I figured that out," Ren whispered and tightened her grip on Dani's hips.

She wasn't made strong enough to resist and let herself go, matching her thrusts to the lift of Ren's hips, long smooth sliding strokes along the length of Ren's hot, firm thigh. Once, twice, until she lost count, and her entire awareness, all she was, centered on the point between her thighs. She sucked in her breath as the hard center of her pleasure expanded, layer upon layer spreading through her, racing down her thighs and cascading upward, stopping her breath, blinding her. Ren's cries cut through the currents of euphoria, matching her own, and the recognition of Ren joining her intensified her release. When at last her muscles loosened and she relaxed with a gasp, remembering just in time to ease to the side and give Ren space to breathe, all she could do was gasp, "Holy hell."

Ren twisted enough to kiss her, then pulled away, her eyes shining, a glint of humor and undeniable triumph on her face. "That was amazing."

"I could start there," Dani said, still trying to catch her breath. "A few more superlatives might be in order."

"How quickly can you recover?" Ren asked.

Dani barked a laugh. "That's my girl. Right to the point. I might need a little while, but I can go again."

"Oh, good."

Dani found the strength to prop her head up on her bent elbow and trace a fingertip around Ren's nipple, watching it tighten, pleased at the sharp gasp from Ren. "But why wait." She skimmed the length of Ren's belly, felt the muscles tremble beneath her fingers, and dipped between Ren's thighs. She was wet and hot and ready.

She got to her knees and slid her fingers lower, watching Ren's face. "Unless you'd rather. Wait, I mean."

Ren's eyes were dazed. "I'd much rather not."

Dani kissed her. "Good."

CHAPTER TWELVE

Ren lay awake listening to Dani breathe. The sound was foreign and fascinating. She'd never slept with anyone else before. Thinking back, the last time she'd had a roommate was in her first year of college, and her roommate, Sarah Fenway, had hardly ever been there. Sarah'd had a group of her own friends whom she'd known from high school. Even then, Ren had recognized that what passed as worldliness and sophistication among Sarah and her friends was really an elaborate disguise to cover insecurity and uncertainty, but that hadn't made their dismissal of her any easier. Ren, feeling out of place whenever any of them decided to spend time in their suite, had taken very quickly to studying in the library. She'd once heard someone refer to her as the little ghost when they thought she hadn't been listening. She supposed she *was* in a way, moving in and out of circle after circle, never leaving an impression on anyone except the teachers and mentors. She'd impressed them for her aptitude, but even they had never seen beyond that to consider what her achievements might have cost. Sax was the only one in her life, until Quinn Maguire, who'd ever looked at her and not thought of her as *special* first.

Ren laughed to herself.

Sax had never found her extraordinary, and in fact had told her point-blank she'd have to be tough and resilient and enterprising to succeed in a career in surgery.

"And you think I'm not," Ren had said, supremely confident at the age of fifteen.

"I think you don't know enough to know what you can do," Sax had said. "Or what you might not want to do."

"I'm not afraid of the competition," Ren said. "I've heard what you've said before, about there always being room at the top."

Sax sighed. "That's an expression that's supposed to be encouraging. But it doesn't mention the cost of success."

"Like what?"

"Like giving up big chunks of your life at a time when you should be enjoying it most—like putting aside relationships until later, if later ever comes."

"You have a relationship with Jude," Ren pointed out stubbornly.

"Yes, and I'm damn lucky I do. If Jude wasn't the amazing person she is—" Sax ran a hand through her hair, and a distant look came into her eyes. "I'm not sure who I might have turned into in another ten years."

"I'm not worried about what might happen in twenty years," Ren said.

"I know. But the sacrifices will start a long time before that— just try to notice, okay?"

"I know what I want," Ren had told her. "And I know what it will take. You've told me. I've been listening."

Sax had studied her for long seconds, then nodded in agreement. "All right then. Let's talk about where you ought to train."

And from that point on, Sax had believed in her. She'd never again warned her of the consequences of her decisions. And Ren had not forgotten.

"What are you thinking about?" Dani said from the darkness.

"My sister," Ren said.

"The one in New York? The trauma surgeon?"

"Yes, Sax. She's the only one—no other sibs."

"What about her?" Dani leaned on an elbow, turning to face Ren. There wasn't enough moonlight for Ren to make out all her features, but she could see the outline of her profile, gilded in silver. Dani's face was strong, the bold contours softened by her perpetual tenderness. Dani was a person who cared.

"You have a great face," Ren murmured.

Dani's laugh was surprised and warm. "First I've heard of that."

"Then you've had strange girlfriends."

"You might be right," Dani said quietly. "So, what were you thinking about your sister?"

"Oh," Ren said, "just thinking about some of the things she warned me about—maybe that's too strong a word. She wanted me to appreciate how hard the training would be."

"Not bad advice. Didn't put you off, though."

Ren snorted. "Or you—or any of us."

"Plenty switched out early on."

"I know. But we're almost done. We've almost made it."

"Until the next round," Dani said wryly.

"You're right. This year is only the end of this step."

"You're not worried about it, are you?" Dani asked. "Getting a fellowship, I mean?"

"Worried?" Ren considered. She never worried—she'd always just planned. Nowhere in her plans, though, had she imagined Dani. Never had she expected to wake up beside a woman and wonder what that meant. "No, not really."

"Good. You shouldn't be. You'll have your pick of places." Dani kissed her lightly. "So you couldn't sleep?"

"I did for a little while," Ren said, trying to set the vague sense of unease aside. "Last night was exhausting in a really nice kind of way."

Dani laughed again. "You have a very interesting way of describing things. But I agree. Exhausting. Basically, you wore me out."

Ren turned on her side to fully face Dani. "Maybe you wore me out too. I usually only sleep a few hours at a time."

"Huh, I didn't get the feeling you were quite done when I finally collapsed."

"I was quite happy, thank you." Ren shivered as Dani skimmed a palm down the curve of her flank and rested her fingers at the base of her belly. A flutter of arousal lifted from her pelvis, and she sucked in a breath.

"How about now?" Dani murmured, her mouth against Ren's breast. "Still totally happy?"

Ren steadied her breathing before she replied. "I obviously have a very rapid recovery time. And I'm definitely not worn out."

"Come here then." Dani wrapped an arm around Ren's waist, turned onto her back, and settled Ren on top of her.

Ren braced herself on her hands to look down. "I've never slept with anyone before."

"I got that idea," Dani murmured, lifting her head enough to kiss Ren.

"No, I mean, in the same space even."

"Oh, not just sex?"

"I think *just sex* is an oxymoron or something similar. But no, I wasn't referring only to sleeping with someone as in having sex with them, but literally sleeping in the same proximity."

"So is it weird?"

"No, it's interesting. Listening to you breathe is nice."

"Nice," Dani said. "Is it nice like sexy, or nice like cuddly?"

"Ah—in your case, I'd go with sexy."

"Mm, good." Dani stroked Ren's back, her featherlight caresses stirring the heat in Ren's depths. "I'm a pretty restless sleeper, usually. I'm not sure you'd like sleeping with me very often."

"I don't know, you've been pretty quiet tonight."

"Like I mentioned, exhausted."

"Oh, that." Ren shifted her hips, fitting herself more closely to Dani's body. She didn't have to wonder if Dani was a good lover. She didn't need any other experience except what they'd shared to know that Dani was everything she could ask for. Dani was attentive, gentle when she needed to be, and not so gentle when Ren needed her not to be. Dani had touched her with confidence, as if she was somehow listening to the rhythms of Ren's blood and body. Dani had given her all she'd dreamed of and more. Ren'd never lacked for confidence herself, and she was quite sure that when she'd touched Dani she'd pleasured her in a way that was satisfying. But she wasn't altogether certain that there hadn't been more that she might've done, and she wanted to do it all.

"What's your favorite thing to do in bed?" Ren asked.

"Um, you know, it depends."

"On what?"

"On what it is whoever I'm with is into."

"Hmm. That's only half the equation, then."

Dani laughed. "I'm not sure you can explain good sex with mathematical theorems."

"I'm unaware of anyone having tried." She'd have to consider that some other time.

Ren scooted down a little bit, and Dani automatically parted her legs. Ren relaxed between them, her middle snuggled into the delta of Dani's thighs. Dani caught her breath and lifted her hips, pressing her center closer against Ren's body. Her heat spread out over Ren's skin, setting off a ripple of sensation though her core.

"I totally see why you thought of the other person first," Ren said. "You're a very perceptive—and I guess the word would be generous—lover. After all, you made me come about 60,000 times."

"Sixty-one," Dani murmured.

"Okay, maybe that many. But what do *you* like? When you think about being touched, what do you imagine? *That's* what I want to know."

"Um, well..." Dani hesitated. The night with Ren had been filled with a lot of firsts—starting way back before they even got into bed. But this was something new she hadn't expected. Talking about what she wanted. She didn't always top in bed, but she did a lot, mostly because she got so much pleasure from pleasuring her partner, and maybe because somewhere in the back of her mind, she knew she hadn't more to give. A conversation like this one just never came up when she'd always been careful to be sure that casual was understood. But, once again, this was Ren—a brand-new game. New rules. Exciting, and scary.

"I promise if it sounds like something I really don't want to do, I'll tell you," Ren said, "but I can't right offhand think of what that might be."

"How do you feel about oral sex?" Dani said softly.

"Oh, I think I feel fine about it. Tell me if I get it wrong."

Anticipating, exhilarated, Ren slid down a little farther and rested her cheek against Dani's thigh. She stroked her softly, tracing the soft, warm contours of her sex, slipping her fingertips over satin-smooth ridges and valleys.

Dani drew a hissing breath. "You have great hands."

"I'll take that as a compliment."

As she stroked her a little faster, Dani's thighs tightened. "*Big* compliment."

Smiling, Ren parted her gently and kissed her.

"Hell," Dani groaned.

She had intended to go slowly, to tease her, to tease herself. To savor every incredible unique sensation, but the yearning that flooded her at the first touch destroyed every plan she'd carefully formulated. Driven by desire, she let the surging hunger carry her beyond thought. She explored, tracing and tasting to satisfy her need, speeding up and slowing down with the rise and flow of Dani's breath. When Dani's hand cradled her head, pulling her tight against her, Ren hurried her strokes to meet Dani's urgent thrusts. Without thinking, she slipped her fingers into Dani's heat, and when Dani broke, clenching around her, the satisfaction was sweeter than anything she'd ever experienced. *Now* she understood how vast the pleasure that came from pleasing.

Ren closed her eyes and let out a long sigh of contentment. "That could possibly become one of my favorite things to do."

"No complaints here," Dani muttered, her voice slurred with satiation.

Ren finally lay beside her and wrapped an arm around Dani's middle. "It's almost morning. I'll have to get up soon."

"Me too." Dani rested her forehead against Ren's. "But I really don't want to."

"I don't know what to say after a night like this."

"You don't have to say anything," Dani said.

"I feel like I do. You were awesome."

Dani laughed. "Okay, I'll take that." She kissed Ren. "I happen to think you're awesome too."

"Even awesome doesn't quite cover it," Ren said, "but I'm just going to say that I really liked being with you last night. And the sex was great."

The predawn light lit Dani's face, and Ren could see her grin. "Okay, that works. Me too."

Ren kissed her, relieved that they seemed to understand each other. She could have said many things, but none would have really relayed how amazing the experience had been. She wasn't ready, literally didn't have time, to think beyond that. She had patients to see, surgeries to prepare for, a paper to finish. Those were her priorities. She sat up quickly. "I'm going to go shower and get to the hospital. Will you be going in now too?"

"I should probably head home for a change of clothes."

"Okay. I'll see you then."

"Ren," Dani said as Ren climbed out of bed.

Ren turned back. "Yes?"

"The other thing, sometimes, after a night like the one we had. One of us says, I'd like to see you again."

Ren paused. "I imagined that was so. I would have said it, if I knew I would have time."

"I get that." Dani swung her legs over the side of the bed and stood. She was beautiful, unselfconsciously naked. "So I'll say, you should call me, when you can."

"All right. I will." She didn't add, *if I can.*

Dani already knew.

Dani met Zoey walking up the front steps.

"Oh, hello," Zoey said. "Just getting in from your hot date?"

"Yup," Dani said. "Just getting home from yours?"

Zoey grinned. "Yep."

They walked in together, and Zoey said, "Dibs on the shower."

Dani edged around her and hurtled up the stairs two at a time. "Too late."

"Make it fast. I'll put the coffee on."

Dani stripped while the hot water actually got hot and stepped under the blessedly strong spray. Eyes closed, she tilted her head back and let the hot needles wake her up. Nothing was going to banish the surreal afterglow of the night before, though. The whole night had been unreal—the anxious craving throughout dinner—so unlike her usual familiar sexual urges, the surprise of Ren taking charge when they'd reached her house and how much she'd liked it, the seamless way they'd fit physically, and the unspoken compatibility of their wants. Ren was completely without pretense in bed—she embraced her pleasure with the same ease as she drew breath. Dani would have been content to spend all night making her come. Just thinking about it now made her hot all over again.

Zoey banged on the door. "Time's up."

Dani started. *Time's up.*

Man, she hoped not.

"Leave the water running!" Zoey, naked except for a towel wrapped around her, hurried in the second Dani opened the door and jumped into the shower.

After she dressed, Dani went downstairs to make toast for both of them.

Zoey arrived five minutes later, her hair in damp strands that would somehow look great when it dried, and plopped down at the kitchen table. "So?"

"No details," Dani said.

"Well, obviously there was sex. You couldn't have been doing anything else all night."

"No details."

"There wasn't?"

Dani slid her two pieces of toast, the last she'd found in the cupboard, across to Zoey along with the Skippy. "Someone needs to go shopping."

"Dani, there's only two of us here."

"I'll flip you for it."

"I'll go this time," Zoey said with exaggerated patience, "and then it's your turn. And you have to get more than Cap'n Crunch."

"There's more?" Dani pulled out the last box of cereal and shook it. From the sounds of it, not even a full bowl remained. With a sigh, she sat down at the table. "We're sad."

"I'm not sad," Zoey said with a twitch of an eyebrow. "I'm sorry if you're sad."

"That's not what I meant."

Zoey pointed with her peanut butter smeared knife. "There *was* sex."

"Zoey," Dani said with a plaintive sigh, "we had a great night together, okay? That's it. No more details."

"All right." Zoey took a bite of toast. "But do you like her?"

"Sure I like her. I wouldn't have—"

"Yes, you would have."

"Hey!"

"I mean," Zoey went on, "you don't sleep with people you don't like. But you don't *like* like all of them, do you?"

"No. Not that way."

"But you do like Ren that way."

"I like her. That's it. Come on, Zoey, we've only known each other a while, and you know, we're residents. You know how it is."

"Um—me and Dec, remember? Anyhow, it's interesting that you bring it up."

"Why?"

"Because I don't think you've ever even thought about it when you, you know, had a night with someone else. You had a night—as I recall, some of them seemed rather…satisfying…" She smirked. "But then it was over, then or maybe the next time. But it wasn't anything you gave any thought to. It sounds like you've given thought to this."

"Well, Ren's different. It wasn't a casual thing. I mean it was, but not…never mind."

Zoey leaned back, her expression softening. "Maybe you'd like it to be more?"

Dani pushed the Cap'n Crunch box away. "I don't know. Sometimes I think yes. But I don't know."

"When's the last time you had a serious girlfriend?"

"College."

"Long time ago. How come, do you think?"

"I had other things to think about, getting into med school for one. Dealing with my parents, and—never mind. Let's just say I didn't have the mental or emotional energy for anything personal."

"I get it. But sometimes you need more than what we get from what we do."

"Maybe some people do," Dani said, tossing the cereal box in the trash. "I'm not sure Ren is one of them."

CHAPTER THIRTEEN

PMC Hospital, 5:30 a.m. on a weekday in August

Ren had to hurry to finish her pre-rounds check on in-house patients for the first time since she'd taken over the service. She hadn't left home in quite enough time, and now she'd have to skip her usual walk through in the emergency room. She always did that around five a.m. and often found a patient from the night shift still waiting on a consult or one who had just been signed in who might need a surgery eval—these were the patients who often ended up sitting around a little bit longer than usual because everything slowed down as shift change approached. She didn't always get a surgery case out of it, but the patients got taken care of sooner, and the ER docs took notice. Sooner or later, they'd count on her coming around. Or better yet, call her. She couldn't make it today. Her disappointment at falling short of her goals sat heavily in her chest. All because her schedule was off.

And it wasn't just her schedule that was off.

She was off, or at least, she wasn't performing up to her standards. Ordinarily, the only thing on her mind was the task in front of her. Her focus, always narrow and intense, allowed her to be efficient and successful. She never made to-do lists—she just always woke with a plan already formed. The execution was a foregone conclusion. She recognized this about herself, took it for granted.

This morning she struggled to find that effortless focus.

Her body felt foreign. She rarely paid much attention to her physical state—good or bad. If she was aware of being ill, she'd take the proper medication. She wasn't often tired, but she did intentionally sleep enough to prevent being impaired at the hospital. Beyond that, her sense of self was rooted in her mind. Except not this morning, and she knew why. Those hours with Dani had definitely felt good, and that wasn't even the word for it. She'd meant it when she'd said the sex had been awesome and amazing and a dozen other accolades. The aftereffects lingered in her awareness, mentally and physically. And something else had changed. She was aware of *having* a body, almost as if new sensory channels had been awakened. She wasn't entirely certain she liked it. The tingling in her extremities and the swirling agitation in her stomach were disruptive and disconcerting. And even more confusing, irrationally pleasant.

One thing was certain. She definitely could do without all the nervous tension. This was no time for her to suddenly be bombarded with new sensations and odd urges. She had less than a year to bring everything she'd ever worked for to a successful conclusion. And to do that, she needed to be her old self. The one she recognized.

Making a final note on the last ICU patient, she hurried toward the cafeteria with a renewed sense of purpose. As if awakening with an answer to a question that had plagued her while she slept, she understood what she needed to do. Despite the unexpected wave of sadness, she sighed with relief. Like so many times in her life, she only needed to will herself to do what must be done. She collected her coffee and a plain bagel with butter and joined her team at their usual table.

"How was your night?" Ren asked as she sat beside the third year resident, who had been on call the night before.

"Okay. No problems." Jezeria, the third year, looked exhausted and very glad to see everyone. Typical after a night of fielding calls from the floors and ER and often needing to make decisions with no safety net if they were wrong. Just a usual night on call.

"Good." Ren already knew Jez hadn't missed anything of importance—she'd made rounds herself. And that's why she did it.

So she could be sure the residents were doing all right without them knowing she was looking over their shoulders.

Once each of the residents had finished reporting on their assigned patients, Ren brought up the list of surgeries for the day. She assigned cases to the junior residents who would assist the attendings, and finished with Zoey.

"Your choice," Ren said. "The fem-fem bypass at eight or the muscle flap to follow."

"I'll take the vascular case," Zoey said. "Every anastomosis counts double on the transplant log too."

"That's where you're headed, after you finish, right?" Ren said.

"Yep."

Ren nodded. "All right. I'll walk up with you and see how the board looks."

Ren wasn't due to scrub until the second case and was about to leave after checking the surgery board for any interesting cases she might have missed when Patty, the OR supervisor, came to the door of the control room.

"Ren, got a minute?" Patty said.

"Of course," Ren answered. "What can I do for you?"

"It looks like room ten is going to be delayed. The patient needs more labs before anesthesia will clear them. Can you see if we can move the muscle flap up there?"

"Absolutely," Ren said. "I'll call Dr. Silverstein right now and let her know that we can start early. She doesn't have office hours, so I think she'll be free."

"Great, can you let me know ASAP?"

"Definitely."

Fortunately, Dr. Silverstein was one of the attendings who actually answered her pages promptly, and within ten minutes, Ren had organized the first year resident to get Silverstein's patient ready to come to the OR early and let Patty know they could go ahead.

"Perfect," Patty said. "Thanks."

"I'll be in the lounge," Ren said.

When she walked in, the OR lounge was mostly empty. The morning cases had already started, and everyone—surgeons, nurses, techs, anesthetists, residents, and students—was in their assigned rooms. Everyone except Dani.

Ren hesitated for just a second before she entered and sat down. She had to be there, and avoiding Dani wasn't possible—even if she'd wanted to. Which she didn't, not entirely.

"Hi," Ren said.

Dani sat in her usual place in the corner of that terribly unattractive mustard-colored sofa, her feet up on the coffee table. Today she had an open journal propped on her thigh. She smiled at Ren. "Hi."

Ren had no idea what to say next. She hadn't expected to see Dani again so soon and hadn't had time to consider what that might be like. The night with Dani was new on so many levels, and she hadn't formulated a follow-up plan. She was without reference points and not certain where to find them. She hadn't expected their next meeting to be awkward, but it felt that way. As if Dani was almost a stranger, when she was anything but. And then there were those troublesome butterflies again. She'd seen Dani sitting in that exact position a dozen times before, but today everything about her stood out in sharp detail—as if someone had turned the lens on the microscope and brought a familiar but vaguely out-of-focus image into sharp relief. The tattoo on Danny's shoulder peeked out a little bit at the neck of her scrub shirt. Ren couldn't stop seeing it the way she had the night before, when Dani had pulled her shirt off. The memory of how Dani looked without any clothes on at all had the butterflies twisting themselves into gigantic knots that pulled tight across the base of her belly. Her fingers twitched at the sleek glide of skin beneath her hands.

"Waiting for a case?" Dani said.

Ren jumped. She'd drifted somewhere. Back to the night before, back to the swirling sensations, into the whirlwind of pleasure that teetered on the edge of pain until it spread like a starburst through every fiber of her being.

"Yes," she said and couldn't think of a follow-up. Dani was watching her, that intense look in her eyes and faintly amused expression that said she knew what Ren was thinking.

But she couldn't, could she? Last night wasn't new to Dani—she couldn't be as displaced, as off-balance as Ren right now.

"I didn't mean to disturb your reading." Ren hurried to a vacant chair across the room from the sofa. The springs—what remained of them—made an odd grinding sound as she sank into the seat.

Dani glanced at the journal as if she'd forgotten it was there. "Oh, nothing to worry about. I'm just killing time. The fourth year is taking a junior through a hernia repair. I wanted to be close if they got into trouble."

"I need to be doing that. Letting Zoey have more teaching responsibilities." Ren winced. "I don't know the residents well enough to be comfortable delegating yet."

"My fourth year came over from Franklin. I know what he can do. You've got plenty of time to—"

Zoey stomped in from the hall and flopped down on the other end of the sofa from Dani. "Hurry up and wait. Every damn day."

Relieved at the interruption and the reprieve from the intimacy that left her so unsure, Ren said, "Problem with the case?"

Zoey rolled her eyes. "Anesthesia had a problem with intubation. Now they want a chest X-ray and blood gases. It's going to be another half an hour at least before we can even prep."

"I'm going to be here," Ren said, "if you have something you need to do. I can page you when they're ready."

"I'd better wait. They might want me for something. What are you still doing here? Something come up?"

"Oh," Ren said, "Silverstein got moved up." She smiled. "So I'm in the hurry-up-and-wait stage too."

"At least getting that case out of the way will make the day easier," Zoey said.

If Ren had been as superstitious as most surgeons, she would have been worried by that remark, but she didn't believe in luck. Good or bad. Relieved of the necessity for conversation now that she wasn't alone with Dani, she pulled out her phone.

She'd do what she always did while she was waiting. Something familiar. Something that let her slip into her private, recognizable self. She texted Axe.

Are you free?
For a while. How have you been? You've been quiet
Oh, sorry. Work has been really busy.
How was Friday night?

Ren stared at the question. What had she said? She mentally recalled the texts.

Got plans?
?
Hey. Friday night. :-)

They'd just been joking, the way they sometimes did when they gamed. They'd never really talked about personal things before. She hesitated. If she'd been herself, she would have ignored the question or answered it with another bit of banter. But she wasn't completely herself, and Axe would know what she meant, even if she didn't.

She texted rapidly before she could change her mind. *It was disturbing.*

Hey! What happened. Are you okay?
Oh no. Not explaining this right. I'm fine just terrible timing
Oh. How come?
Super busy. Can't have distractions
Ha. Distracting. Sounds like it was good then :-)

Ren felt her face warming. Good she wasn't having this conversation in person. She typed, *Not what I expected. Wait. Not what I meant. I didn't know what to expect.*

But you're not sorry? You're okay with how things went with them?

Her. I'm good. It was wonderful. But... Ren paused. If she said more, would Axe still understand? Could she take the chance? She hurried on.

I don't know what to do about that
Huh. Give it some time?
Maybe. I'm not sure—

Ren's phone rang and she swiped out of the message app to answer. "Dunbar."

"Ren, this is Dec Black, downstairs in the ER."

"Yes, Dr. Black." Ren recalled the ER call schedule for the

month and scanned it. A service wasn't on call, but she wasn't going to mention that. "What can I help you with?"

"I know you're not on call, but I thought you'd want to know that Leo Marcoux is down here in the ER. I know you saw him last time he came in. He's running a fever, and he's got belly pain."

Ren shot to her feet. "I'll be right down. Thank you for calling me." She spun around to Zoey. "I need to get down to the ER. Can you get the third year to cover the muscle flap if I'm not back upstairs in time?"

"Sure, Silverstein won't mind. She'll probably even let Jez do some of the case."

"Thanks." Ren pushed out through the doors without a backward glance.

"Well, that was weird," Dani said. "Wonder what that was about."

Zoey shrugged. "I think Ren has the ER staff trained to call her for everything these days."

Dani left her phone open and set it on the arm of the sofa, waiting for a return message. "She's making quite an impression down there."

"Are you worried about it?" Zoey asked.

Surprised, Dani shook her head. "No, why would I be?"

"Well, she probably *is* getting extra cases out of it. And you know, there's the whole Franklin thing."

Dani gritted her teeth. "Man, I think that's a losing proposition for me. Even if I get this paper done, and I'm not sure I will, she's like…a force of nature, you know?"

Zoey laughed. "*Is* she now."

Dani took a quick look around the OR lounge. No one was there. Still, she wasn't going to announce something personal about Ren. "Come on, Zoey. It's not like that."

"I don't know," Zoey said teasingly. "You two looked like you were really into it a few minutes ago."

"What are you talking about?" Dani said.

"The two of you texting. I think the fire alarm could've gone off and neither of you'd have noticed."

"I wasn't texting with Ren."

Zoey's brows drew down. "You weren't?"

"No."

"Oh. Okay. It just…" Zoey shook her head. "Never mind."

"Believe me, I'd be happy for a text from her." Dani dropped her head back to the sofa and sighed. "She's really uncomfortable around me now. I think I totally blew it somehow."

Zoey patted her knee. "Hey, it's just morning-after awkwardness, and come on, she probably doesn't have a lot of experience. I don't know her well enough to ask…yet…"

Dani groaned.

Zoey went on, "But I bet she hasn't had a lot of girlfriends."

"Make that none," Dani said.

Zoey's eyes widened. "Are you guessing, or do you know that?"

"I know that."

"So last night was…like the first?"

Dani nodded silently.

"Well, for crying out loud, Dani," Zoey said urgently. "What do you expect? One of two things is going to happen after a night like that. She's either gonna be after you for sex every other second, or she's going to be really confused about what to do next."

"I'd be good with the sex every other second," Dani muttered.

"And maybe she'll still get there. But you're going to have to be a little patient."

"Oh, look who's talking. How long did it take you to get Dec into bed?"

"Totally different, and quite a while."

"Besides, I'm not even sure that would be a good idea. Getting involved," Dani mumbled. "I need to keep my head in the game around here, and damn it, all I can think about is Ren Dunbar."

"You might not be the only one whose head isn't in the game," Zoey said softly. "Besides, when did you ever meet a game you didn't want to play?"

CHAPTER FOURTEEN

ER, PMC Hospital, mid-morning

Ren hurried to the ER central station, found it empty, and turned abruptly down the adjacent hall where Declan Black—a brunette with bold features and an intense aura surrounding her—talked on the wall phone. Ren waited, trying not to pace, while Dr. Black finished the call. Ren hadn't worked with Dr. Black before—the new attending hadn't been there very long, although Ren was aware that Zoey Cohen and Declan Black were involved personally. For an instant, Ren wondered how Zoey balanced her life as a resident with that, before shunting the thought aside. Regardless of how Zoey managed, the answer had nothing to do with her. A few weeks ago, the question never would have occurred to her.

"Hi, Ren," Dec Black said. "Thanks for getting down here so fast."

"Thank you for calling me. How's Leo?"

"I was just on the phone with the lab. His white count is over 30,000 with a big shift. He's got a temp of almost 102. I'm sending him down for ultrasound. They said they'd send transport as soon as they had a slot open up down there."

"I'll take him down," Ren said quickly. One thing she had plenty of experience with after three years of mostly covering the ER and floors on nights and weekends was how to get patients through the system quickly for imaging and labs. "We're more likely to get him in sooner that way."

"The first year covering transplant is on her way down. She can—"

"No," Ren said quickly. "I assisted on the case. I know him and his family. I'll go."

Dec appraised her, then nodded. "All right. I'll get the first year started on the admission papers. Dr. Ochoa is aware that Leo is here. She's already scrubbed on a case, but give her a call as soon as you see what the ultrasound shows. If the scan's not sufficient, send him right over to CAT scan, but you know there'll be a wait there."

"Of course," Ren said.

"He's in seven."

The same room he'd been in the first time he'd come in with similar symptoms. This time was much different. Ren hurried toward Leo's room, possibilities running through her mind. Sepsis was the obvious conclusion in light of the elevated white count and fever, but that said nothing as to cause. In a transplant patient, one like Leo who was not only medically immunosuppressed but even more impaired due to the trauma of recent surgery, the cause of the infection could be almost anything. What worried her, though, was that Leo was only a few days post-op and had just been released. While he could have pneumonia or some blood-borne infection, the first assumption had to be a surgical complication. And she had not only assisted on the case, she had performed the laparoscopic appendectomy under Dr. Ochoa's supervision. While Dr. Ochoa was ultimately in charge, *she* had been the operating surgeon. If there was a technical complication related to the operation, she was responsible.

Ren's stomach tightened. The feeling and the realization weren't new. She might have spent three years in the lab, but she was a senior surgery resident, and she had, over the course of her protracted residency, assisted on and performed a great many cases. She had been the operating surgeon under the tutelage of staff surgeons, and the attendant sense of responsibility had been instilled in her from the first day she had arrived for her training. If she held the instruments, she was responsible. That's how surgery residents were trained. The attending surgeon assessed a resident's skill and let them do as much as they safely could. Surgery was an apprenticeship in the true sense of the word. A trainee couldn't learn to do the cases by watching a video or operating on a mannequin. The reality was a surgeon could only be trained when they stood at the side of the patient with an instrument in their hand and did the critical parts of the operation. If that wasn't part of their training, when they finally left their residencies to set up practice, they'd be dangerous.

Ren knew all that, as well as accepting that every surgeon at some point or another had an unexpected outcome. Patients were people, individuals, with different anatomy and physiology and nutritional status. Some were like Leo, whose bodies had been ravaged by chronic disease their entire young lives, altered and suppressed by drugs and multiple surgeries. Many times healing was affected by chronic illness. Sometimes tissues were too damaged or unhealthy to heal as expected. Not every complication suggested that a mistake had been made, but knowing that didn't make her feel any better right now. The science didn't ease her mind or lessen her worry. Leo was a young boy, and her patient. It made it harder when they were children, she knew that too. She *knew* all these things—in her rational mind. But as strong and quick as her mind might be, she was not a robot.

With a deep breath, she pulled aside the curtain and stepped into cubicle seven.

"Leo," she said, forcing lightness into her voice. "How are you doing?"

Leo was pale, his dull eyes appearing shrunken as a consequence of the dark shadows beneath them. He looked far sicker than he had when she'd written his discharge orders just three mornings before, when he'd been sitting up in bed and proclaiming with his amazing smile that he wanted to go home because he missed his kitten. Something had happened since he'd been home. Something she should've predicted? Worse, something she'd missed the morning she'd written his discharge instructions and sent him home?

"I pretty much feel like crap," Leo said with a weak voice, and Ren had to smile at the small show of his resilient spirit.

"Well, it's a good thing you're here, then. Any place in particular being the crappiest?"

"I don't know. My stomach maybe."

He closed his eyes, and Ren glanced at his father. Father Lopez, other than his dark shirt and clerical collar, looked much like every other middle-aged man with a slightly receding hairline and barest hint of a thickening middle. His deep blue eyes, however, swam with worry.

"Hello, Father," Ren said.

"Domingo, please, Dr. Dunbar," he said, resting a hand on Leo's thin arm. "I'm glad you're here."

"Well, let's see what we need to do for Leo. When did his condition change?"

"Maybe about twelve hours after he got home? He ate a pretty good lunch, but at dinner he said he was tired and not that hungry. We figured that was probably just normal and put him to bed."

Ren nodded. "That makes sense."

Domingo Lopez pressed his lips together, looking uncertain. "In the morning, he still didn't have much of an appetite, but we took his temperature, and it was less than a hundred. Ninety-nine point nine, I think. Your instructions said to call if he had a temperature more than a hundred, but when things hadn't changed the next morning, we called Dr. Ochoa's answering service anyhow." He shrugged. "We wanted to be careful. A resident called back. They talked to us for a few minutes, asked a few questions, and said that everything sounded normal and for us just to keep an eye on him."

Ren gritted her teeth. She should have given them her number to call. She hadn't thought of it. She should have. Yes, they'd done the appropriate thing. They'd called their attending surgeon. But on nights and weekends, the calls always went to an answering service and then were fielded by the residents on call. Those residents often had no personal experience with the patients and, at times, made decisions with limited information. She hadn't been thinking like a surgeon—the way she should already be thinking, not a year from now. A year from now was too long. Had to be now. She had so much catching up to do before then. But that was a problem for later. Right now what mattered was Leo.

"It's good you called when you did," she said. Leo's parents needed to know they had done the right thing. They were not responsible for this problem. They were devoted, intelligent parents, and nothing they might have done a few hours sooner would likely have changed whatever was happening now. "And you made the right call bringing him in now."

"Thank you," Domingo Lopez murmured.

Ren leaned over and rested a hand on Leo's shoulder. He opened his eyes wearily.

"Leo, I know you don't feel well, and I know that Dr. Black already examined you. I'm just going to take a very quick peek at your belly, okay?"

Leo nodded. His heart and lungs sounded fine. As gently as she could, she listened over his abdomen for any sound of bowel activity, but heard nothing. She'd barely pressed on his small, thin middle before he winced.

"Where does it hurt?" she asked.

"Everywhere."

"All right." Glancing at Father Lopez, she said, "I'm going to get someone to lend me a hand, and we'll get Leo onto a gurney and head down to ultrasound."

"May I come?"

"Absolutely. We're not going anywhere without you." She smiled at Leo. "Right, Leo?"

Leo only nodded.

Ren found Linda hanging IV meds on a patient in the isolation room and waited outside until Linda finished, shed her gown and gloves, and sterilized her hands. "Linda—sorry, I know you're probably swamped. Do you have someone free who can help me get Leo down to ultrasound? If we wait for transport, it's going to take too long."

"Let me check the board."

Ren followed Linda back to the control center while Linda reviewed the active patients and who was seeing them.

"It looks like I've got a PA student who can help," Linda said, "and I think he'd probably want to see the ultrasound. I'll send him down to seven—Peter Holmes."

"That's great. Perfect."

Twenty minutes later, Ren and Peter guided Leo's gurney off the elevator, and Ren checked in with the supervisor in ultrasound.

"Mariko, hi," Ren said, happy to see a familiar face, "aren't you usually working nights?"

"I had to fill in for Adam. His wife is sick, and he's got the kids. I didn't know you actually worked before midnight either."

"I'm moonlighting," Ren said.

Mariko laughed and, when Ren told her she had an emergency peds patient for an ultrasound, said, "Barry is in three. He's just finishing up a routine follow-up on a urology patient. Take your patient back there. I'll call him and let him know you're coming."

Ten minutes later Ren watched over Barry's shoulder as he glided the ultrasound probe over Leo's abdomen. The images appeared on the screen, and after Barry made his first pass over all four areas of the abdomen, he came back to the right lower quadrant, and she could see why. A large echogenic collection occupied the area adjacent to Leo's transplant in the region of the previous surgery. She glanced at Barry, who met her gaze, his wordless, flat stare confirming what she'd feared she would see.

A fluid collection. Possibly blood, but given Leo's fever and elevated white count, almost certainly an abscess. Ren's stomach roiled. Had the clips on the appendix come loose, or had one of the blood vessels been incompletely ligated? Had he bled and then become infected? Was he septic because something had gone wrong with the surgery? The surgery she had been performing? She resolutely pushed the thought from her mind. She didn't have any answers yet, and anxiety would not help her make the right decisions. She edged around Barry's side so Leo could see her face.

"All right, Leo, you're just about done with this test. While Peter and Barry get you ready to go back upstairs, I'm going to call Dr. Ochoa, and we'll see what needs to be done to fix you up."

"Will I have to stay here?" Leo asked plaintively.

"Yes, I think you will. I'm sorry."

Leo's eyes filled with tears. "Can I see my dads soon?"

"Yes—as soon as we get you settled."

The instant she left the room, Domingo Lopez hurried to intercept her. "What do you think?"

"I'll have to talk to Dr. Ochoa," Ren said, "but there's a collection of fluid in Leo's abdomen."

"What is it?"

Ren looked him in the eye. "I'm not sure."

"Well, what will you need to do?"

"That's going to be up to Dr. Ochoa to decide. I'll call her right now. As soon as we've discussed it, I'll let you know."

Domingo let out a long breath. "All right. Should I call Martin?"

"I think that's a good idea. Sometimes these things can be dealt with without surgery, but Leo was asking for both of you."

"And you don't think we can avoid surgery, do you?"

"I don't know." Ren didn't like to admit she had no answers, and in almost every other aspect of her life, certainly in the laboratory, she almost never needed to. But surgery was not an exact science, and giving patients or their families too much information that might end up being wrong, even if it made them more comfortable in the moment, was not doing them any kindness. Making herself feel better by trying to make *them* feel better wasn't fair either.

"I promise, the minute I know what the plan is, I will tell you and your husband."

He smiled wanly. "I know you will. And thank you very much for coming down. I imagine that you're very busy."

"No," Ren said quietly. "This is exactly where I should be."

And that's all she really needed to remember.

❖

Honor opened her Excel sheet with the monthly patient census and sipped her coffee. Tabbing back to the year before, she compared the numbers and shook her head. "I'm going to need to find more staff."

"You know it is sometimes considered a problem when you talk to yourself," Dec Black said from the doorway.

"If you had my job, you'd talk to yourself too."

Laughing, Dec poured a cup of coffee. "You need a refill?"

"I don't think I better," Honor said. "I can already feel my toes vibrating."

"So I thought department heads were exempt from all that mundane record keeping."

Honor snorted. "Even department heads have to answer to a higher power. In this case, several of them. Namely, the COO and the CEO and many other Cs that I don't want to think about."

Dec pulled out a chair next to her and sat down with her coffee. "Things are pretty busy out there."

"I know. Do we have a handle on it?"

"For the moment. The PA program has helped a lot, but it also adds extra work in terms of supervision."

"Every training program does. You should hear Quinn discussing the residency." Honor laughed. "Sometimes I think it's just family dynamics transferred to the workplace."

"Oh, it definitely is."

"So how are you finding it? Still satisfied with the ER?"

"I think if I was in a different kind of emergency room," Dec said thoughtfully, "I might not be happy. But this place? Every day is another challenge. It's plenty enough for me."

"I'm glad. It's not easy to make the kind of change you did."

Dec huffed. "Yeah, especially when I figured I had everything planned out so well." She shook her head. "Boy, did I learn how wrong I could be."

"I'm really glad you're back here," Honor said. "I know I've said it before, but I *think* it at least once every day."

"I'm happy to hear it every day. Feel free." Dec smiled.

Honor had heard some people say that Dec reminded them of

Quinn, but she couldn't see it. Oh, they were both handsome as sin, but Quinn's eyes—no one had eyes like hers. And she really oughtn't to be thinking about her wife's eyes in the middle of what looked like it was going to be a busy day. "And while we're discussing your new circumstances, not to be nosy or anything, but as friends are allowed to be nosy, how's Zoey?"

"Zoey's great," Dec said.

Honor never would've said that Dec Black sparkled, but something in her eyes caught fire, and she was happy for both of them. "She's still living with Emmett and Syd?"

"No, she swapped houses, and she's living with Dani Chan now."

"Any plans to change that?"

"Not right away. I think it's good for Zoey to keep her ties to the other residents. They support each other and validate each other's experiences. They're a kind of family too. We're good with the way things are."

"Well, you could probably move in with Zoey and Dani."

"No way," Dec said. "I'm way too old for that much excitement."

Honor smiled.

Dec let out a breath. "Listen, Leo Marcoux is back."

"Damn." Honor pushed her laptop away. "What's going on?"

"If I had to guess, I'd say he's got an abscess. His chest X-ray's clear, but he's got every sign of having an infectious process. Ren Dunbar took him down to ultrasound just a few minutes ago."

"Ren was on his case when he was here before, wasn't she," Honor said.

"Yes. I paged her because I thought she'd want to know, and I think the family would feel comfortable with a resident they know."

"Good call."

"You know," Dec said carefully, "Ren is an unusual resident."

"That might be your second understatement of the morning. I know she is. Is there a problem?"

"No," Dec said. "I think she's incredibly bright, which is not news to anyone, and intense and determined to do a good job. I'm not sure..."

"Let's pretend that my wife is not the residency director," Honor said, "and we're just talking about a resident who we want to see do well. What's going on?"

"I'm not worried about her work ethic or her skill," Dec said definitely. "I just get this feeling that she's really invested, personally, in the cases that she does. And that's not a bad thing, I'm not saying that. But..." She grimaced. "I remember when I was a surgery resident—it's easy to use patient outcome as the yardstick for judging your own abilities. That can lead some people into trouble."

"It's a thin line, though, isn't it," Honor said. Dec had a different resident experience than she'd had, and she trusted Dec's instincts. "We *have* to judge our actions and our decisions on patient outcome. Otherwise, we'll keep repeating the same mistakes."

"Absolutely," Dec said. "Yes. But that's it—it has to be a balance. We don't start out believing that we're fallible, like everyone else. That we'll never be perfect. When we discover we're not, we still have to maintain a level of confidence in our decisions to be able to make the right decisions." She rose and tossed her coffee cup in the trash can. "I've just got the feeling that Ren's wound pretty tight. And I might be wrong."

"And you might be right," Honor said. "Ren is still finding her feet. I don't think lack of confidence has ever been a problem with her, but I'm glad you let me know. And let me know how Leo does."

"I will. Good luck wrangling those numbers," Dec said as she headed out the door. "Better you than me."

"Thanks," Honor muttered, bringing up a number on her phone. After a moment she said, "Aleisha, hi, it's Honor. Is Quinn around? Can you let her know I'd like to speak to her for just a minute? It's not an emergency."

CHAPTER FIFTEEN

Dani ducked into OR room four and looked over the shoulder of her fourth year resident, Winn Templeton. Carlos, the third year who was doing the hernia repair under Winn's supervision, was just putting in the final sutures on the abdominal closure.

"How'd it go?" Dani said.

"Great," Carlos said instantly, his eyes above the surgical mask practically glowing.

"Winn?" Dani asked again.

"Not bad."

Translated, *everything went fine.* Plus, Winn thought the third year was solid. If he'd said *We'll be done in a few minutes* or some other nonspecific comment, she'd know Winn wasn't happy with Carlos's performance, and she'd need to wait around to talk to Winn in private. Happily, she didn't have to.

"All right, try to finish up in here before your next birthday, would you," Dani said, "and text me when he's extubated."

Leaving them to finish up, she continued on in her search for Zoey. She wanted to know what was going on with Ren. Ren hadn't come back up after her mysterious, urgent call to the ER, and every other moment Dani wondered where Ren was, what she was doing. What she was thinking. And her preoccupation with all things Ren didn't *all* have to do with surgery. In fact, most of it didn't. She really tried to go with what Zoey had said, that Ren was just figuring out what to do about the night they'd spent together. That a little time and patience—ha!—might be a good idea. Zoey made sense, sure, but the trouble was, in Dani's mind, there wasn't anything to figure out.

The time she and Ren had spent together had been great. Just about everything she might want had happened. They could talk to each other, about most anything or not much at all, and the words came easily. The feelings came out too, and for her that was a big thing. Scary, yeah, but…good. Time passed without her noticing it, too quickly. And *forget* about the sex.

That was for sure a problem, wasn't it? She couldn't really forget about the sex, considering that it was not just effortlessly amazing, but they seemed to understand each other physically as well as they did when they talked. They communicated, even when they weren't talking. And Ren was…well, Ren was spectacular.

Why would she want to forget that? Why would she even want to stop thinking about it? Other than the fact that the little flashbacks and instant flickerings of excitement destroyed her concentration and made her a little crazy and—oh, yeah, by the way—borderline horny all the time. Dani blew out a breath. This was not good. She'd never met a woman who'd had this sort of effect on her, and she'd been sleeping with women since she was fifteen. Not that there were an innumerable number, but all the same, enough for her to know what was amazing.

Ren was amazing.

Dani caught sight of Zoey ducking into the OR lounge and followed her in. "Hey, Zoey—I've been looking for you."

Zoey looked over her shoulder and slowed. "Hi, what's up?"

"I was about to ask you that. What's going on with Ren?"

Zoey frowned. "I dunno, what do you mean?"

Dani gritted her teeth. Was she speaking another language? "She went downstairs to the ER in a big hurry and hasn't been back. So what's going on?"

Zoey gave her an odd look. "Oh. You mean the case."

"Well of course I mean the case, what else would I mean?"

Zoey's brows rose. "I don't know, Dani. Are you asking about

Ren Dunbar, senior surgery resident—my chief, by the way—or Ren the extremely hot younger woman who has your ovaries melting? Or possibly your brain. Or both."

Dani ran a hand through her hair. She loved Zoey, she did. But sometimes she could really do without the poking and prodding at her sore spots. "Never mind all that. Just, what's going on in the ER?"

"The kid with the appendectomy, from the transplant service a few days ago? He's being readmitted. In fact, Ochoa wants him up as soon as the room is clear." Zoey took a few more steps toward the locker room. "As soon as I change, I'm supposed to make sure the room is ready. So I gotta go."

"Oh man, that's Leo." Dani followed Zoey into the locker room and leaned against the wall of lockers while Zoey opened hers.

"I guess that's him. Why?" Zoey pulled off her scrub pants and grimaced at the blood-soaked cuffs as she tossed them in the hamper. "Just once I'd like to get through a vascular case without standing in a puddle."

Dani's mind was on Ren and how she'd take Leo being readmitted. "I'm pretty sure Ren did the case with Ochoa. She took care of him while he was here. You know how it is with kids."

"Oh, I get it," Zoey said absently, stepping into clean pants. "That's why they called Ren with the consult."

"Damn," Dani muttered.

Zoey frowned. "What's going on, Dani? It's what happens sometimes. You know that. So what's the deal?"

"I know it happens," Dani said, "but this is gonna really be a tough one for Ren. She really likes that kid."

"We all like our patients. Give her a little credit. She can handle it."

Dani stared at Zoey. "You know something, you're right. I don't know what's wrong with me. Of course she can handle it."

"Listen," Zoey said, a gentle note to her voice edging out her usual hard-edged, tough-love sarcasm. "I know you care about her. And that's...well, I hope it's going to turn into something good, whatever it looks like. And we all need someone to understand us when we're having a hard time, so that's good too. But right now, Ren needs something else."

Dani nodded. "I know. She needs to know she can do what needs to be done. She needs to know how freaking smart she is, and how good she is."

Zoey smiled. "Very good. Just remember that."

"I got it, I got it."

"And if I were you, not that you're asking," Zoey said as she started to turn away, "I'd try to get her into bed again soon. That'll help too."

Dani laughed as Zoey disappeared from the locker room. It wasn't as if she didn't want to get Ren into bed again. She'd been thinking about it since she'd opened her eyes in the morning. She was ready, whenever Ren wanted. She just hoped there would *be* another time.

❖

Ren pushed the gurney with a very sleepy Leo down the hall toward operating room ten.

Peter, the PA student from the ER, who had stayed with the case the entire time, asked in a quiet voice, "Will it be okay if I stay and watch?"

"It should be," Ren said, "as long as Dr. Ochoa doesn't mind. You should ask her when she gets here, though."

"Right, I will."

"Have you ever been in the OR before?"

"Um, no." He looked down, obviously expecting her to say he couldn't observe.

"Okay. Once we get Leo inside, I'll show you where to stand. Do not move, and whatever you do, don't touch anything. If you feel light-headed, sit down."

He grinned. "Right, I got it!"

Ren tried not to roll her eyes. "Great. Put your mask up."

Peter hastily complied, and Ren shouldered open the door to the OR and guided Leo in. The circulating tech met them at the door, Ren motioned Peter to a spot near the anesthesiologist, and in a minute, they had transferred Leo onto the operating table. He looked very small lying in the center of the table, surrounded by the anesthesia machines, the long stainless-steel tables filled with surgical instruments, and the line of equipment carts arrayed along one wall.

Ren adjusted Leo's surgical cap and lightly brushed her fingers down his cheek. "You'll be going to sleep pretty quick, Leo. When you wake up, you'll be in recovery with your dads."

He was barely awake, but as sick as he was, he smiled that brilliant smile. "Okay, Dr. Ren."

His trust was so simple, and so pure, she might have been undone by the enormousness of the responsibility if she hadn't quickly reminded herself that his trust was a gift, and doing her job was the best way to honor it. She glanced at anesthesia and nodded.

"Okay, Leo buddy," the anesthesiologist said as he injected medication into the IV line, "time for you to have some good dreams."

Ren waited until the intubation was over and Leo was stable before she left the room to scrub. She was halfway done when Dr. Ochoa arrived. A woman a bit taller than Ren and built like a rugby player with a thickset, muscular physique, she blew into the scrub area like a hurricane, all rapid motion and swirling energy.

"Everything set to go?" she said briskly, tearing open the covering on a disposable scrub brush and kneeing on the water with the paddle built into the front of the scrub sink.

"Yes. Infectious Disease didn't want us to give him any broad-spectrum antibiotics until we were able to culture him. He's still febrile, but stable."

"How do you suggest we proceed?" Dr. Ochoa scrubbed the antiseptic-impregnated plastic brush over her hands and forearms with rapid strokes.

"From the ultrasound, it looks like there's a large collection around the lower right colon, but it may still be localized," Ren said. "We could try to access it laparoscopically and drain it percutaneously. That would make his recovery a lot easier."

"What's the downside?" Ochoa peered into the operating room through the window above the sink. "Good. Markovic is scrubbed. He's good with the scope."

"Things are likely to be sticky in there," Ren said, "after the previous procedure, and now with an acute inflammatory process, we may not be able to distinguish the tissue planes easily. We could miss a second collection."

"I don't like the idea of trying to do this without direct visualization," Ochoa said, and Ren grimaced behind her mask.

Surgical judgment was every bit as important, even more important in many instances, as the ability to perform a procedure flawlessly. The body was forgiving of small errors, which making the wrong choice of procedure never was.

"But," Dr. Ochoa went on, tossing her scrub brush into the trash, "I agree we should try the least invasive approach first. But I'm not going to spend a lot of time on it. If we can get into the collection, get it drained, and get a reasonable image in here to be sure we haven't missed something else, I'll be very happy." She glanced at Ren. "You get one shot at it."

"I'll get him prepped," Ren said, relieved that her initial plan hadn't been in error. Inside, Ren quickly prepped and draped the field, a small square of pale flesh that encompassed almost Leo's entire abdomen. When she'd finished, Markovic, the scrub tech, held out her sterile gown, and she pushed her arms through the sleeves and then her hands into the gloves he had opened.

Dr. Ochoa, already gowned and gloved, said, "Take the right side of the table, Dr. Dunbar."

The surgeon's side, at least when the surgeon was right-handed.

Ren stepped up to the table. "I think we should try to go through the previous entry incisions. He's not that far out from the last procedure, so the tracts should be easy to open. That might help us avoid opening up new tissue planes to infection."

"Good idea, but go slow. Blunt dissection only. We don't want to get into the kidney."

Ren incised the locations where they had inserted the laparoscopic instruments previously and then carefully spread down through the underlying layers of muscle, opening up the same paths they'd used before. When she'd penetrated the abdominal cavity, she asked for the laparoscope and passed it in.

"Can we turn the camera on, please," she said.

Everyone in the room angled to looked at the monitor mounted at the head of the table. The door opened and closed behind Ren, but she paid no attention to it. People were always coming and going in the operating room.

Quinn Maguire spoke from somewhere right behind her. "What did you find?"

Ochoa said, "Nothing yet. Everything looks pretty hot down here, though."

Quinn grunted. "Lot of inflammation in there. Did you get much of a look at the transplant?"

"No," Ochoa said, "and I don't plan to. We're staying away from it."

Another voice said, "Good idea."

Dr. Doolin, the chief of transplant.

"Go ahead, Ren," Dr. Ochoa said. "Carefully work your way down to the colon, and let's see if we can find the appendiceal stump."

Watching the monitor while manipulating the instruments intra-abdominally, Ren alternately separated tissue, irrigated, and suctioned the blood from the area. Bodies pressed close around the table, several close enough to her to touch her back. Her back wasn't sterile and neither were they, so as long as they were behind her, they couldn't contaminate the field. The impersonal intimacy of the operating room had never bothered her, even when someone put a hand on her shoulder to lean in for a better look. Quinn Maguire. Watching her work. In a second the pressure eased, and Quinn moved away.

"*There*," Ren said. "There's one of the clips on the appendiceal stump, only..." Her stomach clenched. The clip didn't appear to be attached to anything except a tiny strip of tissue. "It's avulsed."

Had she done that after she'd clipped it, while removing the instruments? Had she inadvertently torn the tissue she'd meant to close off, leaving an opening that allowed contaminated bodily fluids to leak into Leo's abdomen? Had her error caused an infection that had now become an abscess?

"Let's see if we can get another view," Ochoa said.

Carefully, delicately, Ren eased the laparoscopic camera ninety degrees, and her fears were confirmed. The stump of the appendix was completely open into the colon.

"Well, that's our culprit," Ochoa said in a calm voice.

"I could have pulled the clip off when I was coming out," Ren said.

"I don't think so," Ochoa said instantly. "If you had, there would've been a lot more bleeding than what we're seeing here. And we would have seen it before we closed. No, I think this is a question of his poor tissue healing."

"Probably chronically infected," Quinn said, "and then, once the clip was on and the appendix was out, the surrounding tissues just fell apart."

"Not surprising with all the immunosuppressants and steroids he's been on," Dr. Doolin said.

Quinn said, "Do you think you can get that adequately drained without opening him up?"

"Let's get it irrigated out first," Ochoa said, "and then we'll see about getting some drains in there."

They worked for another half an hour until Dr. Ochoa was satisfied that the abscess had been drained. They were even able to oversew the opening with some healthier looking surrounding tissue to hopefully prevent further contamination.

"Start him on broad-spectrum antibiotics," Ochoa said as she removed her gown and gloves, "and we'll wait on what the cultures show before we adjust. Don't feed him for at least twenty-four hours until we see how he's doing."

"Of course," Ren said, applying Steri-Strips and dressings to the incisions that they'd reopened.

"I'll talk to the family." Ochoa paused at the door. "Good job, everybody."

Once Ren got Leo settled in the pediatric intensive care unit, she went to see Leo's parents herself. "The PICU staff will let you know when you can see him. It shouldn't be too long. Don't worry, he won't wake up before you get there."

"Do you think this is going to take care of the problem?" Martin Marcoux asked.

"Dr. Ochoa is confident that we were able to drain all of the infection. The best treatment for now is the antibiotics, which have already begun."

Both men studied her, and Father Lopez finally smiled. "You're very good at reassurance. Thank you. What are the chances the infection will recur?"

Yes, definitely intelligent parents. "It's hard to say, but not zero. A lot will depend on his tissue healing and—"

"And he's compromised," Martin said grimly.

"Yes. But," she said firmly, "on the other hand, he's generally been healthy right up until this time, and we got a good look at the area, and his kidney is functioning normally." She caught a flicker of movement out of her peripheral vision. Dani stood in the doorway of the family room. She turned back to Leo's parents and finished, "All of those things are on his side."

"Thanks again," Martin said.

"Of course. I'll check in later, and either I or Dr. Ochoa will let you know if there's any change."

When she stepped out into the hall, Dani was waiting.

"Is there a problem?" Ren asked quickly, expecting some problem with a patient.

"What? No. I wanted to see you."

"Oh." Ren tried to ignore the swift surge of pleasure. Dani was being Dani—kind and thoughtful. Being friends, that's what she'd said. "Thank you. I'm glad you're here."

"So. How'd it go?" Dani said.

"Good, I think," Ren said. "There were a lot of people checking on that case. Quinn was there and Dr. Doolin."

"Not surprising," Dani said as they walked back toward the OR lounge. "Tough cases like that are interesting. Everybody wants to see what's going on with them."

"I think Quinn was there to check up on me."

"Probably not," Dani said.

"I don't know. I'm still not sure it wasn't my fault." Ren glanced at Dani. "The stump's blown."

"Could have been a lot of reasons."

"Yeah, maybe," Ren said uncertainly.

"Listen," Dani said. "I've been there, too. If Ochoa thought you'd made a technical error, she would have told you by now. Probably as soon as you finished the case." After a quick look around, she grasped Ren's hand and squeezed. "Okay?"

Ren smiled and held on for a heartbeat before letting go. "Okay."

"Good," Dani said. "Are you doing anything right now?"

"Um…" Ren glanced at the clock. "Most of our cases should be started already. I should check the board, though."

"Yeah, okay," Dani said, keeping pace with her.

Since Dani wasn't about to leave, apparently, Ren slipped into the hall outside the OR office and checked the board. All the A service cases were underway and covered.

"I should get back and check on Leo," she said.

"The nurses are probably still getting him settled," Dani said. "Come on, let's go grab something to eat."

"I'm not really hungry," Ren said.

Dani said, "You probably are, and even if you aren't, it's never a bad idea to refuel."

She ought to say no. She already knew all the reasons why. But they were in the hospital. Dani couldn't possibly kiss her in the hospital. As if Dani even wanted to kiss her again. And why was she thinking about *that* when she'd already decided there would be no more kissing. Not with Dani or anyone else. She had plenty of time for that later.

"Come on, Ren," Dani said softly. "Just friends, okay?"

"I'm really fine, Dani," Ren said, although she wasn't so sure. The case had been doubly hard, worrying about what she might have done to cause the problem. She couldn't shake the feeling she'd been judged in there, and maybe found lacking. "I think I might like to get out of here for a few minutes, though," Ren said softly. "Just to get some air."

"I know just the place." Dani took her hand again, but before Ren could squeeze back or pull away, she dropped it. "Come with me?"

"Yes," Ren said. That would be safe enough.

CHAPTER SIXTEEN

For just a heartbeat, Dani thought Ren was actually going to hold her hand. But that was crazy, wasn't it? First of all, that just wasn't Ren—she wasn't going to get personal, not here in the hall, even if they were alone. Not anywhere in the hospital, and from every indication she'd given upstairs in the OR lounge earlier, not anywhere. If Dani'd had half a working brain cell, she wouldn't have touched her, not even a casual glancing brush of a hand on Ren's arm, but she couldn't seem to help herself. Whenever Ren was near, every fiber in her body seemed drawn to her, like a stem bending toward the sun. That wasn't her either.

"Sorry," Dani muttered. If she'd had pockets, she would've shoved her hands into them, but all she had on was the stupid yellow cover gown over her scrubs.

Ren looked at her oddly. "For what?"

"I shouldn't have, you know..." She held up her hand helplessly. "Reached out."

Ren frowned at her for an instant, then her eyes widened. "Oh. That's okay. I mean, I didn't mind. I mean..." She gave a helpless shrug, looking a little frustrated and a little unsure.

Just great. Way to make Ren even more uncomfortable. Dani contemplated headbanging, but that probably wasn't going to make Ren feel any better.

"I didn't mean to make you think something like that would bother me," Ren said.

"You didn't. It's me. I'm not right."

Ren cocked her head. "You aren't? Are you…upset about last night?"

"What? No! Of course not!" Dani checked the hall. Still alone. She moved closer, ruthlessly stamped out the urge to touch her. "I'm so totally not upset about last night. It was—you were—just great, okay? Don't even think anything else."

"I don't really want to think about it at all," Ren said. "But I am, and I really don't have any space in my head to do that."

"Look, I know. I do. We ought to talk, and I get now's not a good time."

Ren relieved. "I know. Thank you. I should go. I have—"

"Nope, we're going to get some air." Dani smiled. "I promise, nothing heavy. And you'll be five minutes from anyplace in the hospital. Just a few minutes, Ren."

Ren gave her a slightly wary look, but she smiled, and that smile—well, Dani would probably do anything for that. "All right. Just five minutes."

"Stairs or elevator?" Dani said, leading the way down the hall.

"Um, stairs?" Ren said, making it sound like a question.

"Stairs it is." Dani realized she probably wasn't making a lot of sense or even speaking in complete sentences, but that was the best she could do. She just wanted to keep Ren from changing her mind and disappearing.

They climbed up three flights before Ren said, "Dani?"

"Yeah?"

"Where are we going?"

"Two more flights."

Ren followed silently for another thirty seconds before blurting, "But that's the—"

"Yep." Dani pushed open the door at the top of the stairwell and held it open so Ren could walk out past her. "The roof."

Across the flat expanse of gray concrete, several wide, white swaths of paint denoted several circles within a square. Red flags on slender metal poles at the corners designated the landing area for the medevac helicopters. None of the helos from Starvac and Airmed were housed at PMC. Their home bases and flight crews flew out of two of the other trauma centers across the river in Center City, but all the level-one trauma centers in the city received patients as needed from both air transport systems. Presently the rooftop was empty of everything except the breeze rippling the LZ flags and the midday sun.

"Over here." Dani held out her hand automatically, and before she could take it back, Ren grasped it. When she didn't let go, Dani lightly tugged her across the roof to the chest-high wall facing the four-thousand-plus acres of Fairmont Park, the Schuylkill River bordered by the river drives, and beyond that, Center City, Philadelphia. Cars silently whizzed by on the expressway, just visible beyond the tops of the trees along Lincoln Drive. Up on the roof of the hospital, in the heart of the Mt. Airy residential section, they were far enough from the city that none of the sounds or the scents of an urban metropolis reached them. Instead, the breeze coming across the river through the trees almost tasted like mountain air, fresh and clean in the bright sunlight.

"Oh," Ren said, letting out a surprised breath. "This is beautiful."

"Yeah, I've always thought so. I discovered it a couple days after I started here. Well, I knew about it because I came up for a trauma, but I was looking for someplace to get away for a few seconds, you know? And I thought of here."

"I've been up here when a trauma has come in," Ren said, leaning her forearms on the top of the wall, "but I never looked out. Not really." She turned her head to study Dani. "I think I have a very narrow field of vision."

The way she said it sounded as if she'd just discovered something about herself she didn't like.

"Maybe," Dani said, "that's just because you can focus so well on what you're doing."

Ren pressed her lips together in an almost-smile. "There you go, finding the good side of things. Even if they aren't really there."

"They're there, where you're concerned." Dani chuckled and

shook her head. "Believe me, I don't always. That's what got me up here in the first place—those first few weeks after coming over from Franklin, I wasn't finding much to be happy about."

"Was it tough, starting in a new place like that, when you were almost finished with your training?" Before Dani could answer, Ren grimaced, as if catching an unwanted thought in midsentence. "Well, that was a dumb question. Of course it was. I imagine it was a nightmare."

"Not quite that bad—Quinn made the transition as smooth as anyone could. Still, none of us expected it, so we were pretty much in shock. And yeah, it was scary, but..." She shrugged. "Not much scarier than anything else we've had to do—all of us. Right? First night on call, first emergency room consult, first of a million first procedures. You do what you have to do." She grinned. "Besides, you can do anything for a month."

Ren smiled at the universal mantra of medical and surgical residents worldwide. Rotations usually lasted a month, or two or three months, but somehow it all got distilled down to a month for the purposes of survival. No matter how bad it got, how grueling the assignment, they could all do anything one month at a time.

"I'm sorry that Franklin's program got defunded—that was terrible for all of you," Ren said, catching Dani's gaze. "But I'm glad you're here."

"Me too."

"I would—" Ren caught her breath. "I would be very sorry if we'd never met."

"Ren," Dani said softly, wondering if it was possible for a feeling to grow so large, so intense, she really would drown in it.

When Ren leaned closer, Dani held her breath and stood very, very still. If this moment, fragile as crystal, was to shatter, it would not be her doing. Ren's lips brushed over hers, incredibly soft and somehow even warmer than the sunlight on her face. She kept her eyes open, watching Ren's pupils widen as her lids fluttered, as delicate as a hummingbird's wings above a petal. She ached to reach out, to glide her fingertips down Ren's cheek to rest on the pulse leaping beneath the creamy expanse of her throat. She held back, lest Ren pull away and break the spell.

Ren murmured Dani's name and wrapped her arms around Dani's neck, pressing against her. Dani backed against the wall and gripped Ren's hips, her body aflame wherever they touched. Ren's mouth slanted against hers, and the tip of Ren's tongue darted teasingly over hers. Dani drank in the sensation, her heart beating fast and hard in her chest, her breath not moving at all. Ren eased away with a tiny exclamation.

"I've been thinking about not kissing you all day," Ren said, her arms still around Dani's neck.

"Well, I guess that didn't work very well," Dani rasped, not even surprised her voice was shaking and grateful for the wall at her back. Her legs were jelly.

"Apparently not." Ren smiled a little sheepishly. "Dani?"

"Yeah?"

"You're vibrating."

"Believe me, I know."

Ren laughed. "No, I mean really."

Dani jerked as the buzzing against her chest finally penetrated her muddled brain. "Oh. Hell."

She shoved a hand beneath the half-untied cover gown and pulled her phone out of her shirt pocket. A quick glance and she dropped it back in. "It's okay."

Ren's face morphed from soft and playful to sharply intense in a heartbeat. "ER?"

"What? No." Dani rolled her eyes. "My mother. She never gets that I can't just talk to her whenever she has something new and critically important to advise me about."

"I should get back downstairs anyhow," Ren said just a tad wistfully.

Or maybe Dani just hoped that was what she was hearing. Before Ren was completely out of reach again, Dani said hurriedly, "I'd very much like to do that again. But, you know, maybe not here in the hospital."

Ren laughed, a full-throated laugh, and her eyes sparkled with something Dani had never seen there before. Mischief. "Do you think, Dani? Seeing as how there's nowhere private, and apparently, kissing you does things to my brain? Like shut it off?"

Trying hard not to smirk at the outraged frustration in Ren's tone, Dani said mildly, "Does it? I'm not going to apologize."

"No, that's on me."

"So I guess you didn't like it," Dani said, pushing her luck but wanting to hear it anyway. Wanting, needing to know she wasn't in this all alone.

"You know I did."

And that's all it took to turn everything inside her into a lava flow. "Me too. And it's driving me crazy." Dani took a step closer. "I want to touch you so—"

Ren held up a hand between them. "Stop. If you say it, I'll be thinking about it, and I can't think about it." Ren took a step back, turning to look out across the city, but her words rang clearly. "I can't *not* do what I have to do. And thinking about you, about being with you, makes it so hard."

Dani sucked in a breath. "It's not supposed to do that."

"Maybe not. Maybe not for other people, but it does for me." Ren laughed a little harshly. "But then, I've never been like other people."

"That's not a bad thing—don't think it is," Dani said quickly. "You are you. And however you are, whoever you are, you're terrific."

Ren shook her head. "Maybe that's not quite true. It's not what I know that's important, Dani, it's what I do. It's what I *can* do, and I'm not sure I'll be able to."

To Dani's horror, Ren's voice broke, and the sound almost broke her. She grasped Ren's shoulders. "Ren. It's okay. You're doing a great job. You're way too hard on yourself."

"That's not true," Ren said. "We have to be hard on ourselves. You know that."

"Sure, we have to do the very best we can, but trust me, your best is way good enough."

"Good enough isn't always enough," Ren said.

Dani let out a breath. "I should've expected you to be stubborn."

"Probably." Ren smiled wryly. "All I'm trying to say is that what I need to do in the lab, what I need to do this last year on rotations, is all I have room for. And I'm sorry."

Dani took in a breath. "Don't be sorry. Just…don't be sorry about anything between us." She grimaced when her phone vibrated again. She let it go, her whole being focused on Ren.

"I'm not," Ren said softly.

For now, that would have to do.

"Come on," Dani said, knowing what Ren wanted just then, and it wasn't her. "Let's go so you can check on Leo."

CHAPTER SEVENTEEN

Ren didn't see Dani for the rest of the night or the following day. The surgery schedule was packed, and she was either in the OR, checking patients in between cases, or stopping by the pediatric intensive care unit to review Leo's progress. He was awake intermittently, but his fever was still high despite aggressive antibiotic therapy. Just before she signed out after sending all the residents on her service home except Zoey, who was on night call, she tracked down the infectious disease fellow at home to ask about the antibiotic regimen.

"I'm just sitting down to dinner," he said. "Can it wait till morning?"

"I don't think so," Ren said as pleasantly as she could. It was only six thirty in the evening. She didn't understand why he sounded so cranky. "He's still febrile, and his white count isn't coming down much."

"We still don't have all of the anaerobic cultures results," he said, "but everything else is pretty much covered with what we've got him on."

"Yes, I see that was the treatment plan." Ren ignored his mildly condescending tone as she swiped through the screens on her tablet, correlating all of Leo's recent lab results with his current medications. She didn't mention that *pretty much* was not her idea of good enough. "At least one of these was started pre-op, though, and considering what he's growing out so far, a fourth-generation might have a little more power. What do you think?"

She half expected him to say that he thought he was the infectious disease expert, but after a moment of silence, he said, "Well, I can't see any reason not to make the change. I'll call it in." "That's all right, I'm right here. I'll write the order." She confirmed the appropriate dose with him and put the order through. "Thanks again."

"Uh. Sure."

"Good night." She hung up to let him get back to his interrupted dinner. Now that she finally felt satisfied that all her clinical responsibilities were over for the day, she headed to the research building to finish the much-delayed revisions the editors had requested on several tables for a paper about to be published. She worked steadily for a couple of hours and, after uploading the new PDFs to the journal portal, retrieved her phone from the pocket of her lab coat hanging on the back of her chair to check her texts. She didn't expect to find anything, as she would have heard the message ping, but she still registered a pang of regret to see that there was nothing from Dani. Although, to be fair, she had pretty much told Dani that she wasn't open to a relationship right now. But dinner wasn't a relationship, was it? Even sex wasn't necessarily a relationship, if both people agreed to the limits. Right?

She sighed, not being in the habit of gaslighting herself or anyone else. Dani was only doing what she'd asked, and she appreciated that Dani wasn't pushing. She simply needed to come to terms with the disappointment from having gotten what she wanted...or at least what she thought she needed. She just didn't feel very good about it.

"Enough," she muttered as she punched in a text.

Hi. If you're up, do you feel like a game?

After two minutes with no reply, she didn't expect Axe to answer. Axe almost always replied right away if she was free. Ren blew out a breath. She had no one else to contact to save her from her own introspection, at least, no one she wanted to talk to about any of this. Certainly not Zoey, who was the first person who came to mind. Axe was the closest person she had to a friend right now.

When the phone vibrated, she snatched it up.

Axe, after all. *Sorry I've been out of touch. Traveling.*

I understand. Not a good time?

Can't play. Only have a few minutes. How are you?

That was nice, that Axe was asking, even when she was clearly busy. Axe sounded off, though—usually even Axe's texts radiated energy and high spirits. Tonight she seemed…sad. Ren might not have asked if she hadn't sensed that wistful tone. And she might not have admitted she wasn't having all that great a time either. *Tough few days here. You too?*

Yeah. Personal stuff. Sorry.

Hey, that's all right. Ren hesitated to take the next step, but she cared that Axe was unhappy. Wasn't that what people did when they cared? Reached out? Axe could always just leave. *I don't mind listening.*

It's complicated.

Ren grimaced. *LOL. If it's personal, when isn't it?*

I'm laughing here. True. I haven't laughed in a couple of days. Thanks.

You're welcome. And I really don't mind listening.

Where are you?

Ren paused. *What do you mean?*

I know, weird question. I don't mean in your head. I mean geographically.

That was weird. Although, not really. They'd passed the point of anonymous online gaming handles sometime in the last few weeks, when she hadn't really noticed. *East Coast. You?*

Pennsylvania.

Ren stared. *Really? You're not making that up?*

Nope. :-)

Axe could have only one reason for asking. If they met, what would it mean? Ren had to think about that. Things would change if they did that. Would that be bad? What if they didn't like each other? Would she lose a friend? She huffed. What kind of friends could they be if they didn't actually like each other in real life? Until now, everything was safe and secure. At a distance.

Just the way she liked things. Just like she was trying to do with Dani…

And like with Dani, she only had pieces of a relationship with Axe. But were pieces all she really wanted from another person? She closed her eyes. Axe could be her friend. *I'm not that far away.*

It would be nice to talk in person

Ren gripped her phone. Did she really want another new distraction in her life? Could she afford it? One thing was for sure—she didn't want any confusion. *Hey—I guess I should say I'm involved, sort of?*

Oh, whoa. Yeah. Sorry—I didn't mean to come off that way

Ren hurried to answer. *No. You didn't. I just wanted you to know. And I'm not really*

LOL. You're not sure?

No, Ren texted. *I'm sure. I'm not. But, friends?*

Yes, totally. I gotta go…connect later?

For sure. Have a safe trip. Ren stared at the silent screen a moment longer, wondering what Dani was doing before she slipped her phone away.

❖

Ren finished late in the lab and found an open on-call room where she could spend the rest of the night. She'd just stretched out, still in her scrubs, in the small room with its single bed and the sliver of light sliding in under the door, when her phone vibrated. At this hour it could only be a problem. She rolled over, checked the message. Zoey's name at the top of the screen.

If you're in the hospital call me 911

She hit the return call rather than texting, and Zoey answered on the first ring.

"Ren?" Zoey said, the adrenaline sharpening her voice.

"What's going on?" Ren stepped into her clogs and grabbed her lab coat.

"I'm in the SICU. One of the post-op hearts is crashing. I need to open the chest, and I need a hand."

"Where's the CT fellow?" Ren asked, even as she yanked open the door and raced for the stairwell.

"In the OR with Harkins, doing an emergency CABG. They're having trouble and can't get free."

"What's the situation with the patient?" Ren shouldered her way into the stairwell and consciously blocked out everything except Zoey's voice, including the thundering of her own heart.

"Three-vessel CABG with aortic valve replacement this afternoon. The chest tube drainage was on the high side all evening, but that seemed to have been slowing down. Now it's stopped, and his pressure is bottoming out despite the pressors."

"Harkins want you to open?"

"He said yes, if we can't get his pressure up in the next couple of minutes." Zoey's voice dropped. "I've never done it before in an emergency."

Neither have I.

"I'm a minute away. Have the nurses irrigate the chest tubes again to make sure they're not clotted, increase the pressors, and make sure there's plenty of blood available."

"Got it."

Ren dropped her phone into her pocket, exited the stairwell, and sprinted for the SICU. She had no time to wonder if she was the right person to call. She was the most senior person available, and Zoey needed her help.

❖

Ren didn't have any trouble finding the right patient in the SICU. A cacophony of voices came from behind the closed curtains around a bed in the center of the long row of curtained-off beds. Bright lights illuminated that part of the room despite it being after midnight. Usually, the only sound at that time of night was the rhythmic whoosh of the ventilators and the occasional murmured voices of nurses and PAs discussing patients. Now, as she hurriedly pulled on a cover gown, snippets of terse conversation reached her.

Open it up all the way. Zoey's voice, taut with tension, but still controlled.

We've got no pressure.

Nothing from the chest tubes.

A monitor emitted a loud, steady peal as an alarm went off.

Ren jerked the curtain open enough to get through and hastily yanked it closed behind her. Zoey stood on the patient's right side, her attention fixed on the monitor that registered no blood pressure. The EKG tracing continued to flicker rhythmically, but even as Ren watched, more and more erratic beats appeared.

"Open a thoracotomy tray," Zoey said, glancing at Ren, relief showing above her mask.

Ren tied hers in place and, muttering, "Excuse me, excuse me," pushed her way through the gaggle of ICU staff to face Zoey across the patient's chest. The dressings were off, and Zoey slathered Betadine haphazardly over the surgical incision in the center of the sternum. Ren didn't have to ask for an update. The patient would code any second, and everyone knew it. "Ready?"

"Yes," Zoey said.

"Someone notify Harkins we're opening," Ren said, holding out her hand. "Suture scissors."

A pair of scissors slapped into her palm, and she gave a silent *thank you* that someone knew how to assist. She clipped the sutures at the top and bottom of the incision, grabbed one of the loose ends with a hemostat, and yanked the sutures out.

"Zoey, go ahead."

"Wire cutters," Zoey said.

Ren spread the skin and subcutaneous tissues to expose the breastbone, and Zoey cut the loops of wire that held the two halves of the sternum together.

"Rib spreader."

Ren shoved the wide blades into the gap in the bone and rapidly cranked it open. Blood welled into the incision as soon as she did, bright red and pulsating. Obscuring everything. Somewhere in the depths of the incision, the heart struggled to beat.

"Hang the blood," Zoey ordered. "All lines. Pump it in by hand."

"Suction," Ren said. "We need more suction."

"Hell," Zoey said, looking at Ren. "The valve is loose."

Ren saw the tear in the suture line. "Someone call the OR. Tell Harkins we need him here now."

"He says ten minutes," a voice called an eternity later.

Only they didn't even have two minutes. The patient was going to bleed out through the tear at the base of the aorta if they didn't do something.

"We need a vascular clamp." Ren stared into the depths of the wound as the sound of someone digging through the instrument tray clattered beside her.

"I've got it, I've got it," someone announced breathlessly.

"Zoey, I don't have an angle," Ren said. "Can you get it?"

"I...yes, I think so," Zoey gasped.

"Here, here," a man said and pushed a clamp in Zoey's direction. The fine teeth on the jaws were specially designed not to tear the fragile tissue of the blood vessels when applied.

Ren directed the suction at the base of the aorta where the valve had been sutured in place. It was rocking with every heartbeat, and blood gushed through a half-inch tear. "Clamp it. Clamp it."

"What if I..."

"Clamp it, Zoey," Ren ordered sharply, and Zoey, her hand steady, slid the clamp on either side of the tear and closed it down.

The bleeding slowed. A collective breath went out of everyone standing around.

"Keep the blood coming," Zoey said. "What's the blood pressure?"

"Seventy over nothing," a nurse said.

"Go up slowly on the pressors," Ren said. "We don't want to blow this clamp off."

Thirty seconds later, Zoey said, "It's eighty over fifty, Ren."

Her voice held a note of wonder.

"That should be enough to keep his brain and his kidneys alive." The vise of tension squeezing Ren's chest eased.

Someone shouted, "Harkins is on his way."

"I didn't think to do that," Zoey said, staring at Ren across the table as Ren irrigated the wound and draped the incision with a sterile towel.

"You would have."

"I was going to try to suture it." Zoey grimaced.

"We still might have to." Ren glanced at the ICU nurse next to her. "Load up a four-oh vascular suture, and keep the suctions ready."

"You got it." The nurse shook her head. "What a ride, and no thank you, not again."

Zoey and Ren stood motionless at the patient's side, Ren watching the chest cavity, waiting for the dressings to suddenly bloom and overflow with blood, Zoey staring at the monitors.

"So, what do we have," a brisk voice said after what felt like a week.

Ren glanced at Zoey and signaled for her to go ahead. Her patient, her case.

Zoey half turned to the cardiothoracic surgeon, an impressively large man with a florid complexion, cobalt-blue eyes, and a surprisingly relaxed expression.

"We lost his pressure after the chest tubes clotted. We couldn't get it up again. We…" Zoey glanced at Ren. "We opened his chest."

"How much blood had he lost by then?"

"Almost everything. We've given him ten units so far."

"Huh." As he spoke, he pulled on gloves, asked for suction, and carefully removed the dressings. The clamp was still in place.

"That's one way of handling it," he said. "Who put the clamp on?"

Before Zoey could speak, Ren said, "I made that call."

He glanced at Zoey. "You put it on?"

"Yes."

"Nice job. Tricky, though. If you'd torn the valve out, we would've had a hell of a mess."

Zoey kept her gaze steady. "I didn't think suturing—"

"Trickier still." He straightened. "Call the OR, tell them we're on our way. We need the pump tech to prime the pump to go on bypass. Send all the blood to the OR."

"I'll call," the nurse said.

Harkins looked from Zoey to Ren. "So which one of you wants to come?"

"Both of us," Ren said.

He made a sound that might've been a chuckle.

"There's a surprise. All right, bring him over. I'm going to get a cup of coffee." And with that he was gone.

Zoey looked at Ren. "Oh my God. I can't believe we did that."

"Well, we did." Ren almost wanted to laugh. The relief made her dizzy. And the high—she couldn't think of any other word to describe it—was incredible.

"I've never even seen it done before."

Ren grinned. "Neither have I."

❖

They finished in the OR at four a.m.

"You might as well go home," Ren told Zoey after they got the patient settled in the intensive care unit. "You'll be off today anyway, and there's no point staying for morning rounds."

"I'm staying," Zoey said. "I've got patients on the floor to see."

"I can do that."

Zoey fixed her with a stare as she pulled off her cap. Her hair fell down around her shoulders in a tangle that somehow looked artful as opposed to just messy. Ren ran a hand through her much shorter, wavy hair and had no doubt it was standing out in unappealing clumps. From Zoey's expression, there was no point arguing about her leaving.

"All right, but after that you're out of here."

"I would've been screwed if you weren't in the house last night," Zoey said.

"Thanks," Ren said, "but you would've been fine. You would've figured it out."

"Yeah, maybe, but what if I hadn't figured it out in time, or I'd made the wrong call."

"Then you would've figured out it was the wrong call, and then you would've made the right one."

"I'm trying to thank you here, Ren," Zoey said with an edge.

"I know. That's nice." She paused. "I'd only read about it, and in the largest studies, they clamped if possible. There are other cases where suturing was recommended, but the outcome was at least eighteen percent poorer. I made an educated guess."

Zoey gaped at her. "Tell me you thought that out during the case."

"Well, not all of it," Ren said. "I didn't have time to actually go through all the conclusions."

"You're not kidding, are you?"

"Um, no?"

"It's some photographic memory thing, right?" Zoey said.

Ren nodded, her stomach sinking. They were getting along really well. And maybe they might've been friends.

Zoey laughed. "Oh, well, lucky me that I called *you*. Jeez, Ren, don't keep that thing a secret."

"What?" Ren couldn't quite decipher what Zoey meant. She never told anyone things like that—not when it always produced the same result. Suspicious uncertainty. As if she was somehow dangerous.

"Are you kidding me?" Zoey rolled her eyes. "If you want to save everybody on the service a lot of time, just tell us the facts when we need them. Then we can skip looking up all the studies."

"Who's looking up studies?" Ren scoffed. "We're surgeons. You know, see one, do one, teach one."

"Yeah, but sometimes, you know, we actually have to *know* things."

Ren started to laugh, and Zoey did too.

"I can't wait to tell Dani all about this when she gets back," Zoey said.

Ren grew still. "She's gone?"

Zoey grimaced. "Yeah. I guess she probably didn't even have time to tell anyone. She had to go home. Some kind of a family emergency."

"Oh, is it something serious?" Ren bit at her lip. Was Dani somewhere by herself, hurting? The idea made her ache.

"I don't know any details. I guess it must be, if she left like that."

"I hope she's all right," Ren murmured almost to herself.

"Well," Zoey said with suspicious nonchalance, "you can always text her."

"I…" She shouldn't, should she? But they *were* friends. They'd agreed to that—or at least, she'd given Dani no other choice. "I'm not sure—"

"I am. I'm positive."

Zoey's intensity convinced her not to argue. Especially when she wanted to believe.

"I could do that," Ren said.

"She's in California." At Ren's look Zoey added, "You know, the time difference."

In the morning, *Dani's* morning, Ren thought. *In the morning, I'll text her.*

CHAPTER EIGHTEEN

West Mt. Airy, very early the next morning

Honor sensed Quinn stirring and slowly begin easing to the far side of the bed. In all the years they'd been together, Quinn still apparently hoped she could get up and leave in the morning without waking her. She smiled at her persistence. Whenever she lay beside Quinn, some part of her was always conscious of Quinn's breathing, of her heart beating, of the very miraculous reality of her presence. They lived every day, both of them, with the undeniable truth that life was often too brief, always unpredictable, and eternally precious. She knew that even better than most.

"You've got ten minutes before the alarm," she murmured.

Quinn settled back beside her, pulled her close, and kissed her. "Morning."

Honor curled into the curve of Quinn's body and rested her cheek on Quinn's shoulder. "Busy day ahead?"

"The usual." Quinn stroked her hair. "And the schedule's tight now that we're two senior residents down with Dani Chan out."

"Have you heard when she'll be back?"

"Not yet. We'll manage. The rest of the seniors will just need to take more call for a few days."

"What about Ren—is she doing okay?"

Quinn half turned to face her. "She's doing fine now. I think when the boy with the transplant—Leo Marcoux—was re-admitted, it shook her confidence, even though there's no indication she was at fault. Some residents take everything like it's their personal responsibility."

Honor huffed and thumped her lightly on her very sexy middle. "Just the residents?"

Laughing, Quinn caught her hand and held it. "Yeah, well. As to Ren, I watched her during the case, and she worked through it. That call from Tom Harkins a couple of hours ago was to tell me he wanted her as a fellow next year."

Honor laughed. "How did that come about?"

When Quinn filled her in on the late-night emergency surgery, Honor said, "Next thing you know, he'll want Zoey too. You have to admire his optimism, though."

"Well, Zoey has another year, and as of now, she's still saying transplant. Ren will have her pick of places when she gets ready to decide where to go. But I'm with Tom. We should try to keep her here." Quinn kissed her and moved her hand away from where it had somehow strayed lower as they'd talked. "And I'd better get up—you're starting to give me ideas."

Honor laughed and sat up. "Something to look forward to tonight, then."

When Quinn headed to the shower, Honor pulled on an old T-shirt and a loose pair of cotton pajama bottoms and made her way to the kitchen to start coffee. On her way down the hall, she peeked into Arly's room. The bed had been slept in, but her daughter was not in it. Generally, Arly was not an early riser.

She spied her on the back porch, sitting on the top step in a tank top and shorts, barefoot, holding a mug of what she guessed was tea in both hands. Arly still eschewed coffee. Taking her own cup outside, she said, "Looking for solitude or do you care for some company?"

Arly glanced over her shoulder, tossing her hair out of her eyes with a practiced flick of her head. Somewhere in the last year she had gone from typical angular, loose-limbed teen to very close to the person she would someday become. Someday way too soon. Honor felt a stab of loss mixed with wonder.

"What?" Arly said.

Honor shook her head, knowing she would only embarrass her. "I was just wondering when you'd get the morning coffee bug."

Arly wrinkled her nose. "When it stops tasting like boiled dirt?"

Honor laughed. "All things in time."

Arly returned to gazing out into the backyard. "Yeah. No kidding."

"Hmm. Should I ask?"

Arly lifted a shoulder and said nothing. Honor settled beside her on the top step and sipped her decidedly un-dirt-like coffee.

"How old were you when you first had sex?" Arly said.

Honor inwardly grimaced. Of all the questions she might have been asked about sex, that was the one she really wished she didn't have to answer honestly. But she really did.

"Almost sixteen."

"Terry was your first, right?"

"Yes, she was. My only," Honor said softly.

"How did you know?"

"Oh," Honor said, remembering all the reasons because she'd never forgotten and had never wanted to, "if I had to pick the one, out of all the ways that I knew, it would be that I could always talk to her about anything, and I knew, no matter what I said, she would love me."

Arly half turned. "Couldn't that just have meant she was a best friend?"

Honor smiled. "There *were* other reasons."

She laughed when Arly made a face and said, "No kidding, Mom."

"But I know what you mean. I'm not exactly sure how to describe the difference, but it's about feeling—*knowing*—that someone can see you all the way through, and they love you for that. All the pieces of you, even the ones you never show anyone else."

"I understand." Arly went back to perusing whatever she'd been looking at, which Honor suspected wasn't anything at all, so she waited.

"I'm not having sex with anyone."

"Okay. Is that a problem for you?"

"Sort of."

Honor put her cup down beside her. "Is someone pressuring you?"

Arly shook her head. More silence.

Without looking at her, Arly said, "No, at least not pressure, exactly. But I'm practically the only one who isn't or doesn't want to. And it's like…there's a timetable or something."

"Arly," Honor said gently. "You've got lots of time to be comfortable about having sex. You can wait as long as you want. It's your choice, and you should feel ready, when you really want to."

"What if I'm not in love, like you were with Terry? Or Quinn."

"Everyone is different, honey. For me, well, after Terry died, I didn't want to be with anyone that way, and I didn't think that I ever would. But luckily, I was wrong. At first, though, I was afraid, when I started having feelings for Quinn. Really afraid."

Arly shifted to her look at her again. "Because you were afraid something would happen to her too?"

Honor took a slow breath. "Partly. Mostly I was afraid to feel that much of anything again, and somehow lose it. Even the wonderful parts." She brushed her fingers through Arly's hair and tucked a strand behind her ear. "But I finally saw I was more afraid of not having Quinn, of not having her in my life in every way that I possibly could. With us as a family, with her as my wife."

"I'm not sure I want to wait *that* long," Arly said pointedly, but she was smiling.

Honor laughed again. "Fair enough. But if I had my druthers, you'd wait a few more years. There's no rush, and being physical with someone is complicated. It complicates relationships no matter how old you are. There's a lot of things going on in your life right now, and maybe taking one thing at a time is the best way to do it."

"I guess I'm just gonna have to be the weird one."

Honor slid an arm around Arly's shoulders and squeezed. "No one is going to think that. In fact, I'm willing to bet, even if they don't say so, they're going to think you're pretty amazing for not being afraid to do what feels right for you."

"I guess I'll find out," Arly said. "Thanks, Mom."

Honor gave her one more hug and reluctantly let her go. "All set for the weekend?"

Arly's face brightened. "Totally, we've all got our tickets, and it's going to be so cool."

Yes, indeed. Twenty thousand people converging on Center City, Philadelphia, on the first night of one of the biggest weekends of the summer. Major party time. Honor promised she wasn't going to go over the rules and safety issues with Arly and her friends again. They'd done it at least three times already.

"Absolutely. It's going to be amazing." Honor grabbed her cup and stood. "Quinn's up, and we'll probably be leaving soon. Are you all set for the day?"

Arly rose. "I'm good. I'll go see if Jack is awake."

"Thanks." Honor followed her in. Quinn, with a cup of coffee in her hand and looking ridiculously desirable in plain black pants and a charcoal shirt, leaned against the counter.

Arly said, "Hi, Quinn," and disappeared back upstairs.

Quinn raised an eyebrow and said, "Everything okay?"

"Everything's good. Did you catch any of it?"

"Some. She sounds like she's okay."

"She is for now." Honor wrapped her arms around Quinn's waist. "She's a teenager. Next week, who knows."

Quinn rested her cheek against Honor's hair. "I'm pretty lucky you wanted me enough to take a chance."

"I'm feeling pretty lucky myself," Honor said, and kissed her.

❖

Southern California, 4:30 a.m.

Dani couldn't sleep in her childhood bed. Just something about being home seemed to strip away all the defenses she'd acquired over the years, making her feel like the vulnerable teenager she'd been before she'd left home. Her bedroom was now a guest room, but as soon as she'd entered it, she'd seen the room as it had been when she'd occupied it, and she was catapulted back fifteen years to a time when she'd felt like a stranger even when surrounded by the people who said they loved her. She'd been coming out and coming to realize she was not going to be the person everyone expected her to be. The one everyone insisted on seeing. Catching her reflection in the mirror, a wave of relief came over her that she wasn't who she'd been back then. She just needed to keep reminding herself of that. Even when the reality others insisted upon was a fantasy.

Her siblings had descended en masse soon after she'd arrived from the airport, but everyone had been more concerned with what was happening at the hospital than with her. Her mother had been, if anything, more distant and unapproachable than usual. Dani recognized the defense mechanism. She'd seen it often in the families of patients who coped with fear and anxiety by walling themselves off from an unimaginable truth. Her chest constricted when she considered that in many ways *her* life—as far as her family was concerned—was one of those truths.

But none of that really mattered now. Now she was part of one of those families and faced with more immediate challenges. She was worried, of course, and scared too. All normal reactions, even for someone as informed as she was. When the patient was family, the coping mechanisms her training had instilled dissolved, leaving her helpless and frustrated. She ought to be part of the decision-making processes. She was, after all, the best qualified member of the family to communicate with the medical professionals, but so far she'd been kept at a distance—not by them, but by her mother. She needed to talk with her, alone, and finally make her see that she had something to offer. Not for pride, or vindication. But because she loved her family. If only her mother would listen.

Frustrated with the circular thoughts that chased their own tail through her mind, she abruptly sat up on the side of the bed and grabbed her phone. Everyone back home would either be just getting to the OR or in the middle of rounds.

She'd have to wait until later to try Zoey. Or Ren. She really wanted to talk to Ren. She'd had an excuse, sort of, not to contact her when she'd had to leave so suddenly, but even then she'd known it was an excuse. She hadn't reached out because she was still struggling with Ren's reluctance to even consider a relationship. Dealing with her hurt. And her anger. And her guilt over both. She really did understand Ren's concerns—she knew how hard Ren was working and how much was at stake. For her too. But she had something with her, something rare and exciting that she didn't want to lose. And probably the quickest way to lose it would be to pressure her.

No—she wouldn't contact Ren, not yet. But she took a chance and texted someone who knew her. The irony of that, when she was supposedly surrounded by family, burned.

She texted Raven.

Are you around?

Yes. Hi! How is your trip?

Dani grimaced. How much should she say? How much could she really explain in words, let alone in the limited avenue of a text message? *Hard. Family stuff.*

I'm sorry Anything I can do?

Have time for game? I could do with a good challenge.

LOL Odd therapy, but I get it. I've got a little bit of time.

Dani didn't want to disconnect so soon. *Wait, before we get to that. How are you doing?*

I'm mostly okay.

Mostly?

Raven replied, *Trying to sort some things out. About...This sounds crazy, what I want.*

Oh I don't think it's crazy. Me too.

Yeah?

Dani typed quickly, *Yeah. Is this about your girlfriend?*

I don't think that word applies.

How come?

That's the question. I'm not sure what that means

If you can't decide, maybe it's a no. Dani sighed. Easier to give advice than take it.

I'm not used to not knowing.

Ha. You're lucky

Hey—you okay?

Not so much—but glad you're here.

Me too, Raven answered. *You still up for a challenge?*

Dani laughed. *You know it.*

The game *did* take her mind off things for an intense twenty minutes, and when they'd finished—her win this time—she texted, *Thanks. I needed that.*

I hope things go well with your family.

Thanks. And hey...maybe you should just talk it out with your friend.

I want to know what to say first.

LOL you could probably start with hello.

Raven signed off with a thumbs-up, and Dani stretched out on the bed, her phone cradled against her chest, and closed her eyes. There wouldn't be any more sleep today. She was due to go to the hospital with the rest of her family as soon as the ICU hours began.

Her phone vibrated, and she raised it up to check the screen.

Ren.

She sat up, the phone gripped in both hands, as if that could somehow bring Ren closer.

Zoey told me you were away. Wanted to say hi Hope everything is okay.

Dani sucked in a breath and quickly texted, *Hi. My father had a stroke. Things are iffy.*

Oh So sorry!

Thanks sorry I left in a rush

No—that's...wait

Dani stared at the screen.

ER paging. Text me sometime?

Dani expelled a relieved breath. Sometime meant one more time, at least. *For sure*

Then Ren was gone. The brief contact left Dani aching for more. For so many things.

CHAPTER NINETEEN

West Mt. Airy, several days later

Dani dozed in the back seat of the Uber, only vaguely aware of time passing in the unnatural coolness of the air-conditioned interior. She hadn't slept much on the plane, or much of any time at all while she'd been home, and despite being used to working long hours on not much sleep, she'd finally surrendered once the trip was over. She drifted on the edge of total slumber.

"The pink one in the middle of the block, lady?" the Uber driver asked, a pleasant guy who had mercifully not talked to her on the forty-five-minute ride from the airport.

"Yeah, but that's salmon not pink," she muttered.

"Like the fish?"

Rubbing her face, she said, "Yeah. Like the fish."

"You're home then." He sounded happy as he pulled to a stop, and Dani guessed she was too.

Home. Yeah, this was home, the place where she belonged. Where she knew who she was and so did the people who mattered. Wearily, she pushed open the door and glanced up at the house she shared with her friends. She froze, half out of the big black SUV. She knew she wasn't asleep, so she couldn't be dreaming, but she still had trouble grasping the reality.

Ren slowly rose from where she'd been sitting on the top step and smiled.

Dani came instantly awake, as if she'd just answered a stat

page in the middle of the night. Her brain kicked in and her body followed. She swung around to the rear of the vehicle and grabbed her duffel before the driver'd even gotten it out of the trunk.

"Thanks. Thanks a lot," she said and was halfway up the sidewalk before he'd closed the trunk. Ren was real, and she was waiting. Dani stopped at the bottom of the steps and stared up at her, drinking her in, imprinting every detail. Ren looked fantastic. Cream-colored shorts that came to midthigh, bare legs ending in strappy sandals, and a tank top that reminded Dani of mint ice cream. The color, not the taste. Her dark hair was a little windblown and sexy as hell.

"You're here," Dani said. A brilliant understatement but the best she could manage when her throat was so dry and mostly blocked by her heart trying to beat its way out of her chest.

Ren smiled. "You're here too. I hope you don't mind me showing up unannounc—"

"Are you kidding?" Dani bounded up the stairs and tossed her duffel onto the porch. She barely resisted throwing her arms around Ren and pulling her close. It just felt so damn good to see her, she ached to touch her, but she couldn't breach the few inches of distance between them uninvited. Even when every superheated atom in her body vibrated on the brink of explosion.

"Zoey told me when you were coming home." Ren looked down for a second and then met Dani's eyes. "I really wanted to see you."

"Ren," Dani murmured. "I'm so fucking glad you're here."

Ren hurried on, "I know you're probably tired, so I won't stay, but—"

"Are you kidding?" Dani grabbed her hand at last, to hell with caution. "No way are you going anywhere."

Ren's hand closed around hers. "If you're sure."

"I'm more than sure. You're exactly the person—the *only* person—I want to see right now."

"How are you?" Ren said softly.

"Oh man," Dani said with a sigh. "Long story. Let's sit down.

No, wait. I need a beer for this. God, I hope there's a beer. I know you don't want one, but—"

"No, I'll try one. I have to get used to the grown-up drinks."

Dani grinned and almost kissed her then. "That's what I like. An adventurous woman."

"Oh yeah, that's me." All the same, Ren flushed as if she liked the idea.

"Wait right here." Dani pointed to a spot on the top step. "Right here. Promise. I'll only be a minute."

Ren nodded. "I won't go anywhere."

Dani grabbed her duffel and hurried to the door, glancing back once over her shoulder just to be sure. Ren was watching her, a look on her face that mirrored everything Dani was feeling. Happy, anxious, excited. Yeah, she needed to hurry.

"Zoey?" she called as she charged down the hall toward the kitchen. No answer. Seven o'clock at night, Zoey might be at the hospital, or with Dec. But right now, the house was empty. She grabbed two beers, thanking all the powers that be that half a six-pack of Heineken sat on the top shelf. Beers in hand, she sprinted back to the porch. Half fearing Ren would be gone.

She wasn't.

Sitting on the top step, Ren leaned back on her arms with her legs stretched out in front of her. She was gorgeous, and Dani was having a little trouble concentrating. "Um, I forgot a glass for you."

Ren swiveled to see her. Her gaze moved slowly from the cans in Dani's hands up her body to her face. "I can drink out of the can. It's just like soda."

"Uh-huh, yup. Just like." Dani handed her a can and sat beside her, their thighs not quite touching, and sipped her beer. "I'm really glad you're here. Did I say that yet?"

"You did. I wasn't sure it was the right thing—"

"It was. Just the right thing."

"I just couldn't wait any longer."

"I thought about you—all the time."

"Me too." Ren tried the beer, wrinkled her nose a little, and took another sip. "I think I can get used to it when I stop expecting it to taste like anything I recognize."

"Give it time."

"So how are you," Ren said, watching Dani with that look in her eyes that made Dani feel as if Ren was seeing something deep inside her. Her instinct was to say *fine*, but she wasn't. She wanted to talk, and she needed to talk, and she wanted Ren to be the one to hear her. Right now she only wanted Ren.

"My father's still in the intensive care unit," Dani said, "but out of immediate danger. He had a middle cerebral bleed, left side, and he's got some major deficits." She didn't have to explain the details to Ren, who would know how debilitating something like that was, and how long the recovery, if the recovery ever happened. She blew out a breath. "The family is in shock. He's never been sick. My mother's still in denial, I think. The neurologists speculate this may be partly due to a fall he took six months ago when he was running. He tripped and hit his head on the curb. No one thought much of it at the time. Such a stupid thing."

Ren took her hand. "I'm sorry. That has to be even harder when it's so unexpected." She hesitated. "How did things go with your family?"

Dani shook her head. "The same—and completely different, at least for me. I guess that sounds pretty strange, doesn't it?"

"No," Ren said simply.

Grateful for that unspoken encouragement, Dani took a deep breath. "I told you how my family, my mother especially, has always been after me to come to my senses and give up medicine for pure science."

"I remember." Ren slid her fingers through Dani's.

Dani rested their joined hands on her thigh, and Ren moved a little closer until their shoulders touched. The contact strengthened her as much as it soothed her. "I've never realized how much it made me feel like an outsider, knowing that my whole family disapproved of what I was doing and secretly thought I'd let them down somehow. I hate that it took something like my father practically dying, and almost certainly having his entire life altered forever, for them to see some value in what I do."

"You interpreted for them at the hospital," Ren said.

Dani nodded. "After I got past needing my mother's approval or permission, I corralled my father's doctors, and we had a family conference. I went over everything with them, looked at the scans, talked to them about potential treatment, rehab, all of that. My whole family was there."

"Your helping them to understand your father's situation must have been such a relief for them." She squeezed Dani's hand. "And a comfort."

Dani swallowed around the tightness in her throat. "It was, I think. I guess that's how people in my family deal with fear. They can't conquer it until they understand what's happening."

Ren's gaze met hers, warm and tender. "You too."

"Yeah, me too."

"Did it help, knowing that your family finally understood what you do? Seeing how good you are at it."

Dani laughed. "I don't know if they got that out of it, but I could see something in my mother's eyes for the first time. Maybe not exactly pride, but appreciation."

"I'm glad."

"So am I," Dani said. "But you know what I'm really glad about?"

"What?"

"I'm okay now with them not getting it. They're never going to completely accept my choices, but there's nothing I can do to change that. But *I* know I'm doing the only thing I can do. This is what I want." Dani tipped her head to Ren's and sighed. "This right here."

She didn't even try to pretend she was talking about surgery anymore.

"Dani," Ren said gently, "you need to go to bed and get some sleep. And you need to get another day off."

Dani shook her head. "I don't think that will work, not on a

Friday before a holiday weekend. Besides, I'm okay." She grinned. "Seeing you made me forget all about being tired."

"Really," Ren said, her tone playful. "I definitely should've waited to come over, then."

"Oh no. No way."

"I should go, though, because you really do—"

"I'll tell you what. You fill me in on everything I've missed, and then maybe I'll consider it. Otherwise, I'll have to call Zoey, and then I'll never get to bed."

Ren studied her, her eyes narrowing. "Only if you agree to go right to bed after."

Dani rose and tugged Ren toward the door. "I need a minute to shower, and then we can talk. And I promise when we're done, I'll go to bed."

"Okay," Ren said as Dani held the door for her. "But just a little while."

"Deal. Come upstairs."

Before Ren could argue, Dani led her upstairs to her room and pushed the door open. Thankfully, she'd left it semi-neat, and the bed was mostly made. "You can sit anywhere—I'll be right back."

She was in and out of the shower in under sixty, toweled off, and pulled on a cutoff sleeveless T-shirt and a pair of baggy workout shorts in another minute. She hurried back to the bedroom and stopped in the doorway, watching as Ren studied her gaming console, the fingers of one hand lightly skimming over the joystick and keyboard in the kind of unconscious movements that only a gamer would make.

Ren heard her and looked over her shoulder. "This is a really nice setup."

"You play?" Dani asked softly.

"When I can, you know how it is. A little bit here or there. Not as much as I used to." Ren shrugged. "How about you?"

"Every now and then, whenever I can fit in a quick game," Dani said. "Helps to get away from it all for a while."

"For sure."

For sure.

Zoey's voice echoed in her mind. *What were you and Ren texting about?*

Her and Ren. Only it hadn't been Ren she'd been texting. It had been Raven. Raven, who was always around at the same strange, odd hours she was—dead of night, early morning, bits and pieces in the middle of the day. Raven, the gamer who lived somewhere close. Raven, who'd blown off work for a dinner with someone new. Raven, who had just met a woman, *unexpectedly*, a woman who might be her girlfriend—only Raven wasn't sure how she felt about her. Raven—who she'd been talking to about, hell, everything. What the hell had she told her?

"You know what you were saying, about not being sure what you wanted," Dani said softly.

Ren's brows furrowed. "When?"

"The other morning—when we texted."

"I didn't say that, Dani," Ren said carefully.

"No, but Raven did."

Ren went completely still.

CHAPTER TWENTY

Dani couldn't read anything from Ren's expression. For a few seconds she wondered if she was wrong. She'd made a few leaps in deduction, but everything fit so perfectly, like puzzle pieces that you could never seem to find, and then, after picking up one piece, a dozen fell into place. Looking back, she could see how their paths had crossed and recrossed for months, but each encounter had been defined by her misunderstanding of the reality. Funny, now that she knew, she had no trouble believing Ren and Raven were one and the same.

"How long have you known?" Ren said, her expression still a cipher.

"About a minute. Does that matter?"

"Oh, I think so," Ren said, an undertone of suspicion making Dani's spine stiffen. "From the minute we met, I've told you every single thing I've felt about what was happening. I revealed every single uncertainty and...other things, only I didn't know I was telling the person I was having those feelings *about*."

"That street runs both ways," Dani said reasonably, but she understood Ren's reaction. People—*she*—said things to friends she might not say to someone else, especially when those things were *about* that person. But they couldn't undo what they'd said, either of them. "And besides, you told Axe."

Ren waved a hand. "I don't think it's the time for semantics."

"Neither do I," Dani said, surprising herself at the temper in her tone. She hadn't realized she was angry, and she wasn't entirely certain why she was. "You haven't actually told *me* very much at all. But you told someone else, a stranger."

Ren leaned back against Dani's gaming table, one hand resting on the surface, a few inches from her main console. "That's not exactly the case, is it? Raven and Axe are not strangers."

"They're not real," Dani said, even as she inwardly protested that was not true.

"Of course they're real," Ren said with maddening calmness. "We're real, and they're part of us."

"You trusted her more than me."

Ren smiled, and the light returned to her eyes. "Dani, I trusted Axe because she *is* you. I might not have known that, but I know Axe is funny and kind and a good listener. And she looks at both sides of an issue. She's fair. And...she likes me. She never once found anything I said or thought strange."

"You feel that way about me?" Dani asked softly.

"Of course. I haven't told Axe anything that I haven't told you."

Dani let out a long breath. "I can't believe I'm jealous of... myself."

Ren laughed and looked pleased. "You're jealous?"

"Well yeah. I can't remember everything precisely that Axe and Raven have discussed, but you know, you've been hanging out with her for months, when it could have been...me."

"Dani, it was you." Ren caught her bottom lip for an instant, the little habit she had when she was struggling to sort out her feelings. "It's always been you."

"But I didn't know it."

"Do you now?"

Dani took a deep breath and all her anxiety melted away. Ren was incapable of subterfuge or half-truths. The consummate gamer never played games. "I believe you, and I'm very, very glad."

"Good." Ren tilted her head, a teasing note in her voice. "So, how do you feel about Raven now?"

"Are you kidding me? Raven is amazing. Besides Zoey, she's

my closest friend." Dani stopped and stared. "I've felt that way for a long time—before we, you know, found each other. Found out more about each other. I don't want to lose that."

Ren pushed away from the gaming table and draped her arms carefully around Dani's neck. "We won't. We can't. We're *us*, Dani. We just learned some things earlier than we realized. And we'll learn more every day."

"Yeah, we will." Dani kissed her softly. "Raven's the best gamer I've met. *You* are the best. How come you never said anything?"

"Because it's not part of what we do every day. It hasn't been what I do every day for more than ten years, I guess."

"You think we'll ever game again?"

"I hope so. I mean, you know, I really like Axe."

The teasing note was back in Ren's voice, and Dani couldn't find a single thing to worry about. She settled both hands on Ren's hips, letting her thumbs rest along the crest of Ren's hipbones. Slowly, she traced the delicate curves beneath the stretch of her linen shorts. "You like Axe a lot, huh? More than me?"

Ren leaned into Dani's hands and met her gaze. "I've never liked anyone as much as you."

Dani eased away, and a question came into Ren's eyes. "I'm going to close my bedroom door now. Unless you want to leave, when I'm done, we should lie down on the bed."

Ren dropped her arms and backed toward the bed. "You should get the door, then."

In the ten seconds it took Dani to get to the door and turn back around, Ren had settled on the edge of the bed, her sandals off already, in the same pose she'd been in on the porch—leaning back on her arms, legs casually stretched out before her, an appraising expression as if she was saying, *What do you plan to do next?*

Dani moved over to her, one slow, deliberate step at a time, and eased between Ren's thighs, leaning down until her torso and Ren's nearly touched and her arms rested on the bed, framing Ren's body. Ren's cheeks colored ever so faintly, and her breath hitched. Dani whispered in answer to the unspoken question.

"I intend to kiss you, for quite a long time. Then I intend to help you out of your clothes, and then I intend to explore with my hands and my mouth all the places you like to be kissed. *Then* I'll do whatever you want."

Ren grabbed the bottom of Dani's T-shirt and tugged it up, exposing Dani's stomach. She pressed her palm flat against her midsection, making Dani's muscles quiver. "Those are a lot of intentions, and it sounds like that might take a long time. I had something a little faster in mind."

With her other hand, she pushed Dani away and tugged Dani's T-shirt up all the way. Dani automatically lifted her arms and found herself naked before she was entirely certain what was happening. Grinning, she grasped Ren's forearms and pulled her upright. So much for going slow—there were other ways to tease. She kissed Ren exactly the way she'd intended—with deep, devouring kisses that said *I want you, I can't get enough of you, I might not stop until you can't think...breathe...remember your name*—all the while undressing her, her hands moving on autopilot as her mouth coursed over Ren's. Her fatigue vanished, replaced by hunger as Ren kissed her back with fierceness of her own, her teeth scraping over Dani's lip, one hand spread in the curve of her spine, pulling her closer until their legs entwined.

Dani lifted Ren's tank up over her arms and freed her of the last bit of clothing. She took in what her hands had explored, and places deep inside her quivered. "You look...amazing."

"So do you." Ren pressed her mouth against Dani's breast, her lips like silk. Her mouth so soft, so almost not there...until she skimmed Dani's nipple with her teeth.

The heat was a torch setting Dani on fire. Her head snapped back, and she swallowed a groan. She stayed upright as long as she could, her legs trembling, pressure coalescing in the pit of her stomach, throbbing between her thighs. "You're making me crazy hot, Ren. I need...hell, I need you to..."

"I need something too," Ren said in a husky voice Dani barely recognized. Ren went to her knees by the side of the bed, her forearms clasping Dani's hips, holding her upright, and kissed Dani's stomach.

"Ah, hell." Dani closed her eyes.

When Ren kissed her way lower, all the way lower, and skimmed her lips over Dani's clit, Dani swayed. Her vision tunneled, and she grabbed Ren's shoulder to steady herself. "I don't think I can stand up if you do that."

"Should I stop?"

"Fuck, no—just—wait a min—"

Ren might've heard, but if she did, she didn't seem to care. Her hands floated up and down Dani's back, shaping the curves of her muscles down her back and butt, all the time pulling Dani ever tighter against her mouth.

"Oh damn, Ren," Dani moaned, and the hard core of her sex shattered, sending a thousand shards of light cascading outward, spearing her senses with pleasure. She sagged forward and just managed to catch herself with one arm outstretched against the bed, nearly pinning Ren beneath her.

"Sorry," she mumbled and rolled onto her side, finally managing to get all the way onto the bed. She lay on her back, gasping as Ren stretched out beside her. She turned her head and met Ren's satisfied gaze. She grinned, still riding the last crests of a very awesome climax. "That was...most excellent."

Ren laughed. "I believe the phrase is *Atta girl. Nice job.*"

Dani laughed at the standing OR joke and wrapped an arm around Ren's shoulders, drawing her against her side. "Better than that, even. You destroyed me."

"Mm. Very excellent then." Ren ran her fingers through Dani's hair and whispered, "As soon as you catch your breath, I'd really like you to make me come." She traced a line down the center of Dani's body with one fingertip, stopping just below her navel, leaving Dani's skin ablaze. "If that's still your intention."

"Oh yeah. It so totally is." A jolt of adrenaline brought Dani upright, and an instant later she knelt on the bed, slipping her hand between Ren's thighs. "I want to watch you come."

"It won't be long," Ren said, raising her hips.

Dani kissed her and kept kissing her as she filled her. Silk and flame surrounded her, engulfed her, drawing her deeper with every stroke. Ren gripped her sides, her nails pressing crescents into her skin, each point so erotic Dani's stomach clenched. Ren rocked to meet her every stroke, until with a sharp cry, her back bowed and she shuddered.

The sound stole Dani's breath. She didn't breathe again until Ren grew soft around her and smiled.

"Thank you," Ren murmured.

Dani laughed unsteadily, still nearly breathless. "Oh, believe me, I'm the one who's thankful." She relaxed beside her and looped an arm around her middle. "You are so sexy. I want to do that again. I love making you come."

Ren grinned. "That works for me. Making you come makes me want to come."

"We could keep that going for a while, then." Dani pulled Ren closer and fought to stay awake. "Just a minute."

"You should sleep," Ren said. "We can wait."

"Don't leave," Dani mumbled.

Ren rested her palm on Dani's chest and her cheek in the curve of Dani's shoulder. "I won't."

❖

Ren's internal alarm woke her about four. The room was dark, and the house was silent except for the rhythmic sound of Dani's breathing and the steady cadence of her heart beating beneath Ren's cheek. She lay with her head on Dani's chest and an arm around her middle. She'd never slept in such an intimate position before. The first night they'd spent together, they'd hardly slept at all, and the unnaturalness of actually sleeping next to someone had kept her restless and on the verge of waking. Last night, she'd slept soundly, a dreamless sleep. Dani's skin was warm beneath her palm, and she slowly traced the curve of her side until her hand rested on Dani's hip.

"Hi," Dani said in the darkness and brushed a kiss against her hair.

"I'm sorry, did I wake you up doing that?"

"I don't think so," Dani said. "If you did, I don't mind. I like it when you touch me."

Ren smiled. "Do you? I like touching you. Especially like this, when we're in bed in the dark. It's as if there is no one else in the world except us."

"What about the rest of what we do in the dark? Do you like that too?"

"The sex?" Ren chuckled. "Yes, I like that quite a lot. I just assumed you could tell."

"I was hoping…" Dani blew out a breath. "I don't want this to be the last time we wake up together. I like you, more than *like*. You're pretty much all I think about."

"Do you think that's a good thing," Ren asked, "because I spend a lot of time thinking about you too. And that's…different. And sometimes I worry."

"You know, one of the things I like about you," Dani said, turning on her side so their bodies touched, front to front. Her arm came around Ren's waist, and her hand drifted down to the curve of Ren's spine, her touch familiar and still so new. "You say what you're feeling, and you don't worry about how I'll take it. At least, you don't try to make it into something you think I'll want to hear. Or not hear."

"That sounds terrible," Ren said. "I don't mean to act like I don't care. I do. I never want to hurt you, and I'm afraid I might."

"You can't hurt me by being honest, Ren," Dani said. "Disappoint me, for sure. Because I will be really, really, *seriously* disappointed if you don't want to see me again. I already have a lot of feelings for you, and it would be hard for me to get past those, if it turns out you don't have any kind of feelings for me. But I still need to know what you feel."

"I would be very unhappy if I didn't have a chance to be with you like this again," Ren said, inching her way through the tangle of fears and uncertainties, like she would in a darkened hallway with her fingers lightly tracing the surface of the wall to orient herself. She could so easily get lost in the not knowing, but she'd been in those places many times in her life. She'd never shied away from the not knowing. This time was different, but what she needed to learn felt every bit as important as every other pivotal moment in her life. "I need to learn how to be comfortable with this other thing in my life."

"Other thing?" Dani said gently.

Ren laughed. "You. You are the thing."

Dani kissed her. "I like being your thing."

"Dani," Ren said, "I'm serious here."

"So am I. If anybody's going to turn your world upside down, I want it to be me. But only in a good way."

"I think it's a good way," Ren said. "You understand me, what I need to do. What the future looks like, because you're living it too. You know how hard this year is going to be. And the next year. And maybe every year after that."

"I know we both made decisions a long time ago that got us to this point. Some things will be hard, and sometimes we'll be challenged." Dani shrugged. "That's nothing new."

"Being in a relationship will change things," Ren said. "Not just for us personally. There's still the Franklin to think about."

Dani blew out a breath. "Yeah, well, we're in the same year, which makes us competitors, and we can't change that. At least we know we're evenly matched."

"Axe and Raven might be," Ren said softly, "but I'm not sure we are, not in this."

"Are you saying you want to wait until this year is over to…be with me?" Dani asked cautiously.

Ren sat up and pulled the sheets up to her chest. "I don't want to make a mistake, and I'm not used to not being sure."

"I understand. I didn't figure on this. Neither did you." Dani pulled Ren closer and kissed her again. "I'm not going anywhere. Just so you know."

Ren let herself drift in the warmth of Dani's body and the quick surge of arousal that followed her kisses for a few minutes before she drew away. "I need to get to the hospital."

"You start early," Dani said, but she made no move to draw her into another kiss.

"And you should probably catch another hour of sleep."

"Maybe, but I think I'd rather have coffee. I need to check in with my residents too. We can go in together."

Ren smiled as she searched for her clothes. "There might be talk."

"Yeah. Do you mind?"

She heard the uncertainty in Dani's voice and hated that she'd caused it. She wished she could just...be, but when she looked ahead, she couldn't see a clear path. Not the way she always had—but then, she'd always been the only one on the road. But maybe sometimes, there was more than one path to follow. Maybe. Dani sat on the bed, watching her intently. Ren kissed her. "I don't mind at all. Let's go to work."

Chapter Twenty-One

"Do you want to grab a quick shower?" Dani stood by the door, looking as relaxed naked as she did fully clothed. Was she clueless as to how amazing she looked, or was this some subtle form of torture Ren needed to learn about?

Although torture wasn't the right word. Temptation. Definitely temptation.

"Yes." Ren looked away and gathered her clothes into her arms. "That'll save some time, and I can just change into scrubs when I get to the hospital."

"I've got a bunch of clean scrubs here."

"Even better." Ren joined her and valiantly kept her gaze above shoulder level.

Dani held out her hand and pulled Ren's attention into the danger zone again. "Come on, let's go."

Ren hesitated. "Together?"

Dani grinned. "I've already seen you naked. In fact, you're still naked."

"Yes. Well." Ren could feel the flush flow halfway down her body. Not embarrassment. Most definitely not that. "Okay. Why not?"

She took Dani's hand and followed her out into the hall, quickly scanning up and down to see if they really were alone. Silence greeted her, but she had a sense the house wasn't empty.

The bathroom was bigger than she expected, with the walk-in shower where a tub had obviously once been, now brightly done in white subway tiles. Dani had the water going, and in a couple of seconds, steam filled the rest of the room and clouded the mirror above the sink. Dani slid the glass door open and stepped in, her hair instantly wet and sleeked around her face in dark tendrils. She brushed water out of her eyes. "You coming in?"

Ren started. "Oh. Yes."

She dropped her pile of tangled garments on the floor and slipped into the shower. Her breasts glanced across Dani's chest as she found her footing, Dani's arm came around her waist, and Dani kissed her. Kissing Dani was as natural as it had been since the first time, although the spray of warm water enclosing them turned these kisses into something new. Soft and velvety, gentle, and tender.

"I wish we had more time," Dani murmured against her mouth, their bodies, warm and slippery, pressed together.

"I'm not sure there's enough room in here for what you're thinking," Ren said.

"We'd probably find a way." Dani slid her hands down to Ren's hips and eased her back an inch, breaking their contact. Her eyes beneath misty lashes held Ren's. "But you need to get to the hospital. We both do."

"I wish we didn't have to," Ren said, surprised by the truth of it.

Dani nodded. "Me too."

"I think that's a first time for me. You're...distracting."

Dani grinned. "I remember Raven mentioning that."

Ren smiled. "I recall. Can you try not to be quite so much for a little while?"

"I'm on my best behavior."

The way Dani said it, her voice low and husky, did little to relieve the tension pulling Ren's mind from what she had to do, but true to her word, Dani made no move to continue the kisses. Ren pushed aside the pang of disappointment and hurried to finish her shower.

She circled Dani in the falling spray, washing quickly. Dani stepped out, and she followed, watching as Dani leaned down to dry her legs and then her abdomen and chest. Muscles rippled that

Ren hadn't seen in the near darkness of their hours of lovemaking. She toweled off automatically, absorbed, until Dani said, "I feel like you're touching me all over and you're just looking at me."

"You're beautiful," Ren said. "I love your body."

"You're not helping us get out of here," Dani whispered and leaned forward to kiss her. This was not the slow, warm, tender kiss they'd shared in the shower. This one was hard and demanding and possessive in a way Dani hadn't kissed her before.

Ren backed up a step, pulling Dani with her, until her back touched the closed bathroom door. Dani pressed hard against her, and everywhere she touched, Ren's body flared. She put both palms flat against Dani's chest but didn't push her away. "Unless you can make me come in thirty seconds, you need to stop kissing me."

"Can you come in thirty seconds?" Dani asked hoarsely. She didn't even wait for an answer but slid her hand between Ren's legs and stroked her.

Ren leaned her head back and closed her eyes, the orgasm so close already she could only let it take her. Dani pressed her face into the curve of Ren's shoulder, holding her as she came. Ren gasped. "You do things to me I can't even describe."

"Only seems fair, since you make my brain melt." Dani backed away and wrapped a towel around her torso. "I'll get those scrubs."

Ren rested her hips against the vanity and caught her breath. She barely recognized the reflection in the mirror, her face flushed and her pupils still wide with the rush of her orgasm. She smiled, satisfied not just physically, but in some primal place that nearly purred with contentment. How very odd. And wonderful.

The door opened, and Dani came in, already dressed in scrubs, and handed her a set. "These are mediums, so probably be a little bit big, but...okay?"

"Yes. Fine." Ren took the scrubs. "They'll do. Thanks."

Dani lingered in the doorway for a second, desire plain in her eyes.

"Do not come in any farther," Ren said.

Dani grinned. "It's not my fault you make me crazy."

"I'm not complaining." Ren flicked a hand. "Just...out."

Laughing, Dani closed the door, calling, "I'll be downstairs in the kitchen. Come get coffee."

Ren dressed quickly, folded her clothes into a neat bundle, tucked it under her arm, and stepped into her sandals.

Zoey sat at the kitchen table and looked up when Ren walked in.

"Morning," Zoey said, as if Ren's presence before dawn was a normal occurrence.

"Morning," Ren said with what she hoped was equal nonchalance.

"We don't have anything to eat," Zoey went on. "We never do, not unless you're good with toast and peanut butter or, God forbid, Cap'n Crunch."

Dani held out a box designed to capture the attention of a five-year-old, and Ren made a face. "Is that even food?"

"Dani's major form of sustenance," Zoey said.

"Toast and peanut butter sounds fabulous." Since Zoey sat with only a cup of coffee in front of her, Ren added, "Can I make you some?"

"I'll love you forever." Zoey smiled up at her from beneath her blond fall of curls.

"Hey," Dani protested.

Zoey smirked. "Ooh, possessive."

Ren looked back and forth between the two of them and laughed. "Wishful thinking."

"Ha." Zoey pointed a finger at Ren. "I knew you had a sense of humor hidden somewhere beneath all of that seriousness."

"It's a newly acquired talent." Ren took the quarter loaf of bread that Dani held out to her. "Thanks. Are you really going to eat that stuff for breakfast? I can make you toast too."

"Too late to change my habits." Dani hopped onto the counter, dug into the box, and swallowed a handful of cereal.

Grimacing, Ren slid the toast into the toaster and, when it was done, added the peanut butter and passed a piece to Zoey along with half a piece of paper towel to use as a napkin. She leaned against

Dani's hip and bit into the toast. Dani dropped a hand onto her shoulder. She'd never enjoyed breakfast more.

"We're heading over to the hospital," Dani said once the toast had disappeared.

Zoey stood and stretched. "I still have to shower. I'll catch up with you at rounds, Ren."

"See you later," Ren said.

The predawn light turned the sky from pale gray to blue as they walked the few blocks to the hospital. Just as they approached the entrance, Dani grasped Ren's hand to slow her. "Last night was great. This morning was amazing."

"I know," Ren said. "The peanut butter and toast was incredible."

Dani laughed and kissed her quickly. "I'll catch you later."

"For sure."

Ren ran into Zoey in the stairwell twenty minutes before rounds were due to start.

"Did you finish seeing everybody?" Zoey asked.

"Yes, but I want to stop and see Leo before I head down."

"I'll go with you," Zoey said, "if you don't mind."

"Sure." Ren started up to the next floor and said, "Is this where you do the best friend talk?"

"Huh?" Zoey asked.

"You know, aren't you supposed to say something about how great Dani is and how you hope I'm not going to break her heart or something?"

Zoey laughed. "And here I thought you didn't know anything about girlfriends."

"I didn't actually have girlfriends, but I did live with a lot of girls in college and was always hearing them talk. I never needed to pay that much attention. It didn't apply until now."

Zoey stopped and leaned against the wall. Ren faced her on the same stair.

"Well," Zoey said, "since you are both friends of mine, I'd have to give the talk to both of you, and that's too much trouble. Dani is a big girl, and so are you. Plus, I happen to think the two of you look really cute together, and it's about time you both figured that out."

"That's a very accurate assessment," Ren said. "I mean, the part about it's time we both figured it out. We're working on it."

"In the meantime, my suggestion is to have a lot of great sex and enjoy each other and whatever happens, happens." Zoey dusted her hands, shrugged, and started back up the stairs.

Whatever happens, happens, Ren thought as she followed Zoey up to Leo's floor. Maybe she could learn to live without a plan. That might even be a plan in itself.

❖

Leo was sitting up in bed when they arrived, looking more energetic than Ren had seen him since the day he'd come in critically ill. His face brightened even more when he saw them. "Dr. Ren! Hi! Hi, Dr. Zoey."

"Hi, Leo," Ren said.

"Hey, kiddo," Zoey said, joining Ren at the bedside.

"So, Leo," Ren said, "I hear a rumor that you're going to go down to the regular pediatric floor today."

He bounced in the bed. "I'm ready. It's very boring up here with just grown-ups. I'm really ready to be around kids."

"I can't say as I blame you a bit." Ren smothered a smile.

"How do my numbers look today?" he asked.

Ren held up the tablet and scanned his latest labs. "Absolutely excellent. Your white count is normal, and your renal function looks great."

"That's really good," he said in all seriousness. "My dads are really worried. Can you tell them to stop now?"

Ren squeezed his hand. "I will. We have to get to work now, but I'll come see you again later today or tomorrow."

"Can you tell them I want to go home soon too?" he called as they reached the door.

"I'll pass that along," Ren called back.

Out in the hall, Zoey said, "You're really good with him."

"He's a really smart little boy," Ren said. "And a very brave one."

"Ever thought about kids?"

Ren stared. "No. Why would I?"

Zoey laughed. "Just wondering. People often do."

"Do you?"

"I do, actually. Hopefully, one day."

Ren shook her head. "I'm just trying to figure out how to have a relationship."

Zoey gave her a friendly squeeze. "Good luck with that."

Luck. She'd never counted on luck, but maybe that was just part of the plan too.

CHAPTER TWENTY-TWO

Ren had an hour free before evening rounds, and when she stopped into the OR lounge, looking for Dani or Zoey or any of her residents, she found it empty except for a med student asleep in a chair in a position likely to cause permanent nerve damage. Neither Dani or Zoey were scrubbed—she'd already scanned the OR board to see what cases were still running. With a sigh, she dropped onto the couch, pulled out her phone, and checked to be sure she hadn't missed any pages. Nothing. She knew what she would have done at a time like this a week ago. She would have checked with Axe to see if they could get a game in progress.

And why not now? Some things had changed in very important ways, but reminding herself of the logic she'd argued with Dani, fundamentally they were still who they'd always been. They knew each other now on many different levels, experienced each other intimately, but given time, they might have ended up in the same place. She smiled and imagined how that might have come about. All in all, she was glad they'd fast-forwarded. For now, though, she enjoyed playing their game. She opened Raven's message app and texted.

Any chance you're free for a game?

Axe texted back right away. *I wish. You know that project I mentioned? I'm working on it.*

Oh, points for you. How's it going?

Slowly.

Ren hesitated. Crossing boundaries was still something new,

and maybe Dani felt differently than she did. Her next question would mean one more barrier coming down between the way things had always been and the way they might become. But that would be Dani's choice, and Dani couldn't choose if she didn't give her the chance.

Want company?

This time, Axe didn't answer right away.

Ren tugged at her lip.

Yeah I'd really like that. Sorry about the game.

We can always play some other time.

For sure.

Smiling, Ren texted, *Be right there.*

She hurried through the hospital, across the bridge to the research building, and down the hall to the conference room. Dani was in her usual place, but the stack of charts that had sat beside her last time had dwindled to almost only a few.

"You're making progress."

Dani pushed back in her chair. She was in scrubs, like Ren, and her hair was ruffled from what Ren suspected were many frustrated thrusts of her hand through her sleek dark waves. She looked a little tired and awfully sexy.

"I don't know when it happened," Ren said, "but sometime in the last little while I've started thinking about sex every time I see you."

Dani grinned. "I can do this stuff some other time."

Ren held up a hand. "Nuh-uh. We have to learn restraint."

"We do? Why?"

Dani sounded so honestly perplexed, Ren laughed and kissed her. "Because we both have work to do—I still haven't made sign-out rounds yet."

"All right. But I'm not letting you forget what you just said."

"I won't forget. So, tell me where you're at with this."

Dani sighed. "I've got everything extracted and organized, but I'll be damned if I know quite what to do next."

Ren pulled out a chair next to Dani and sat down. "Tell me your research questions again. What is it that you're trying to show?"

Dani gave her a long look. "Okay."

She talked for a few minutes, and Ren automatically sorted information, formulated questions, mentally organized the data. When Dani was finished, she said, "Can I see what you've got so far?"

"Are you sure you want to be helping on this?"

"It's an interesting question," Ren said. "The study hypothesis, not yours. And yes, I'm sure. If you want my opinion, that is."

"Are you kidding?" Dani snorted. "You're the research expert, but you know why I got into the project in the first place, right?"

"I know," Ren said. "I'm not sure you need it to be competitive for the Franklin. It's mostly a clinical award. And you're a really, really good resident, Dani."

"But not all that well-rounded," Dani said without rancor, "and not that well known."

"Well, neither am I. And you know what," Ren said, her words coming as almost as much of a revelation to her as they probably would be to Dani, "I don't really care about the Franklin. I thought I did—I thought it would say something about who I was or maybe whether or not I belonged." She shook her head. "Now that I think about it, that sounds a little crazy. It's not that I don't think the award's important, I do—at least what it stands for. And it's not that I wouldn't like to be recognized and be rewarded for doing well, because I would. But it won't prove what I thought it would."

Dani studied her for a long time without saying anything.

"What?" Ren said.

"I think I'm falling in love with you."

Ren took a deep breath and then couldn't find any words. She took Dani's hand where it lay on the table, squeezed, and didn't let go as their fingers locked. "That's...huge."

Dani smiled, a soft, nearly shy smile. "Yeah, it pretty much is. I'm not trying to scare you away."

"I'm not scared," Ren said quickly. "Just tell me, is that a good thing for you?"

Dani leaned across the space between them and kissed her. "It's a very *very* good, amazingly good, totally completely good thing."

Ren laughed. "Okay, that sounds pretty definite."

"That too."

"I don't know if I know what love feels like," Ren said, wishing she'd thought of something else to say. Like how Dani's words and the look in her eyes opened up places inside her that brimmed over with excitement and happiness. But what mattered even more was that Dani not get hurt—that *she* not hurt her when she didn't mean to.

"There you go, being honest again," Dani said.

"I'm sorry."

"Don't be. Don't ever be. But I'm pretty sure you'll know when you are. In love, I mean."

"I know I wish we weren't here right now, that I could be as close to you as I possibly could be, maybe even inside your skin." Ren took a deep breath. "I want to touch all the places inside you that you touch in me."

"Ren," Dani said, her eyes darkening in the way that Ren knew meant desire, "that's about the only thing you ever need to say to me to make me happy."

"I think I'd rather show you. I have to make rounds in twenty minutes, but then I'm not on call," Ren said. "Right now, though, maybe we should look at your data."

"I'm not on tonight either. So will you come home with me?"

"Yes," Ren said instantly.

Dani let out a long breath and turned the computer toward her. "Then let's do this."

Focusing on the numbers helped Ren clear her head of the swirl of emotions, and after she scanned the columns of data, she looked at the notes Dani had made. "I think…Can I change a couple things?"

"Go ahead," Dani said, her gaze still fixed on Ren.

"You should watch, then," Ren said, and Dani laughed. Smiling as Dani leaned closer, Ren reordered the columns and ran a quick statistical program. "This is just a different way of looking at the data and analyzing it. I think this might—"

"Yeah, totally," Dani said excitedly, pointing to a column on the spreadsheet. "I don't know why I didn't see that before."

"You would have, it just takes practice. And I've been looking at this sort of thing for years."

Dani kissed her. "Thank you! That's really just what I needed to—"

Both their phones went off simultaneously. Ren checked hers as Dani retrieved hers.

Code red 911

Ren jumped up, and Dani slammed her computer closed.

"ER," Dani said as they started to run.

Mass casualty alert.

Arly jumped up as the opening band hit the crescendo of their closing number. The twenty thousand fans packed into the Wells Fargo Center screamed and stomped and waved their arms in the air, bodies spilling out into the aisles and crammed into the space in front of the stage, thirty deep. She and her friends had really super tickets, way down front, and they *still* had to stand on their seats to see. Janie was next to her, her arm around Arly's waist, and Arly balanced herself with her other arm around Eduardo's shoulders. They swayed and sang and shouted with everyone else, the sound vibrating through the floor into her bones, and Billie Eilish hadn't even come onstage yet. But the band opening the show was awesome, and everyone was already beyond excited. Arly barely registered what reverberated like a boom of thunder and figured the quick flash of light she saw toward the back of the stage was part of the show until red lights began flashing all around the perimeter of the cavernous building and a filmy gray cloud drifted over the stage.

Nothing happened for almost a minute, and then the crowd, like a threatened animal breaking cover, began to move, a tidal wave of people surging away from the stage.

"What is it?" Janie screamed, her voice nearly lost in the rising roar of the crowd, panicked now, fear replacing adrenaline-soaked elation. "What's happening?"

"I don't know!" Arly searched frantically for any sign of Jackie and Raymond and Zaisha. They'd jumped out into the aisle to dance and chant with all the other people in their row just a few minutes before, and now she couldn't see them. "We need to go."

"How?" Eduardo yelled.

Arly searched desperately for some direction. The packed aisles were out—even as she watched in horror, people fell and others ran over them as if they weren't even there. That way was suicide. She turned on her seat and pointed to the far right end of the stage, ten rows down and fifty seats away from where they were. "There. An exit."

"We'll never get there," Janie screamed.

People were climbing over the seats, pushing each other to get away from the front of the stage where the smell of smoke was more powerful now. And everyone was coughing.

"On the seats," Arly ordered, "go on the seats!"

"We'll never make it." Tears streaked Janie's face.

"Yes, we will. Take my hand." Arly grabbed Janie's and reached back for Eduardo's. "Don't let go no matter what. *Go go go.*"

CHAPTER TWENTY-THREE

Honor careened into the lot opposite the emergency trauma entrance and pulled her car into the first free spot she could see. As she ran across the lot, helicopters circled overhead, descending to the trauma landing zone atop the building. The distant sirens of approaching emergency vehicles grew louder. *Many* sirens, their mingled screams like those of a panicked herd rushing from a pack of predators. The double doors at trauma admitting swept open as she barely slowed enough to clear them. Dec turned from the central station at the far end of the wide hallway, saw her coming, and strode toward her.

"What is it?" Honor said, barely catching her breath. She'd faced mass trauma alerts before, and every one was different. And every one brought tragedy—unless she and her staff were prepared, and maybe a little lucky. "I was almost home when I got the alert."

"We don't have much in the way of details," Dec said. "Something about an incident at a concert downtown. All we're hearing is multiple injuries at this point. We're expecting at least a couple dozen, the extent—"

Honor lost the words beneath the roaring in her ears. She swayed, suddenly dizzy, and spots danced before her eyes.

"Honor. Honor?" Dec's worried voice cut through the screaming inside her head.

Honor struggled to focus, looked around, and saw that Dec had drawn her out of the main corridor where nurses, PAs, residents, and techs from every area of care raced back and forth, preparing rooms, organizing emergency equipment. A dozen gurneys already lined the length of the hallway, all the way to the entrance—sentinels waiting to collect the casualties as they arrived.

"I…" Honor swallowed around the terror in her throat. "Dec, Arly's at that concert. I…oh my God."

"I'll find Quinn," Dec said. "Let's go to your office."

"No, no." Honor took a deep breath, forcing down the nausea and panic. "I can't sit somewhere and wait. And there's work to do." She willed her mind to work, and despite her soul-searing panic, she planned. "I need to call her. Just let me call her. Once I know she's all right, everything will be fine. Fine."

"Right, go ahead. I'll be just down the hall getting the residents assigned." Dec squeezed her arm. "Let me handle this part, Honor."

"Of course." Honor pulled out her phone as Dec walked away, already talking on hers.

She checked first for a text—nothing. She called Arly, and the message went to voice mail. She called back instantly, knowing that sometimes Arly would catch her call the second time around. Arly didn't answer the third time, or the fourth. Honor leaned against the wall and closed her eyes. Arly would be fine. There were thousands of people there, and it had to be chaotic just trying to get people to safety, let alone clear the roads for their vehicles. The phone lines had to be jammed, or down altogether. It would take Arly a while to call. No word only meant Arly couldn't get through. But she would. Of course she would.

"Honor," Quinn said and pulled Honor into her arms.

Honor pressed her face to Quinn's shoulder. "I can't reach her."

Quinn drew her down the hall away from the bustle of equipment carts rolling by and people calling instructions. "I know, I can't either. But she'll call as soon as she can."

"Yes, I know. I know." She stopped abruptly and looked into Quinn's eyes. "We have to take care of the patients coming in. Raymond will bring them home, or Arly'll come here. She'll know to do that. Or she'll call us. And if she doesn't, we'll go find her."

Quinn took her hands, as solid and steady as she had ever been. "We will. Can you work?"

"Yes," Honor said, the strength returning to her body as she focused on the next step. She would take that step, and the next, and the next—until everyone who needed her was taken care of. "Arly knows where we are, and there's nothing we can do right now to find her. We'll do what we do, what we have to do here, and then..." She straightened. "Then we'll know what to do next."

"Where's Jack?" Quinn said.

"I called Phyllis from the car on my way back here. She'll keep him there with her as long as needed."

"I'll call her," Quinn said, "and get her trying to trace Arly's phone. She can call other kids' families too. She knows them all. Someone will have heard."

"Yes, yes." Honor grasped Quinn's arm. "And after that, we'll need to contact the other ERs."

Quinn nodded. "If we don't hear. But we will. I'm going to be in the OR. You call me the minute you hear from her. No matter what, you call me."

Honor cupped her jaw, drawing strength from the certainty in her eyes. "I will. I love you."

Quinn kissed her. "I love you too. She's going to be all right. She's the smartest kid I know."

Honor heard the catch in Quinn's throat and loved her for it. She put her arms around her. "It's going to be all right."

For an instant, Quinn clung to her as Honor had clung to her a few minutes before. Then Quinn stepped back and smiled that smile that said everything Honor needed to hear. "I'll see you as soon as I can."

Honor found Dec, and between them, they organized the ER and the trauma unit as the first of the patients rolled through the door. Then she got to work.

❖

Emmett stood in the center of trauma admitting, directing residents as they raced in. She signaled to Dani and Ren when they arrived. "Dani, run trauma one. Ren, you've got trauma two. Here's the drill—time is everything—we can't let them get backlogged.

Once a patient is stabilized, hand them off to your junior resident to take them the rest of the way. If you need to clear anything with an attending, grab one or one of the staff PAs. Keep the patients moving through as quickly as you can. We don't know how many we're gonna get, but what I'm hearing right now, it's at least twenty. Smoke inhalation, crush injuries, the usual blunt trauma stuff."

"What about coverage for procedures?" Dani said.

Emmett shook her head. "The seniors are acting junior attendings tonight—you supervise the juniors, take over where needed. If you run into trouble, look for staff." She shrugged. "But don't count on that."

"Right," Dani said flatly.

Ren glanced at Dani, her heart pounding unnaturally fast. She'd handled traumas before, but never what was coming. Patients with multiple traumas, all arriving at once, who would have to be triaged within minutes and stabilized enough so their noncritical injuries could be treated later. And with that many patients, the staff would be fully involved, and her call would be the final call.

"Okay then," Dani said. "I'll take Sadie and Roberto."

"Where's Zoey?" Ren said.

"She's running an ER room. You're going to have to work with one of the juniors. Sorry."

"Yes, fine," Ren said and, catching sight of Jez, signaled her over. "Trauma two. Let's go."

Jez nodded, almost running to keep up with Ren. "What are we doing?"

"Whatever we have to," Ren said.

And then there was no more time to talk. Or prepare.

The patients came through the doors in a steady stream, some of them in wheelchairs pushed by staff, but others by friends who had somehow gotten them to the hospital. Some walked in under their own power, and some, the critical ones, arrived on gurneys with EMTs and paramedics running along beside them, calling out the status to whichever staff hurried along beside them. As soon as the staff took over, the medics raced back outside or up to the helo pad to head back out for another run. The medivac helos landed continuously, bringing the critical-level ones to the trauma unit. Smoke inhalation, multiple fractures, crush injuries, head injuries, spinal damage. The signs of a crowd out of control.

Ren lost track of time, moving from bed to bed, assisting residents putting in chest tubes, applying splints, ordering X-rays, starting bloods, grabbing the neuro fellows or the CT fellows or whoever she could find to take the worst cases to the OR. When the arrival of new patients had slowed to the point that some of the residents had no new patients to see, she finally stepped back, drew a deep breath, and took in the evidence of chaos throughout trauma admitting. Empty equipment carts pushed haphazardly up against the walls, gurneys with rumpled sheets hanging askew, scattered bandage wrappers and intravenous lines and IV bags, a crash cart with empty drawers standing open outside room three. All evidence of the many patients they had evaluated, treated, and stabilized in the last—she glanced at the big clock on the wall—fifty-two minutes. Fifty-two minutes that felt like fifty-two hours.

Dani came out of a room down the hall, saw her, and walked to meet her. Her cover gown was bloodstained, and her usual brisk step slowed.

"Are your rooms pretty clear?" Dani said.

"Yes," she said breathlessly. "Jez has it under control."

"Good. Emmett just called. They need us in the OR."

Ren pulled off her cover gown and grabbed a clean one. "Yes, right."

They rode up in the elevator together, barely speaking.

"I have no idea if I made all the right calls," Ren finally said.

"Did anyone die?"

"No, at least not down there."

"Then you made the right calls," Dani said. "They need somebody on the ruptured aortic aneurysm. You want to take it?"

Ren stared at her. "You have to ask?"

Dani grinned and looked like her old self. "Just checking. I'll take the exploratory lap. I think it's gonna be a splenectomy."

"I'll see you later?" Ren said.

"You better."

❖

Trauma admitting, 3:00 a.m.

As soon as the splenectomy was off the table, Quinn tossed her gown and gloves into the bin and raced back down to the emergency room. She saw Dec first. "Where's Honor? Has she heard anything?"

Dec shook her head. "I don't think so. She's calling the other hospitals right now, but it's a mess. We don't even have IDs on half the kids we've admitted here tonight."

Quinn ran a hand through her hair. "I'm not even sure where to start."

"You start by not going anywhere," Dec said. "Arly'll call or she'll come here or we'll all work the phones and call every ER in the city until we find her. But the chances are she's okay."

"I don't believe in chances," Quinn said. "I gotta find—"

"Quinn!"

At the sound of her name, Quinn spun around, and for an instant she was almost afraid she was dreaming. Arly ran toward her, her clothes disheveled and grimy, but moving under her own power.

"Get Honor." Quinn catapulted forward and scooped Arly into her arms, trying not to crush her to her chest the way she wanted. "Are you hurt?"

"Arly," Honor called and suddenly the three of them were entwined.

"I'm fine I'm fine I'm fine," Arly chanted. "But Janie's hurt. They took her in the ambulance, and I went too. Her arm is broken, I think. They're bringing her, Mom." She shivered. "There were so many people. She fell but she never let go of my hand."

"I'll take care of her, honey." Honor stepped back and grasped Arly's shoulders, studying her from the top of her head to her toes. "Why are you barefoot?"

Arly stared down at her feet. "I don't know. I lost my shoes, I guess?" She looked back up at Honor and burst into tears.

Honor wrapped her up and looked at Quinn. "I've got her. Can you find Janie?"

"On it. I'll see to her and then find out about the rest of the kids. It'll be all right." Quinn kissed Arly's head and then Honor. "We're together. We'll always be all right."

❖

OR lounge, PMC, post-mass-casualty alert

Later turned out to be three in the morning before they'd finished repairing the ruptured aorta in a seventeen-year-old who had shoe marks on his chest from where someone had run over him. His ribs were fractured, as was his sternum, and he'd nearly bled out from a traumatic tear in his aorta. Ren scrubbed with Harkins, who remembered her from the surgery she'd done with him on the ICU patient.

"You're planning on CT, right?" he said as they placed the sternal wires at the end of the case.

"Yes." She twisted them down with the wire twister, and he cut them one by one.

"Not planning on wasting your life in the lab, are you?"

She glanced up and couldn't read in his eyes if he was kidding or not. "I don't think it's a waste, but no, I plan on primarily clinical surgery. But I hope to oversee a lab at some point."

Harkins laughed. "Smart answer. I would be very positively inclined should you decide to stay here."

Ren smiled. "Thank you for saying that."

"Is that a yes?"

"I'm not sure I'm supposed to say anything about that."

He shrugged. "I'm going to consider that a yes. If for some reason something makes you want to change your mind, come see me first."

"Thank you. I will."

When she got the patient settled, Ren returned to the OR lounge to wait for Dani. The last she'd heard, they were finishing up in her room too. She looked up at the sound of footsteps, and Zoey came in.

Zoey flopped down on the far end of the sofa and said, "Nobody tells you it's gonna be like that."

"I thought it was just me," Ren said.

Zoey gave her a look. "You mean the panic? The pee in your pants terror?"

Ren laughed. "Well, that too. But I kind of meant how fast it is, how little time there is to make a decision, and how many of them there might be. But everyone was amazing. The juniors handled it, though—Jez especially. She's really good."

"She says the same thing about you," Zoey said.

"Really." Ren smiled, the praise coming from a resident meaning more than the invitation she'd just had from Harkins. "That's good."

"What's good," Dani said, squeezing in between Zoey and Ren on the sofa. "Other than, you know, an amazing incredible night like this…and, you know, an awesome girlfriend."

Zoey groaned. "Don't even go there."

Dani slid her hand over Ren's where it rested on her thigh. "Case go okay?"

"Good," Ren said. "Harkins sort of said I should stay here for CT."

"That's my girl. Awesome in every way."

Zoey got up. "Okay, I'm leaving before this gets any heavier." She paused at the door. "Are you two planning on coming back together tonight? Because if you are, I'll find Dec and stay with her."

Ren answered before Dani could. "Yes. But we don't make that much noise."

Zoey burst out laughing. "I'm sure I'll have plenty of opportunity to find out. But I'm feeling a little noisy myself, so I'll go find Dec." With a wave she disappeared.

"I really like her," Ren said.

"Yeah, me too. Let's check downstairs in the ER," Dani said. "Then let's get out of here. Because that sounded like a promise to me."

Ren held Dani's hand as they rose. "It is. And I like what you said, about me being your girl."

"I was serious," Dani said quietly.

"I know. Me too. And you know what you said earlier, about knowing when you know?"

Dani drew a breath. "Yeah?"

Ren kissed her. "I know."

CHAPTER TWENTY-FOUR

One year later

"Are you worried about today?" Ren asked.

Dani turned on her side and slid an arm around Ren's waist. "Morning. I'm not worried about anything right now."

Ren laughed and kissed her back. "Sorry. I wake up and my mind starts working."

"I've noticed that a time or two hundred."

Ren snuggled closer. No matter how many times she woke up with Dani, her first sensations were always brand new again. Surprising, exciting, comforting. And then came the rightness of being exactly where she was. "I know my mind isn't the only thing that's working right now."

Dani chuckled and stroked the length of Ren's belly in such a possessive move Ren instantly quickened. A few minutes later, Dani said, "How's your mind doing now?"

Ren sighed and wrapped her arms around Dani's shoulders, holding her as close as she could. With her cheek pillowed on Dani's chest, she murmured, "Can't think of anything particularly important. Right now."

"Good. Are *you* worried about today?"

"No, not at all. Well," she added, "I want you to win, of course. But that's not a worry."

"You know I'm good with it if you do, right?" Dani said.

"Of course."

Dani kissed her. "It's all kind of irrelevant, anyhow. No matter what happens, it's not going to change anything between us."

"No, nothing ever will." Ren kissed her. "I love you."

"I know, and I love you back."

"So," Ren began carefully, "I think I should move in here."

Dani pushed up on her elbow. "Really? What about your house?"

"I can rent it. If Zoey is going to move out, we'd have this place all to ourselves. And Syd and Emmett are right next door. It's nice to have other people around sometimes. Just not..."

She broke off at the sound of footsteps passing in the hall outside the bedroom.

"Just not," Dani agreed, stifling a laugh, "someone always in line for the shower."

Ren looked up. "That is, if you, you know, want me around twenty-four hours a day and not just for the awesome sex when we can manage the time."

Dani raised her brows, her eyes sparkling. "Hey, I like the booty calls. But I'd also really like having you here all the time, even if we probably wouldn't see each other half of it anyhow."

"All right," Ren said, mentally preparing the to-do list, "I'll contact a Realtor to rent the house and find a property manager. And then we'll need to schedule a mover, and coordinate our schedules, and—"

"Baby," Dani murmured, "I think we better get to the meeting, or we won't have jobs and we won't have to worry about the rest of it."

"Oh!" Ren sat up. "That's a much better plan."

Zoey waited while they showered and dressed, and the three of them left for the hospital together. Along the way they met Syd and Emmett, and when they reached the auditorium, Jerry and Sadie were waiting.

"Hey," Syd said, "we're all together. That almost never happens."

Jerry smiled, and even Sadie seemed glad to see everyone. "Seemed like something we should do as a group."

They took seats in the second row, and promptly at seven, Quinn came in, gave them the results of the surgery match, and let them all know that once again the incoming first year residents were a good crop.

Quinn surveyed the hall filled with residents. "Tomorrow all of you fourth years will be chief residents. You'll be responsible for guiding the junior residents through the upcoming year. Zoey Cohen"—she shot a fleeting smile in Zoey's direction—"will be the chief surgical resident, seeing that all of you make the most of your last year of training. Congratulations, Zoey."

Zoey gasped and searched the far side of the room where Dec sat as those around her turned to congratulate her. Even Sadie gave her a quick shoulder bump.

"We're also," Quinn continued, "very pleased to announce that the recipient of the Franklin Surgical Award, given each year to the outstanding chief resident who demonstrates proficiency in surgery…"

Ren reached over and grasped Dani's hand.

"…is Emmett McCabe."

"Whoa," Emmett blurted loud enough to make everyone laugh.

Ren and Dani simultaneously called, "Hey, way to go, McCabe. Go get your award."

Syd kissed Emmett and pushed her to her feet. "Go. Congratulations, baby."

Ren glanced at Dani as Emmett made her way to the stage. "Emmett was a good choice."

"Yep. Totally cool. And totally right." Dani smiled. "You would have been too."

Ren said, "You know, I already have all I want. I have you. I love you."

"Funny," Dani said, "I'd say it's a win-win for both of us then, since I love you back. So, about those plans…"

About the Author

Radclyffe has written over sixty romance and romantic intrigue novels as well as a paranormal romance series, The Midnight Hunters, as L.L. Raand.

She is a three-time Lambda Literary Award winner in romance and erotica and received the Dr. James Duggins Outstanding Mid-Career Novelist Award by the Lambda Literary Foundation. A member of the Saints and Sinners Literary Hall of Fame, she is also an RWA/FF&P Prism Award winner for *Secrets in the Stone*, an RWA FTHRW Lories and RWA HODRW winner for *Firestorm*, an RWA Bean Pot winner for *Crossroads*, an RWA Laurel Wreath winner for *Blood Hunt*, and a Book Buyers Best award winner for *Price of Honor* and *Secret Hearts*. She is also a featured author in the 2015 documentary film *Love Between the Covers*, from Blueberry Hill Productions. In 2019 she was recognized as a "Trailblazer of Romance" by the Romance Writers of America.

In 2004 she founded Bold Strokes Books, one of the world's largest independent LGBTQ publishing companies, and is the current president and publisher.

Find her at facebook.com/Radclyffe.BSB, follow her on Twitter @RadclyffeBSB, and visit her website at Radfic.com.

Books Available From Bold Strokes Books

A Long Way to Fall by Elle Spencer. A ski lodge, two strong-willed women, and a family feud that brings them together, but will it also tear them apart? (978-1-63679-005-3)

Forever by Kris Bryant. When Savannah Edwards is invited to be the next bachelorette on the dating show *When Sparks Fly*, she'll show the world that finding true love on television can happen. (978-1-63679-029-9)

Ice on Wheels by Aurora Rey. All's fair in love and roller derby. That's Riley Fauchet's motto, until a new job lands her at the same company—and on the same team—as her rival Brooke Landry, the frosty jammer for the Big Easy Bruisers. (978-1-63679-179-1)

Perfect Rivalry by Radclyffe. Two women set out to win the same career-making goal, but it's love that may turn out to be the final prize. (978-1-63679-216-3)

Something to Talk About by Ronica Black. Can quiet ranch owner Corey Durand give up her peaceful life and allow her feisty new neighbor into her heart? Or will past loss, present suitors, and town gossip ruin a long-awaited chance at love? (978-1-63679-114-2)

With a Minor in Murder by Karis Walsh. In the world of academia, police officer Clare Sawyer and professor Libby Hart team up to solve a murder. (978-1-63679-186-9)

Writer's Block by Ali Vali. Wyatt and Hayley might be made for each other if only they can get through nosy neighbors, the historic society, at-odds future plans, and all the secrets hidden in Wyatt's walls. (978-1-63679-021-3)

The Business of Pleasure by Ronica Black. Editor in chief Valerie Raffield is quickly becoming smitten by Lennox, the graphic artist she's hired to work remotely. But when Lennox doesn't show for their first face-to-face meeting, Valerie's heart and her business may be in jeopardy. (978-1-63679-134-0)

Cold Blood by Genevieve McCluer. Maybe together, Kalila and Dorenia have a chance of taking down the vampires who have eluded them all these years. And maybe, in each other, they can find a love worth living for. (978-1-63679-195-1)

Greener Pastures by Aurora Rey. When city girl and CPA Audrey Adams finds herself tending her aunt's farm, will Rowan Marshall—the charming cider maker next door—turn out to be her saving grace or the bane of her existence? (978-1-63679-116-6)

Grounded by Amanda Radley. For a second chance, Olivia and Emily will need to accept their mistakes, learn to communicate properly, and with a little help from five-year-old Henry, fall madly in love all over again. Sequel to Flight SQA016. (978-1-63679-241-5)

The Hummingbird Sanctuary by Erin Zak. The Hummingbird Sanctuary, Colorado's hottest resort destination: Come for the mountains, stay for the charm, and enjoy the drama as Olive, Eleanor, and Harriet figure out the meaning of true friendship. (978-1-63679-163-0)

Journey's End by Amanda Radley. In this heartwarming conclusion to the Flight series, Olivia and Emily must finally decide what they want, what they need, and how to follow the dreams of their hearts. (978-1-63679-233-0)

Secret Agent by Michelle Larkin. CIA agent Peyton North embarks on a global chase to apprehend rogue agent Zoey Blackwood, but her commitment to the mission is tested as the sparks between them ignite and their sizzling attraction approaches a point of no return. (978-1-63555-753-4)

Something Between Us by Krystina Rivers. A decade after her heart was broken under Don't Ask, Don't Tell, Kirby runs into her first love and has to decide if what's still between them is enough to heal her broken heart. (978-1-63679-135-7)

Sugar Girl by Emma L McGeown. Having traded in traditional romance for the perks of Sugar Dating, Ciara Reilly not only enjoys the no-strings-attached arrangement, she's also a hit with her clients. That is, until she meets the beautiful entrepreneur Charlie Keller, who makes her want to go sugar-free. (978-1-63679-156-2)